CIRCA
NOW

CIRCA NOW

Amber McRee Turner

SCHOLASTIC INC.

ISBN 978-0-545-84349-2

12 11 10 9 8 7 6 5 4 3 2 1   15 16 17 18 19 20/0

Printed in the U.S.A.   40

First Scholastic printing, March 2015

For that spectacular fifth brother,
Great-Great-Great-Great-Uncle Bryan

Studio Monroe

Circa Monroe's walk home from school was so gusty, she thought the wind might very well snatch the books from her backpack and rearrange their pages.

"See you tomorrow, Circ!" said her best friend, Nattie, pulling her hat down over a mess of braids and veering off at her own driveway. "If the school doesn't get blown to Botswana."

"Yeah, we wish," said Circa. "See ya, Nat."

Circa continued a few doors down and steadied herself at her own mailbox. Even from the curb, she could hear her dad's poor attempt at singing, the warm-cool April wind giving a lift to every sour note. Circa smiled, grabbed a fistful of photography catalogs from the mailbox, and made a run for the door, just fast enough to avoid being blown off course. She straightened the crooked Studio Monroe sign next to the entrance and walked into the big, cozy room at the end of her house.

"I'm home," she called to her mom, whose legs jutted out beneath a giant tropical photo backdrop. The wind that snuck inside pressed the backdrop up against Laurel Monroe's short, slight frame, making her look like a dancing palm tree.

"Hey, babe," said the mom behind the tree. "Glad you made it. I was about to send your dad out to fetch you."

"My bags are packed . . ." Dad sang out super loud and twangy from his swivel office chair at the other end of the room. He had headphones in his ears, and his back was turned to the door.

"So how was your day?" Mom asked.

"Okay," Circa said, tossing her backpack onto the floor.

"My guitar too . . ." Dad sang.

"*Truly* okay?" said Mom, lowering the backdrop enough to show her skeptical eyes. Circa knew well that Mom knew well that many school days had been less-than-stellar this year, thanks to a couple of what Dad liked to call "persistent nasties" in Circa's class.

"Medium okay," answered Circa, sneaking catlike across the room toward Dad. She crouched behind his chair and got set to pinch the headphones from his ears.

Dad threw back his head and crooned even louder. "Taxi's coming. Nothing I can do."

Circa stealthily reached up toward his headphones. Then, in a flash, Dad spun his office chair around and shouted, "Well, I'll be! Lookee who's home!"

Circa stumbled backward. "Dad!" she gasped. "I thought I had you."

"Nope." Dad unplugged his headphones. "Saw your reflection in the monitor," he said smugly. "Not to mention that an eleven-year-old ought to know by now that three thirty is her dad's favorite time of day for one reason and one reason only."

Dad reached out for Circa and wrapped her in a big, solid hug. This coffee-smelling, corduroy-soft start to an afternoon in the studio made three thirty a pretty good time of day for her too.

"Got any homework?" Mom said as she tacked the big backdrop to the wall.

"Just some Spanish vocabulary is all," said Circa. "But I can practice that with Nat on the way to school tomorrow."

"Well, then, by all means, come on over and join me," said Dad. He pushed a plate of apple slices across the desk toward Circa and picked the topmost sliver for himself. Circa settled herself onto the tall wooden stool near his chair and grabbed the next slice.

"Check it out," Dad said, admiring his piece of apple. "Thinnest ever."

Circa held her own slice up between her face and Dad's iPod screen. It was so thin she could make out the shapes on the album art on the little screen through it. It was the head and shoulders of a man wearing a big hat.

"This is *for real* thinnest ever," Circa said, making her dad puff up with pride. Slicing apples superthin was one of his best food tricks. "Um, Dad, you do realize you were listening to that exact same song when I left this morning."

"I know," he said. "I keep waiting for it to end. It must be the longest song in the world."

Dad opened wide and placed another slice of apple on his tongue, then backed it into his mouth. "Good thing it's my favorite, huh?" he said as he chewed.

"Maybe not a good thing for the people who have to hear you sing it," said Circa, grinning. Mom snorted out an amen from across the studio.

Circa picked through the apple stack to find the flimsiest

one and surveyed the room to test what shapes she could see through it. Through the apple, Studio Monroe was a mushy blur of shadowy shapes. Behind the apple, Studio Monroe was a cavey-comfy place with low ceilings, wood-paneled walls, and squishy tan carpet. Halfway down one of the long walls was a door that led to the kitchen, with the living room just off of that, but truth be told most of the Monroe living was done right here. The place was lit by a scattering of mismatched lamps made from antique camera equipment. The north end of the room, where Laurel Monroe ran her portrait business, was full of neatly arranged tripods and props. Down there, the walls were decorated with smiling portraits of folks of all ages: school photos, engagement pictures, anniversary shots.

The south end of the room, where Circa sat, was where Dad worked to restore damaged photos to their original luster. To do this, all he really needed was a scanner, his computer, and a printer, but his desk was still a mess of papers held down by coffee mugs. The walls on his end of the studio were crowded with a magnificent display of befores and afters, framed duos of faded, torn, or scorched images from the past married up with their patched and revived counterparts. These were the things that made up Studio Monroe, and it was all beautiful to Circa, even distorted through a piece of apple.

Dad wadded up the cord to his headphones and tossed them aside as Mom yanked another tightly rolled backdrop from a long cardboard box across the way.

"How's Mom feeling today?" Circa whispered to Dad.

"Quiet," he said. "Kind of teetering on the edge of a blue funk, but I'm keeping an eye on her."

4

Circa watched Mom unroll the backdrop and smooth it out onto the floor to check for flaws. Mom had once described depression as carrying a wet bag of sand everywhere you go. Heavy and messy and hard to shake. Circa knew Mom had tried at least three different doctors in the past for her bouts with sadness and anxiety. There was one who insisted she take a medicine even though it gave her awful nightmares, another who totally creeped her out by hugging her too close, and another who said all she really needed was to go out and get some sun. "Quacks," Dad would call them each time that Mom came home upset by a visit. Then he would just work harder to help her get by. Sometimes just his company was enough, but for particularly anxious times, she had tiny pink tablets of some kind of store-brand medicine he'd buy for her.

"So tell me, Circ, what was the best part and worst part of your day today?" Dad said.

"Let's see," said Circa, turning her attention back to the plate of apple. "Best is hard to pick, because I aced my history test *and* my math quiz."

"That's my girl." Dad nodded.

"Worst is easy though," she said. "Chad Betts called me Circus Monroe again."

Circa held her left hand up and folded in all the fingers but the one that wasn't there.

"Chad Betts?" said Dad. "You're telling me the kid that once peed his pants inside this very studio was making fun of *you* for not having a pinkie finger?"

"Yeah," said Circa. "Nat told him to quit it, and then we

joked I should just call him something right back. Like Chad *Wets* or something."

This prompted a look of concern from Dad. He started tapping on his front teeth with his fingernail.

"Don't worry," Circa continued. "I handled it all nice, just like you would have told me to."

Dad quit tapping and gave her his usual one-sided smile.

"But then Chad still sang circus music every time he passed me today," she added, killing Dad's smile.

"Well, Circ, sometimes we don't get the results we want right away," he said, jiggling the mouse to wake up the computer. "And just because doing the right thing can be prickly, that doesn't make it any less right."

"Sure felt extra prickly today," said Circa.

Dad patted her on the knee. "I will tell you this," he said. "I'm even more proud of you for how you handled Chad Betts than I am about the quizzes."

"Thanks, Dad." From the corner of her eye, Circa could see Mom remove Chad Betts's sixth-grade picture off her gallery of portrait work and drop it into the trash can. Her own tiny revenge.

Dad double-clicked to open his Photoshop program.

"Whatcha working on today?" Circa asked, leaning onto her elbows to get a close look at the screen. "Any Maple Grove stuff?"

"I wish," Dad said. "You and I need to pay a visit to Maple Grove sometime this week, so we can pick up a new batch of photos to scan. There's a ton of work to be done by August."

Dad's suggestion gave Circa a stir inside. She loved to visit the Maple Grove Residence. Her own great-aunt, Ruby, had been one of the first people to move into Maple Grove when it opened a couple years back, and Circa and Dad had been going there every other week since then. Circa loved getting to drink glass-bottle Cokes and play hair salon with Great-Aunt Ruby.

After Ruby died, Circa got to know the other people who lived up there, like Miss Rempy and Hank-not-the-Mayor and Maki Lee, each of whom sometimes knew her right back and sometimes didn't. Ever since Dad had explained to her what the residence actually was—a place for people who have sicknesses like Alzheimer's and dementia that cause them to forget things—Circa appreciated her new friends even more, knowing how much they enjoyed sharing found bits of stories with other people. "After all," Dad had always said, "just because the book's too high up on the shelf to reach, doesn't mean the story's not there."

"How many do you have left to work on?" asked Circa.

"As it stands, still dozens," Dad said. "After our next visit, maybe a dozen more."

In the past year, Circa and Dad had been to Maple Grove a bunch of extra times to help plan the details of their big "Memory Wall" project. Pictures of things like old school buildings, local restaurants, climbing trees, parks, and picnics—either from the residents of Maple Grove or from local archives—would soon hang together to fill a whole wall with sparks of memory . . . and Studio Monroe would be restoring all of it.

She and Dad loved to look at the big empty wall in the Maple Grove lobby and daydream about the finished project, and how, come August, it would be a magnificent showcase of the missing pieces of their friends' lives. It made Circa feel proud that Studio Monroe was going to do something good for people whose actual memories were as torn and faded as their paper ones. To help them reach their stories.

"I can't wait till you fix up some of the Nelsons' pictures," said Circa. "Lily said they used to win swing dance contests."

"I can picture it in my head," Dad said as he clicked FILE: OPEN to bring up a fresh photo. "I'd rather be swing dancing myself than working on this one here."

"Not a Maple Grove picture?" said Circa.

"Unfortunately, no," said Dad. "It's the Linholt family reunion one."

"I thought you were finished with that," she said.

"Yeah, I thought I was too," said Dad. "But that nitpicking Mrs. Linholt called today in a huff about the last proof I e-mailed her. Seems I hadn't made the skin coloring 'pink and healthy' enough, and she thought I'd stretched the photo out and made everybody—namely herself—look fatter."

Circa laughed, accidentally spitting a fleck of apple onto the screen. "Oops, sorry," she said, getting even more tickled.

"Anyway," Dad said, wiping the monitor dramatically with his cuff, "I have to tweak the picture right now. Mrs. Linholt wants to pass out the prints at tonight's reunion."

"Where is it?" said Circa.

"The same park that this one was taken," said Dad.

"Even if it's stormy?" said Circa.

"Yeah, Todd, can you pinken up that sky too?" Mom interjected as she tacked a field of yellow tulips to the wall.

"Nope, changing the weather costs extra," Dad said. "But you've got a point there. . . . Since no one's been in to pick this up, all I can figure is they must have rescheduled."

Circa leaned closer. "So are you going to make Mrs. Linholt look skinnier?" she asked.

"Nope," Dad said with a smile. "Plastic surgery costs extra too."

He dug around on his desk for the original, damaged Linholt reunion photo. "Do you know, I've spent more time on this than on any one picture before." He held up the damaged reunion pic and compared it with the skin tones on the computer.

"Looks the same to me," said Circa.

"Me too," he said. "But if the Linholts want to be pinker, I guess I'll make the Linholts pinker."

Circa finished off the apple stack while Dad worked, watching each careful pixel-by-pixel edit. She loved watching him edit a picture, studying his every click and drag and cut and paste and brushstroke, memorizing his techniques in hopes of having her very own swivel chair and computer right next to his someday. Plain and simple, Todd Monroe was the best photo restorer there ever was. He claimed he'd gotten that gene from his own aunt Ruby, who was once a whiz at doing photo touch-ups back in a time when all the restoring was done with tiny brushes and colored ink. He even kept a collection of her dried-up ink bottles on a shelf above his desk.

As Circa watched, she wondered how anyone with just brushes and ink could make photo magic happen like Dad and his computer. With the Linholt Reunion photo, like all his others, she could hardly tell where the original photo ended and his work began. And like always, thinking about Dad's talent soon turned Circa's mind to the one thing that he did even *better* than photo restoring. She reached across the desk to a disheveled collection of file folders and pulled out a well-worn folder labeled simply SHOPT.

That one word alone instantly brightened her pixels.

The Shopt

"Is there anything new in here?" Circa asked in a half-singy way, hoping Dad had found some time in the midst of Linholt pinkening to add something new to the Shopt file for her.

Dad got a serious look. "Isn't it past your bedtime, young lady?"

Everyone in the room knew good and well that four twenty-one was *not* past Circa's bedtime, but for as long as she could remember, Dad had made this dumb joke at least once a day. Rolling her eyes at him, she laid the Shopt folder open across a small, clean portion of desk and began to thumb through the large stack of photo prints. There were dozens of them, each one a copy of a picture that Dad at one time or another had worked his restoration magic on. They came into Studio Monroe as ordinary pictures in need of repair, but this particular collection of prints had since been turned into something extra special just for Circa. Dad had begun by scanning the original photo, and then, on his computer, had made his own custom version by Photoshopping extraordinary things in, sometimes snagging pieces from other pictures, sometimes simply drawing things in fresh. Like fish floating in soap bubbles. Or clouds shaped like trumpets. Even once, a giant glowing hamburger. These whimsical creations he'd nicknamed simply "the Shopt."

Dad's changes somehow made the pictures even better than they ever could have been before. Scenes that started out as big snoozers, like a class picture or yet another wedding shot, seemed to undergo a magical transformation with the Shopt additions. And yet the pictures were only the half of it, for Dad would also always make up a fantastical story to go along with the stuff he'd put in. He'd scribble the story underneath the picture, sometimes continuing onto the back with his crazy tale.

Circa flipped quickly to the last piece of paper in the folder and was thrilled to find that there was indeed a newly Shopt photo. She was surprised to discover that it was the Linholt Reunion pic. "You did a Shopt version of *that* one!" she said with delight.

"I had to, to keep my sanity," he said. "It was good therapy to be able to goof on that family while dealing with crabby Mrs. Linholt."

Circa's eyes darted all around the picture to find what Dad had snuck into the new version. She called out to him every bit she discovered, and each new thing gave her a sharper thrill inside. There was a huge stern-looking potato peeking out from behind a tree, a pocket watch big as the sun on a chain entangled in the branches behind the family, and, of all things, a beaver playing a bugle right into a Linholt's ear. When she thought she'd discovered all there was to find, Circa started to restack the pics and stuff them back into the folder. But then Dad interrupted her.

"Hold up," he said. "I think you may have missed something."

Circa flipped back to the Shopt reunion pic and scanned it slowly, glancing up at Dad's screen again and again to compare it to the original version of the picture. It took her three solid looks before she noticed.

"Dad, are you kidding me?"

"You found it," he said.

"A baby?!"

"Diaper and all," said Mom.

"He's pretty cute, don't you think?" said Dad.

Sure enough, right there in the front row of the family picture, Dad had Photoshopped in a baby so real-looking, you'd never know it wasn't really part of the Linholt festivities. Circa could hardly believe what she was seeing, and how very real he looked.

"I told your mom we needed to celebrate the arrival of a new little bundle of Shopt joy," said Dad.

Circa looked across the studio. "Mom, you saw this?"

"Pretty amazing, huh?" Mom said with a grin. That was another powerful thing the Shopt could do. They could *always* make Mom smile.

"Dad, how did you sneak a whole 'nother person in?" asked Circa.

"It took a while to get it right," he said. "But get this. I copied some features from our own family pics and pasted them in. Then I just blended and tweaked until I'd built a little baby."

"Unreal," said Circa as she studied the chubby Shopt infant, plopped right there at the feet of an unsuspecting Linholt.

"Convincing, no?" said Dad.

Sure enough, the baby did bear a strong Monroe family resemblance.

"So what's the story?" Circa asked. "About the baby, the potato, and the big watch? Oh, and um, the beaver with a bugle?"

"Yes, do tell us," said Mom. "I'm particularly curious about the baby. I dearly hope he didn't ride in on the back of that beaver without wearing a tiny Shopt helmet."

"Or maybe he swung in on the watch chain," said Circa, focused so intently on the little Shopt guy, the harsh ring of the studio phone almost startled her off her stool. Dad pulled the phone from under a stack of papers.

"Oh boy, that story's a real doozy," he said. "Hang on a minute."

"Hello? Studio Monroe," Dad answered. "Oh, hey, Mrs. Linholt." He rolled his eyes when he said her name.

After that, it seemed he wasn't given the opportunity to squeeze in many more words at all. Beyond a couple of *No*'s, a couple more *Sorry about that*'s, and a *Just give me some directions*, Dad remained silent, looking quite huffy.

"Dad, someday will you teach me to do that? To put a baby in a picture?" Circa said once he'd hung up.

"Sure," Dad said as he clicked to save the changes on the non-Shopt Linholt photo. "Just bear with me for a bit, if you will. Mrs. Linholt claims, and very harshly I might add, that I was supposed to deliver the prints to the reunion. Apparently, she's three counties over pacing ruts in the grass waiting for me."

Dad clicked FILE: PRINT and typed *30* in the quantity field, as Mom took a fretful look out the studio window.

"Like I'd ever promise to drop off a stack of photos two hours away," he said irritably. "But I guess they say the customer is always right, huh?"

"Unless she's way wrong," interjected Mom.

"Let's just say the customer is always right when that customer threatens to not pay you for the umpteen hours you've spent on her project," Dad said. "And especially when said customer keeps throwing around that she has some important government job."

"But seriously, Todd, with all this crazy weather?" said Mom.

"Yeah, well," said Dad. "What is it that supersmart guy that we know always says? That sometimes doing the right thing is prickly?" He gave Circa a wink, and she promptly closed up the Shopt folder and returned it to its spot. She had a feeling the new story would have to wait awhile.

As the thirty prints rolled out into the tray on Dad's big printer, he said, "Circ, if you want to, while I'm gone, you can tinker around with making your own addition to the Shopt family."

"For real?" she said. "Like a baby?"

"Why not?" he said. "You know, I'll venture to say that the day you can seamlessly add a fresh person into a pic, then you can do just about any kind of photo restoration."

Dad clicked down into a couple of folders and found a file called DONE AND DELIVERED. Within two more clicks, he'd located a black-and-white picture of a big group of soldiers from 1942.

"Here. These guys look like they could use a baby around," he said. "Just be patient with yourself, and practice using some of the techniques I've taught you."

Dad stacked up the reunion prints and slid them into a big padded envelope.

"And don't be scared to experiment," he added. "You know you can always click 'undo.'"

"Got it," said Circa.

"And hey," he said. "If the weather does get worse and your mom says it's time to hunker down, then no arguing, okay?"

"Okay, Dad."

Circa was no stranger to hunkering down. The year had so far brought with it the worst storm season that Wingate, Georgia, had ever seen. In fact, the Monroes had sat in a dry bathtub surrounded by pillows so often that spring, they'd nicknamed the downstairs bathroom "Hunkerville."

Dad already had his keys and wallet and a wrinkled plastic poncho gathered when another call came in on his cell phone. He groaned when he saw that it was Mrs. Linholt's number again.

"Studio Monroe," he answered flatly.

Circa stopped and listened intently, hoping Mrs. Linholt had changed her mind and that Dad could stay home. Mom got still too. But Dad didn't look relieved by the call at all. He didn't even make googly eyes. He just kept saying "Who is—" and "What are—" and being interrupted. The only complete thing he got out was a quick "I'm on my way." And that was it. When Dad hung up, he looked to be shaking some kind of weirdness from his head.

"What was that?" asked Mom.

"I don't know. I don't even know *who* that was," Dad said. "But I've really got to go."

"Well, just make sure you get back soon as you can," she said as she gathered cushions for Hunkerville from off her studio couch. Circa and Dad exchanged a look. They were always making fun of Mom for setting up Hunkerville way too early.

"And Todd, please, whatever you do . . ." Mom began, looking at Dad so seriously. "Don't sing to them," she said with a grin.

"Yes, ma'am. You got it," Dad chuckled. He gave Mom a big hug all the way around both her and the cushions.

"Have fun with the Shopt, and we'll exchange baby stories soon," he said to Circa. "But don't stay up past your bedtime, young lady."

Circa pretend-snarled at Dad as he smooched his finger and touched it to the tip of her nose. Then he tucked the puffy envelope under his arm and dashed for the door.

"Taxi's coming . . . nothing I can do . . ." he wailed into the murk of the afternoon.

From her stool, Circa saw the incoming wind whip Dad's hair into a total mess as Mom crossed the room with another load of cushions for Hunkerville.

It was their first time to climb Umbrella Rock, and the family was having second thoughts about trusting a gorilla as a tour guide. Little did they know, the silverback and his fearless assistant Elaine had a very balanced approach to their work.

3

Undone

Three weeks, three days, and nine hours later, Circa stood barefoot on her own driveway with a sleeping bag in her arms and her face to the sky. She had never seen a night so dark. She grabbed the handle on her rolling suitcase as Mom rattled the doorknob at the entrance to Studio Monroe. It seemed like ages since they'd slept at their own house.

"I could have sworn I locked this," Mom said, pushing the door open so easily she almost stumbled over the pile of mail at her feet.

"Must not've," mumbled Circa, remembering that she herself had forgotten to lock it the last time she'd snuck away from the Boones' for a good cry in Dad's chair.

Mom gathered up the mail, took one step into the studio, and flicked on the overhead light. It buzzed out dead instantly.

"Oh baby, I just don't know about this." Mom put her hand across her chest and faltered in the doorway. Circa knew that Mom had been psyching herself up to come back to the house all day long. Up the street, the Boones had already fed them dinner, dessert, and even a bedtime snack.

"We couldn't stay at Nattie's forever," said Circa, bumping her suitcase over the threshold, gently nudging Mom in. The room was so very musty, the thick air smelling of dead flowers and things left behind in the kitchen. The scene made Circa feel like faltering too. Maybe they could stay at Nattie's just a few days longer.

"Hold on," said Mom, putting her arm out in front of Circa. "Do you hear that scuffling noise?"

Circa sure enough heard the scuffling noise. In fact, it had been cutting her secret visits to the studio supershort, even after Nattie had theorized about the noises at the Boone house one night, suspecting that a fat raccoon was hopping from garbage can to garbage can all the way down Delp Street.

"Just a raccoon," said Circa. Dad's desk was already calling to her.

Mom began to make her way slowly around to turn on the lamps, stopping short of Dad's side of the studio like there was some kind of force field dividing the room. Circa went straight to the dark end of the room and settled into the dents of the big office chair. She turned on Dad's iPod, which still had his favorite song displayed. Circa pressed play. *It's way past midnight.* That's how the song began. Circa stared at the glow on the little screen. The music was so full of bittersweetness. Even so, she let it go on, like there was a sore spot on her soul she just couldn't stop picking at. It actually *was* past midnight, a part of Sunday morning that eleven-year-olds and their moms don't often see together. But Circa had hardly even noticed the time. What did it matter anyway, the knowing whether it's 12:06 that your heart is breaking, or 12:07?

Circa swiveled the chair around slowly. In the generous lamplight, she could see the same familiar features of the room. Unbroken walls. Undamaged furniture. Unleaky ceiling. Unwobbled pictures. Slow-motion mom. She thought about how Studio Monroe and their home—the whole town of Wingate, for that matter—had miraculously been spared from destruction. And yet somehow, this room was totally different than before, completely drained of its comfort and charm. Photographically speaking, Studio Monroe had become a low-contrast, monochrome version of the room it was just three and a half weeks ago. Weeks ago, before most people knew what "Category EF5" meant. Before towns like Smithville, Mississippi, and Tuscaloosa, Alabama, had almost left the map. Before countless Hunkervilles had saved countless lives, but couldn't do anything for one very important life.

Circa found herself longing for a thinnest-ever apple slice to look at the studio through. The only moving part of the scene was Mom shuffling from one corner to another, stacking and restacking pictures and papers, like mindless tasks were the glue that kept her from crumbling into a heap on the floor. Circa considered how Mom hadn't really even had to be a mom for the last three weeks. Mrs. Boone had been mother enough for them both while Mom lay in the bed and Nattie entertained Circa with an endless string of board games, craft magazines, and nature shows. But now here Circa and Mom were, just the two of them, fumbling around in a half-lit room full of smells that didn't belong.

Circa turned back toward Dad's computer and gazed at the picture that was taped to the edge of his screen, the one of Dad and Mom and baby her. Then her eyes traveled to the carved wooden box full of ashes sitting on top of the monitor. She thought of all the undeveloped memories that must be inside there, and it made her chest ache with sorrow.

She pulled out the Shopt folder and laid it open across her lap. Starting at the beginning, she looked at every fanciful picture, lingering on her favorites. The basketball team with elaborately styled mustaches. The bride and groom squeezed together by a plump, green octopus tentacle. The Grand Canyon, flowing with alphabet soup. Each one had a short story scribbled underneath in Dad's messy handwriting. And each one was its own much-needed spark of joy.

Once Circa made it to the Shopt version of the Linholt Reunion picture, though, the sparks fizzled. At first, she could hardly stand looking at that place, possibly the very same place her dad was killed. She was tempted to tear the paper into tiny pieces. But then, for some reason, she just couldn't bear to get rid of it. She suddenly felt connected to all the good things Dad had added into that picture and again longed to know their story, the story he'd never gotten to tell her. About the watch, the potato, and even the musical rodent. But mostly, about that baby.

Fighting hard to contain the tears that threatened to stain the image on her lap, Circa tucked the Shopt baby and his family safely back into their folder. As she slid the folder back into its spot, she bumped the mouse and woke up Dad's computer, where the portrait of Dad that Mom had printed for his memorial service was still open on the screen. Circa knew it was Mom's favorite picture of Dad, taken at least ten years before

Mom got her first-ever good camera. Seeing his face—his crinkly brow, sparkly brown eyes, and broad smile—made Circa feel like she just couldn't bear to keep the sadness in any longer. But then she caught sight of Mom in the monitor's reflection. Mom was sitting in the beanbag with a lap desk across her legs and holding her face in her hands. She was silent, but her shoulders shook like she was crying hard enough for the both of them. Circa had just that morning overheard Mrs. Boone tell Mom she was going to have to be Circa's "rock." But it looked like the rock was sinking fast.

Circa wondered what to say to Mom, wondered what Dad might have said, what he might have done to help. She looked to his face on the screen for inspiration. Then, without hesitation, she grabbed the mouse and clicked the paintbrush icon on the Photoshop toolbar. She opened up a color palette window and chose a bright purple. Then, as best as she could, she painted some silly purple star-shaped glasses right onto Dad's face. They were uneven. They were cartoonish. But she felt like they might still do the trick. As she worked to smooth out the jagged lines of the glasses, the song played softly on Dad's iPod. It was called "A Prayer Like Any Other." She listened to the chorus: *"Oh Lord, keep an eye on this place."* It was the first time she'd ever paid close attention to that part of the song. Three weeks and three days ago, it was just about taxis and guitars and the long, old road. Today, it was *being gone* and *praying* and *saving grace*. She wished that God had listened to Dad's singing and counted it as a prayer worth answering.

Circa struggled to focus her thoughts on putting some final touches on her Shopt work. Once the glasses were complete, she printed the picture and carried it over to Mom, who sat writing a check to the funeral home for more money than Circa ever imagined them having. Circa slowly handed the picture to her and said, "Here you go. Dad and I made something for you."

Mom stopped and gave Circa a puzzled look. She sniffled and took the picture from Circa's hand. She sniffled again. Circa wondered if she had done the wrong thing. How was she even supposed to know the right thing? Weren't parents supposed to know all that?

Then, finally, Mom cracked a slight smile. "I should be the one trying to cheer you up," she said. "Not the other way around."

Circa couldn't have agreed more.

"I never knew your father to wear purple star glasses," Mom said. "But I must admit he does look kind of handsome in them." She maintained the little smile for a few moments, but Circa could tell it was as fake as the sunshine backdrop pinned to the wall behind her. Dad had once made up a secret code name for Mom when she was trying to fake being okay for people despite feeling miserable. "Sunny Backdrop," he would say to Circa, as a signal that both of them would do what they could to minimize Mom's stress.

"You've got his sense of humor for sure," Mom said, handing the picture back to Circa. Then she dabbed her face on her sleeve and turned back to business.

Flipping through the checkbook, Mom let out a sigh as Circa walked back across the room.

"Circ," Mom said, "I— I mean, things— I mean, well, my schedule is going to have to change a bit now. I'll need to do a lot more portraits in order to make ends meet, especially since the restoration half of the business will be closed down."

Circa's heart began to race. She steadied herself down onto Dad's chair. That was not a Sunny Backdrop thing for Mom to say.

"That means this space might have to change a bit too. . . . We may need to sell some of this equipment," Mom continued, her words soft, but cutting as barbed wire. Circa felt breathless. The big, empty wall at Maple Grove flashed into her mind. The stories out of reach. She gazed at the flaky insides of Aunt Ruby's once color-filled jars and thought about Dad's beautiful work drying up just like that.

"But what about the Memory Wall?" she said.

Mom's shoulders dropped with the added weight of the question. "I guess they'll have to find someone else to do it," she said.

"But it's not someone else's thing. It's *our* thing," argued Circa. "And no one else can do that stuff like Dad does . . . I mean, like he did."

"Then they might have to make other plans," said Mom.

"But they *can't* do that," said Circa. "What about Miss Rempy and Maki and Hank and the others? All those pictures that were going to help them remember?"

"I don't know what they'll do," said Mom, clapping the checkbook shut. "But I just can't worry about that right this minute, sweet girl."

Circa suddenly felt herself spinning into a panic, like the whole picture of what used to be was fast crumbling into yellowed paper bits at her feet. Unrestorable bits. She turned to look at the picture of Dad again, for any inspiration that might be left there. She found a faint flicker of an idea in the eyes behind those purple glasses.

"Then let *me* worry about it," Circa said with such conviction she surprised herself.

"About what?" said Mom.

Circa swiveled around. "Dad's been teaching me stuff for a long time," she said. "Let *me* do the work."

Mom sat still in the thick silence.

"But, Circa, you don't know enough—" she said. "You can't expect— I mean, you're a child."

"I can at least try, right?"

"No, Circa."

"Why?"

"Because . . . because you just can't."

"Please, Mom," she begged. "Just let me *try*."

"Circa, doing photo restoration requires a lot more than being able to draw silly glasses on somebody," Mom said. "I'll allow you to use Dad's computer to tinker around if you want, but the answer is no on the Maple Grove thing."

"But why? You won't even have to go up there," said Circa. "I can pick up the pictures myself."

"Circa. I can't do this right now. I said *no*," Mom said, fanning her face with an envelope.

"Okay, fine," said Circa, spinning back toward the desk indignantly. "Then I'll just *tinker*."

Mom's *no* had dropped like a heavy curtain between them, only feeding Circa's need to prove herself. As soon as Mom turned her attention back to her paperwork, Circa pulled up

26

the old soldier picture that Dad had opened for her weeks ago. She had not gotten up the nerve to work on it after he'd left that day. Only now, she replayed Dad's words again in her head. *The day you can seamlessly add a fresh person into a pic, then you can do just about any kind of photo restoration.*

So Circa set to work adding a baby into the picture. With fierce determination, she copied features from their own Monroe family pictures and pasted them in with the soldiers. Then she painted, sized, blurred, smudged, and clicked UNDO a hundred times until she thought her brand-new little Shopt person actually looked very human, somewhat cute, and maybe even printable. Circa swiftly printed the picture, only to feel utter disappointment when she held it in her hands. It looked like a baby sure enough. But it was so very obvious that someone had faked it. So very opposite of seamless. So opposite of Dad. She was embarrassed to see she'd even forgotten to put a right arm on him. Circa crumpled the picture and let it fall at her feet. She turned to see if Mom was aware of what she'd done, only to find her curled up on her side in the beanbag chair. Clearly, the glue was not holding. Mom was coming apart, and thanks to Circa's failure, so was Dad's legacy.

Circa closed the old soldier picture. Then she closed Dad's portrait.

Would you like to save your changes? it said.

No, she clicked.

Then Circa gazed at the blank background of the monitor, wondering how in the world she and Mom were going to make it. Wishing she could just curl up inside this empty, Dad-shaped hole in the room and disappear. Longing for the power to change other things with just the click of a mouse.

Dad leaving to deliver the reunion photo. UNDO.

Tornado. UNDO.

That tree, that stupid Jeep-wrecking tree at the park. UNDO.

All of April twenty-seventh. UNDO.

Every last bit of this. UNDO.

Surely after that whole mess of undoing, Circa Monroe would no longer be rocking herself nauseous in an office chair that was too big for just her. And Laurel Monroe wouldn't be crumpled up in the middle of tear-spattered bills and sympathy cards on the studio floor. And most important of all, Todd Monroe would not be just a collection of ashes inside a wooden box on top of a computer monitor. Instead, he'd be right here filling these chair dents and reminding his daughter that one forty-nine a.m. is oh so very past her bedtime.

Paper Flowers

It seemed like mere moments later when the sunshine streaming through Circa's window stirred her awake. She was surprised to be lying in her own bed, since she had absolutely no recollection of walking to her room. In fact, the last thing she remembered were the hazy letters of Dad's keyboard as her head bobbed over it. How *had* she gotten upstairs? Circa wondered. It couldn't have been Mom that did it. Mom always had to ask Dad to help her with carrying even just a few sticks of firewood. "A little help over here, sweetie?" she'd always say after a little grunt of effort, and Dad would come running.

Circa rolled over. She suddenly felt so very alone. It was the first morning in weeks she'd woken up without Nattie one sleeping bag over. The Boones had been so generous to let them stay until the shock of Dad's accident had worn off. In that time, Circa had grown accustomed to the routine at the Boones' house. A home-cooked breakfast every morning, the noise of a busy bustling family all day long, and a best friend who pretended not to notice when Circa needed to sneak home for a cry. All these things had made the giant gaping hole in her heart feel a little more bearable. In fact, many things had been more bearable at the Boones', Circa realized now that there was no smell of bacon wafting up the stairs.

Circa climbed out of bed. Her head was swimmy with exhaustion as she padded to the bathroom across the hall. Tired or not, she had to get herself ready as quickly as possible. Circa had something to prove, and today was going to be the day to do it.

Circa quickly brushed her teeth, wiped her face with the cleanest washcloth available, and then smoothed her thick brown hair over into its usual sloppy side ponytail. She hurried back to her room to get dressed in the one thing that could do without ironing, then finished off with sandals and a small purse slung across her. She felt a sense of victory when the purse fell into place right as Mom's phone sounded its wake-up crickets down the hall. As Mom fumbled around to silence the chirps, Circa quickly made her way down the steps and through the foyer, passing sympathy plants in various stages of shrivel.

Circa had been dreading going into the kitchen, the source of all that stink. She held her breath, pushed the narrow doors open, and threw as much fuzzy fruit and green bread as she could in the garbage before exhaling. Then she checked the fridge. There was the milk. That definitely had to go. But then where was all the rest of the food they'd left behind? Almost everything was already gone. Maybe Mrs. Boone packed them all up, Circa figured, as she found herself one nonmushy pear on the door of the fridge.

From above, she could hear the squeak of the water turning on upstairs and felt relieved that Mom was okay enough to get up and shower. Despite staying bedded down at the Boones' for the last two Sundays, church was something her family didn't like to miss, because the people there were always so sweet to them, especially when Mom was having a hard time. Aside from the doctor visits and a couple of attempts at grocery shopping when Dad was in bed with the flu, church was the only place other than the Boones' that Circa had ever known Mom to go. If Mom ever felt panicky there, she could just go sit in the room at the back of the auditorium where people rocked their babies. The Cry Room, they called it. Circa felt sure that's where they'd be sitting this morning.

Even for Circa, church was a place so different from school, where kids whispered junk about her family and how weird they were for "hiding out" inside their studio most of the time. It didn't help things any that Circa also had a funny name and only one pinkie finger, small facts that had added up to a measure of difficulty in finding friends at Wingate Elementary School. Normally to Circa, it would be heaven that all the schools around had closed early for the summer because of the damage in the areas where buses ran. But she would have gladly been a fifth grader all year-round if it would take back that storm.

Circa grabbed the sharpest knife from the wood block and tried to cut the pear into a stack of thinnest-evers. Mom had left the air conditioner running all night long to make things less musty, and the house was awful chilly for May. Not to mention awful quiet without Dad's precoffee Sunday morning hymn, a racket that Circa had never really appreciated before this moment.

"Ooch!" Circa winced. At the end of the pear, she'd nicked her own thumb just enough to produce a squirt of blood that made her go a little woozy. Composing herself, she carefully wrapped a paper towel around the cut and carried her breakfast into the dark studio, which was even colder than the rest of the house. Circa didn't turn on the lamps in the studio, but instead woke up Dad's computer and ate the pear slices by the monitor's glow until the tiny red soak-through spot on her thumb wrap grossed her out too much to finish. Then, with her good hand, she set to work.

Circa wanted to try another Shopt addition to a photo, and definitely something easier than yesterday's soldier baby. Instead of exploring Dad's files, Circa decided to start on something fresh. She looked around the studio and found Mom's small point-and-shoot camera. The camera was a little hard to maneuver with the paper towel on her thumb, but Circa managed to snap a picture out the studio's front window, a great upward shot of the pine tree growing next to her bedroom.

Circa popped Mom's memory card into the slot on Dad's computer and opened her picture up in Photoshop. Then she began to work. Quickly, but carefully, Circa added the one thing she thought she could pull off in a short amount of time. She added a scraggly nest full of blue speckled eggs tucked into a gap in the top of the tree. This time, her addition was scruffy where it needed to be scruffy and smooth where it needed to be smooth, and somehow, just seeing that little Shopt nest in there made the dim, lump-throated day a bit more bearable. She even started to conjure up a Shopt story about how those eggs had been laid by some kind of time-traveling bird, when suddenly, she heard Mom bellowing upstairs.

"Circa! Get up and get ready, okay?"

Circa didn't bother to tell Mom she was already dressed and in the studio. She just kept improving the little nest right up until she heard Mom thunking down the steps in her flats. Then she rolled the chair backward to get a good look at her work. Her little addition was nestled enough, it was pretty enough, and, on top of all that, it actually looked *real*.

"This one will do the trick, Dad," she whispered, then clicked PRINT. She fanned the ink dry, folded the picture over twice, and stuffed it into her purse. It would be kind of soothing to have it along with her for the morning.

"Circ? You coming?" Mom called again.

Circa quickly closed the nest picture without saving it, deleted the tree pic from the memory card, and returned the card to Mom's camera. Then she walked into the kitchen, startling Mom when she entered from the direction of the studio. Mom sat at the table steeping a little teabag into a cup of hot water. Circa noticed that her hair was pulled back soaking wet into a ponytail. She'd put on a little bit of lipstick, but no other makeup, and her eyes were bloodshot and swollen all around. It was clear Mom was going to have a hard time being Sunny Backdrop today.

"I was just messing around in the studio," said Circa, trying not to stare.

"Okay, baby," Mom said, hovering her eyes over the steam. "You look nice this morning."

"Thanks," said Circa, hearing a light rapping at the front door.

"Oh me," said Mom. "Circa, will you . . . never mind," she said, patting her damp face with a napkin.

"It's okay," said Circa. "I got it."

Circa made her way to the front of the house, closing the narrow double doors between the kitchen and foyer behind her. She opened the front door and breathed a sigh of relief when she saw that it was Nattie. Sweet Nat, standing on the front porch holding an armload of paper flowers.

Nattie smiled and held the flowers out to Circa, who noticed right away that they'd been crafted out of at least a dozen kinds of old wrapping paper. "It's kind of like a whole year's worth of leftover happy," Nattie said cheerfully, looking fancy as ever in her favorite church hat. Circa had never known Nattie to not be pretty. Especially today, the way her dark skin contrasted against the pale yellow of her dress. Circa recognized it as Nattie's Easter dress, but modified somehow. Like she had snipped off a doodad here and there to make it more suited for a regular Sunday.

"These are amazing," Circa said, grabbing the bunch of flowers and catching herself almost sniffing them. "Thanks, Nat. Mom'll like these too." She stepped inside to grab a vase from the living room, plunged the flowers into it, and set the arrangement in the middle of the coffee table.

"Want to walk to church?" asked Nattie, shuffling her shiny white sandals around. "It's real nice outside."

Nattie was four months younger than Circa but was an inch taller and far wiser on any given day. The two of them had been in class together since kindergarten, but in the fall, Nattie would be going to the North Georgia Academy of Science Charter School, which Mr. Boone had said would be better for Nattie's "fascination with the intricacies of the earth." In

Mrs. Boone's words, it was because gophers made her laugh and grammar made her cry.

Circa considered Nattie's walking idea a no-brainer. Some fresh air sure would be a welcome thing.

"We don't have to talk a lot if you don't want to," added Nattie.

That sweetened the deal even more. Circa wasn't up for much conversation.

"Hey, Mom, can me and Nat walk?" Circa called out toward the kitchen doors.

"I suppose so," Mom said. "Just be careful and be on time."

Circa pressed on her purse to check on the folded nest picture.

"Hi, Mrs. Monroe," said Nattie to the double doors. "And bye."

"Bye, Mom," said Circa.

"Love you girls," said Mom. "See you there."

Circa and Nattie stepped outside and headed up Delp Street in the direction of the old town square. Circa knew that such a sunshiny, beautiful day should make her feel better, but as they moved along, she felt more and more like it was everybody else's beautiful day *but* hers. At first they walked in silence, just like Nattie had offered. Then after they passed Nattie's house and a couple more, Circa became vaguely aware of her friend asking a question, only she wasn't quite sure what it had been. She was distracted by how all the giant oak trees around had thickened up green and lush. It was normally such a beautiful thing, but today it somehow felt threatening, like they were flexing their muscles at her. Like they all might have been brothers to the one that got Dad.

"How was last night?" Nattie said a little louder. "My mom wanted me to ask if you guys need her to get some groceries or anything."

"Oh. It was okay I guess," said Circa. "Kinda weird, though. I think it's just going to take my mom a while to get used to doing house things."

Circa looked to the sky, wishing she could find a trumpet-shaped cloud. "Plus the fridge is empty, so maybe yes on the groceries," she said.

The entire walk to church was only four blocks, made up of mostly sidewalk, then a drainage ditch with a little bridge over it, and a railroad track. Nattie was kind enough to fill in the many empty spaces in conversation with random wildlife facts. Because it was the only noncussing channel on their TV other than the one with the snoozy antique specials, Nattie was allowed to watch as many shows as she wanted on the Animal Wonders Network. On any other day Circa might have teased Nattie that part of the reason she knew about outdoorsy stuff is because of the goofy crushes she got on all the swamp-exploring, cave-diving hosts of those nature shows. Today though, hearing about how the hummingbird has the largest brain of all birds and how very rare it was to find a nine-spotted ladybug was just the sort of temporary distraction that Circa needed.

Nattie stopped along a fence to grab a plump white honeysuckle bloom, eased the stringy part out the bottom, and held it out to Circa to slurp the tiny clear bead of sweet. Circa plucked one honeysuckle after another to try to return the favor, but had a hard time finding a juicy one. So Nattie found another one for her.

"Hey. Pretty cool we don't have to see Chad Betts's mean face, thanks to—" Nattie stopped herself short. "I don't mean the storm is cool. Just the no school part . . . oh . . . you know what I mean, right?"

"Yeah, Nat, I know. Extra cool for you. You won't have to see him ever again."

Circa's gaze dropped to the ground. It had only just occurred to her that part of the unofficial storm damage included that terrible windy day being the last official time she'd get to walk home from school with her best friend.

"I guess when you start your new school, you guys will have to drive," she said.

"Let's not even talk about it," said Nattie. "Sorry I even mentioned all that, Circ. I'm a major shmoo."

"It's okay, Nat. I knew what you meant."

"Besides," Circa said, "it's good that summer started early, because now I'll have more time for the Maple Grove project."

"Oooh," said Nattie. "That wall of pictures thing? You mean *you* get to work on it?"

"On the whole rest of it," said Circa. "My dad's been teaching me how."

"Wow, cool, Circ," said Nattie as she waved a mosquito off. "I bet you'll do great."

"Thanks," said Circa, smiling at the big drip of sweet that was Nattie. She thought about how extra tough it was going to be in the fall when she had to move to middle school without Nattie by her side. She'd still have her close by at home and church, but for so many reasons now, that just didn't seem like enough.

The girls walked the fake-grassy carpet up to the church building's main entrance.

"Nat?" said Circa.

"Yeah?"

"What in the world is a *shmoo*?"

The two of them squeezed through the glass doors in a stifled fit of giggles.

The cash prize for the most flapjacks eaten at the country store was five dollars. Sadly, Flora Mae had been cursed with a tiny stomach. Not one for giving up, Flora thought of her own contest. Fortunately, she simultaneously befriended a robot drifter named Jimbob 3000, who was content with doing nothing all day except for keeping Flora Mae's tower of flapjacks from tipping over. Three hours later, discouraged by the lack of interest in her contest and suffering a fierce headache, Flora ate the stale flapjacks and sold Jimbob for five dollars to the proprietors of the dangerously leaning Umbrella Rock.

5

The Boy

After that, church services were a two-hour blur of hugs and nods and lingering eye contact from adults who'd never spoken directly with Circa before that summer. Circa was glad to sit in the room at the back with Mom this time. It was a good break from the overdose of pity. Plus, this time Nattie's family was in there with them, which made the three-pewed room full of snoring old people and crying brand-new people a lot more pleasant. Mrs. Boone leaned over and said she'd bring some milk and bread and eggs over to the house tomorrow. Circa secretly hoped she might even throw in a peanut butter pie.

Once worship service was over, everyone filed out into the lobby like always, only this time Circa stood quiet and still next to Mom, who seemed to lean against her daughter more and more with every handshake. This must be what it's going to be like for me to be the rock instead of Mom, thought Circa. As she irritably shuffled through a stack of tracts on the visitors' desk, the secretary from the church office approached Mom and handed her a baggie with what looked to be an old photograph inside.

"It's the original church building in 1929, on the very day it was completed," the lady explained to Mom. "I'd told your husband I would give it to him this week to include on the wall at Maple Grove. It's got a few small worn spots, but it should still fit in nicely with the photos he's already spruced up." She held on to Mom's hand and patted it. "I'm so sorry for your loss," she said. "I'm grateful that the wall will be a showcase of Mr. Monroe's legacy."

Circa felt a sudden glimmer of hope for the project. She watched Mom's face. Unfortunately, Mom's expression remained flat.

"Thank you for the thought," Mom responded. "But you should probably hang on to this."

She handed the baggie back to the lady. Circa felt a twitchy urge to grab it.

"I'm sorry to say that Studio Monroe won't be involved with the Memory Wall after all," Mom explained. "There was so much still left undone when the accident happened."

"Oh," said the lady, fanning herself with the photo. "Oh my. It seems that I've been terribly insensitive. Please forgive me. I thought—"

"It's okay," said Mom. "Really. It's okay."

Mom nudged Circa slightly as if to herd her across the lobby. Then, at once, Circa was overwhelmed with a sense that her arms were no longer under her brain's control. She reached out and snatched the baggie from the woman's hand. "I'll keep it," she said.

Mom stiffened. The secretary blushed and gently took the photo right back. "That's all right, sweetie; it was rude of me to assume. I'll just tuck it back into the church scrapbook."

"No!" Circa raised her voice. She grabbed at the baggie again, squeezing it so firm this time, she felt the little picture crinkle inside. "CAN'T. YOU. HEAR. ME? I. SAID. I'LL. KEEP. IT," she demanded.

Even Circa was surprised at her own words. Apparently her arms weren't the only thing she'd lost control of. Mom stood there looking stunned. And so did the woman, and so did the Boones. Why in the world did everyone in the whole lobby have to stand there looking stunned? Circa thought as she let go of the photo. Then, of all places, of all moments, it happened. For the first time all weekend, she broke down in tears.

The woman backed away with the retrieved wrinkled baggie, saying again more quietly, "That's okay, hon. Like I said, it was rude of me to ask. I'll just return it to the scrapbook. Don't you fret. No harm done."

"Circa Monroe, you are riding home in the car," said Mom under her breath, taking hold of Circa's elbow and leading her toward the exit like she was escorting some kind of major shmoo. A shmoo who'd just totally lost it in front of her mother *and* her best friend. A shmoo who'd just crumpled an old photo *and* talked ugly to an old lady. A shmoo who could think of nothing more than how her dad would have hated *every*thing about all that.

Circa felt herself quivering at the knees. Nattie shuffled to catch her and Mom at the door.

"Um, can I ride too, Mrs. Monroe?" she said. "So me and Circa can talk some more?"

Mom looked from Nattie to Circa to Mrs. Boone and then back to Nattie. "I suppose so," she said with a sigh.

"Nattie," said Mrs. Boone. "You just be sure and come on home after that, so you can help me with Durret while I make lunch, you hear?"

"Yes, ma'am," said Nattie, following Mom and Circa out the door.

Mom grabbed Circa's arm again as Nattie climbed into the backseat. "Look, I know you're hurting, Circa," she whispered. "We all are. But you cannot be acting like that to people who care about you, okay?" Circa noticed that for such fussing, Mom had a good dose of pity in her voice. The two of them joined Nattie inside the car, where Circa buckled her seat belt and dried her face on her sleeve.

"Okay?" Mom repeated.

Circa nodded as she stared at a stain on the floor mat. Nattie began to chew on her longest braid. Circa felt a bit sorry for her friend, who surely already regretted coming along.

"I could have fixed that picture," Circa said, super quiet, knowing full well that she was on thin ice.

"You almost *ruined* that picture," said Mom, pulling to a stop at the lowering railroad crossing arm.

Nattie made a *quit it before you get in big trouble* face at Circa.

"Can we maybe go visit the Maple Grove people today?" asked Circa.

Since church services were pretty much the extent of her outings, Mom had never been to Maple Grove. But Circa secretly hoped it might sway her a bit if she got to see that empty wall and meet those people and want to help them reach their stories. To feel the Dadness that was still there.

"Not today," Mom said.

"Then when?" said Circa.

The train seemed to last forever. Mom put the car into park.

"Forgive me, Nat," she said. "But I have something serious to say to Circa right now."

"Yes, ma'am," said Nattie, without even dropping the braid from her mouth.

"Circa, listen to me," Mom said. "You know I loved your dad's life more than my own, just like I love your life more than my own. I don't want all of that stuff to go away either, but I simply have no choice about it. I've got nothing against the people at Maple Grove, Circa. You know that. I pray for them every day." Mom squeezed hard at the steering wheel. "But I'm not Dad enough to fill those shoes, Circa," she said. "And neither are you."

Mom looked at Circa in the rearview mirror. "And that's all right," she said.

But it's not all right, thought Circa. It was far from all right. How did Mom know Circa couldn't fill Dad's shoes if she wouldn't even let her stick her toe in?

Circa stared out the window at the heaps of coal zooming by. She imagined the splendid Shopt graffiti Dad could have added to that train. "But I don't want to *be* him," she said stubbornly. "I just want to be *like* him."

Mom puffed out her cheeks like she was full up with something. Nattie chewed a second braid.

"Circa Monroe, you are eleven years old," Mom said. "You deserve to be a kid . . . to have recess and kick a ball around and wiggle your loose molars. That's your job. You are just not able to pick up where your father left off, nor should you feel like you have to."

Circa felt the ugliness welling up inside her again. She wanted to say, *Well, somebody's got to pick up where he left off because you're sure not gonna.* But then she looked at Nattie, who was about to squirm right out of her seat, and she softened her tune a bit.

"Not *have* to," Circa protested. "*Want* to."

Drop it drop it drop it, signaled Nattie. But Circa was unfazed. She unsnapped her purse and pulled out the edited picture. As the train rushed past, she unfolded the photo and held it up for Mom to see.

"Bet you can't find the Shopt thing," she challenged.

Nattie was so puzzled she froze her chewing. Then Mom sighed big and pointed right to the top of the tree.

"The nest, baby. The nest," she said before the caboose could even pass them by. And with those measly five words alone, a thousand-pound realization came crashing down hard on Circa. That nearly all the good stuff in her life was speeding away from her even faster than that train.

As the striped arm went up, signaling that it was safe to cross over into the rest of the Monroes' miserable life, an oblivious Nattie poked her friend on the leg. "Shopt?" she mouthed.

"Nothing," said Circa. She'd never shared Shopt stuff with Nattie before, or with anyone for that matter, because Dad made her promise she would keep it in the family. He didn't want anyone outside the studio to know about the Shopt stuff, in case customers found out and thought he was goofing on them or their ancestors. Besides, Circa sure didn't feel like explaining herself under these miserable circumstances. She suddenly felt pinched by two guilts at once, for almost letting the secret slip in front of Nattie and, in turn, for excluding her

45

best friend in the first place. In utter frustration, Circa tore the photo to bits and let them drop at her feet, vowing inside to plant herself in Dad's office chair and set to work again as soon as this wretched drive was over.

There was so much sadness and quiet stuffed into the car, Circa thought Nattie might never ask to ride anywhere with them again. Then, suddenly, at the end of the drive, something happened that instantly distracted the three passengers from their funk. They saw it as soon as they turned onto Delp Street. There, climbing clumsily out of the Monroes' backyard over their own wooden fence, was a stranger. A boy, who struggled hard to free his shirt from between the planks.

"Mom," said Circa, her heart racing. "Look."

"I see him," Mom said. "What in the world is he doing?"

To Circa's surprise, when the boy freed his sleeve and caught sight of the car, he didn't run. Instead, he just froze there by the fence like it didn't even occur to him to take off. The lanky boy just stood right there looking all worn out and sweaty, like some guy who'd cut the grass and was waiting for his glass of lemonade and a twenty dollar bill.

"Circa, do you know that kid?" said Mom.

"Uh-uh."

"Nattie?" she said.

"No, ma'am. Never seen him."

"Then what was he doing in our backyard?" said Mom, riding right on past the driveway.

Then, as if the car was on some kind of autopilot, Mom drove it all the way around the block. When they came back around, the boy had sat down on the front porch step, settled in like he'd been waiting there for an hour. Circa wondered what Mom was expecting to see the second time they approached the house. Like if she hoped to find that the boy had figured out he was at the wrong place and skedaddled, or maybe even that they'd imagined him all along.

By the time Mom finally pulled into the driveway, slow as she could make the car crawl, Circa had been able to observe quite a bit about the mystery kid's appearance. Wearing a green-sleeved baseball shirt, torn jeans, and a great deal of dirt, the boy sat facing forward on the doorstep with his knees bent up high and his elbows planted on them, his arms crossed in front to make a resting place for his chin. He had longish sun-bleached hair that lay kind of wavy across one eye, and he looked as if his one and only task was to keep tabs on the few cars that passed this way and that on Delp Street.

"He must be lost," Mom said. "That's all I can figure."

"He's kind of wild looking," said Nattie, tucking a moist braid behind her ear. "Like a swamp boat pilot or something."

Circa wanted to pinch Nattie for saying such a ridiculous thing, but instead she stayed quiet, finding herself more and more captivated by the strange boy's presence.

"I wonder," she said, pressing a tear-striped cheek against the car window, "if maybe he's here on purpose, Mom."

Often when we are distracted by other things, we tend to leave our container of magic lidless and unattended on the front step. Usually, nothing comes of this. But every now and then, a little something catches the wind and lands in the wrong, or maybe even the right, hands.

Now don't you go saying you haven't been warned.

6

Miles

Mom struggled nervously to free the keys from the ignition. Nattie arranged the chewed braids back behind the neat ones. Circa stared out the window at the porch. The stranger there looked down at his hands and rubbed them together in a slow-motion dusting off. Circa noticed there was a backpack slumped behind him.

"Well, I guess let's get on out," said Mom, unbuckling. "He doesn't really look dangerous."

The girls followed her lead, climbing out and approaching slowly up the walk. As soon as they got within speaking distance of the stranger, Circa considered looking away to save the boy the embarrassment of people seeing him tremble, but for some reason she couldn't take her eyes off him. The boy quickly pushed his hands up under his legs to steady them.

"Hi," said Mom, in a gentle, puzzled way. "Are you lost? Can we help you with something?"

Nattie was suddenly contemplating her own shoes, but Circa fanned out from behind Mom just enough to study the boy's face. She couldn't put her finger on what it was, but something about him was familiar. Not like kid-at-your-school familiar, but more like a foggy, weird déjà-vu kind of thing. Like that animal instinct stuff Nattie talks about.

"Yes, ma'am. And I hope you can," the boy said. His voice rasped like he was coated with dust on the inside too. As if he'd either been talking nonstop for a week, or hardly at all. The boy looked up at Mom and had to squint from the blazing sun. It made him look like he was in pain. Or maybe he really *was* in pain. Circa had never seen someone look like he needed so many things all at once.

"Come on in the house," Mom said. "Let's get you a drink of water, and then we'll talk."

As Mom reached out a hand to help the boy to his feet, Circa greeted him with a slight nod and slighter smile. Nattie glanced up and gave a bashful shrug. Mom fumbled for her house key as the boy picked up his pack and slung it over a shoulder. It looked as though Mom had caught a case of the trembles from their unexpected guest.

"Nattie," Mom said, "your mother said she wanted you home right away to help with your brother while she makes lunch. How about you run on over?"

Nattie lingered for a few seconds, studying the mystery boy from head to toe and back up again.

"*Okay*, Nattie?" said Mom.

"Oh, um . . . okay." Nattie snapped out of it. But before she left the porch, she tugged at Circa's sleeve and leaned in.

"You better call me later," she said.

Circa nodded.

"Bye, uh, everybody," Nattie said, walking slowly across Circa's yard toward her own.

"See ya," murmured Circa, herself now mesmerized by the weary stranger's movements. The boy leaned against a column, patient, like an old dog waiting to be let in. Even leaning, he was a good head taller than Circa. She couldn't help noticing the smell of hot car vinyl and Windex around him.

Mom pushed the key into the front door at the very same moment a surprised yelp came from the front yard. Circa turned to witness her best friend in the midst of a stifled dance of disgust. Nattie exclaimed in a most flustered manner that a bird perched high in the tree next to Circa's bedroom window had just freshly "done his business" on the brim of her church hat. Then, with one last humiliated glance at the spectators, Nattie ran the rest of the way home, her Bible and purse clutched tight in one arm and the poor hat held out far as the other arm could stretch. Circa exchanged a *yeeks* face with Mom and then watched to see how the boy would react. He was unfazed, though, focused on the opening door.

Inside the Monroe house, the air was cool and damp and still smelling like an abandoned grocery store flower department.

"You can set your backpack anywhere," said Mom, but the boy just held tight to his pack and shuffled through the foyer, clumsily bumping some of the shriveled petals off a daisy. Nervous about what he might be hiding, Circa tried to decipher the bumps and bulges of the backpack as they made their way single-file into the kitchen. She wondered what in the world he'd been doing in their backyard. It was such a jungle. No one had even been back there in a month.

Mom pulled a chair out from the kitchen table and told the boy to have a seat. Circa settled into her usual spot while Mom unstacked two plastic cups.

"I'm Mrs. Monroe," she said, setting down water for the kids. "And this is Circa."

Circa realized that she hadn't yet spoken a single word to the stranger.

"Hi," she said, nodding shyly toward him, suddenly embarrassed by her sadness-swollen face spotlighted under the kitchen light. But the boy had such a glazed-over look of his own, if he'd noticed her puffs and streaks, he sure didn't seem to care.

"I'm, um . . . my name's Miles," he said, like he wasn't real certain of it. He turned the cup up and downed his water in three gulps. Mom studied the boy as he drank. Before he could even set the cup down, she was swiping it from him to refill.

"Miles?" she said. "Do we know you from somewhere?"

"I don't know. *Do* you?" asked Miles. Were it not for the hopeful look on his face, Circa would have thought he was being a smart aleck.

Mom handed him his second cup of water. "Miles *what*?" she said.

"What?" he gurgled through his sip.

"What's your last name?" she said.

"Oh," Miles said, putting down his cup. "That."

The water dripping down the boy's dirty chin made tiny mud trickles. As the two, maybe three, of them waited for an answer to Mom's question, Miles quickly surveyed every inch of the Monroe kitchen, darting his eyes across each dirty bowl, musty dishrag, and empty canister. Circa wondered if he was scoping it out to steal something, if that backpack was maybe full of someone else's silverware. She finished off her own water, and then secretly stared at Miles over the rim of her cup. Judging by his knobbly tallness and his cracked voice, the boy seemed to Circa to be thirteenish. He had at least a couple layers of dirt on him, mosquito bites on every finger, and that kind of sunburn that's already peeled, letting the new shiny skin show through.

"My last name, well, uh," he said. Miles squirmed, letting the backpack slide off his lap to the foot of his chair. To Circa's relief, it didn't clank.

"It's just," he stammered. "It's just that I really don't know that."

Circa's still-raised cup pressed against the top of her nose.

Without turning her attention from the boy, Mom reached toward the counter behind her for a decent piece of fruit.

"Circ, you want something to eat?" she asked.

"No thanks," said Circa, her voice echoing in her cup. "I'll have something later."

Mom grabbed up a whole pineapple from a basket, sawed it crudely into wedges with a bread knife, and sat down at the table with a few pieces on a paper towel. "Miles, are you all right?" she said. "Are you injured in some way?"

The boy nodded, but Circa didn't know if he was nodding to the all-right thing, or to the hurt thing. He looked like he was trying to figure it out himself.

"Um. Can I have the pear instead?" he said. "The one in the fridge?"

Mom and Circa puzzled at each other. Mom leaned back in her chair to check the refrigerator. "There isn't a pear," she said, "And anyway, how would you—"

The boy's face went even redder. "I meant, *if* there's one in the fridge," he said.

Circa got chills all over. She knew good and well there had been a pear in the fridge before that morning. The question was, how did *he* know that?

Mom put her chair back down on four legs. "Miles," she said slowly. "What were you doing in our backyard?"

Circa slid to the edge of her seat, as Miles hung his head.

"Living there," he said.

Circa's eyes grew wide.

Mom leaned in closer. "*Living* there?" she said.

"Yes, ma'am."

"For how long?"

"A few days."

"Why? How? Why?" stammered Mom. "Did you run away?"

"Sort of," said Miles.

Mom patted her pockets and looked around the room. "That settles it, then," she said. "We've just got to call your parents."

Miles nodded. "I think that would be good," he said.

Mom excused herself to find the phone. "Holler if you need me," she said, leaving Circa and the boy sitting in awkward silence. Miles tore into the hunk of pineapple, as Circa set down her cup and focused in on the wooden door directly opposite her. She briefly considered making a fast break for the studio, locking the door, and settling in at Dad's computer until Mom had all this weird boy stuff figured out. But one thought alone kept her glued to that chair.

"You're the raccoon," she said.

"Where have you guys been?" Miles said at the same time. "Wait. What? Raccoon?"

54

"The scuffling noises I heard," said Circa. "It was you."

Miles chewed longer than an aged pineapple needed chewing and gulped bigger than well-chewed pineapple required. "You were *here*?" he said, suddenly sounding frustrated.

Circa knew that her sudden suspicions about the boy should be giving her a major case of the heebie-jeebies, but for some strange reason they didn't.

"Did you sneak into our house?" she said. "And eat our casseroles?"

Miles nodded sheepishly. "I was only in the kitchen," he said. "And that bathroom there. That's all, I promise. And the casseroles were furry. So I ate the chips instead."

"No way," said Circa. "How did you get in here?"

"Why do you have so many dead flowers?" Miles said obliviously as he bit off hunks of rind that nobody eats unless they're starving.

"They were sent by people," said Circa. She was suddenly distracted from her own unanswered question by the inevitable sadness of what had to come next. "My dad was killed," she said, keeping her voice low. Circa glanced toward the foyer and could see Mom sitting at the bottom of the steps clearly *not* searching for a phone, but instead trying to keep herself together with what looked like slow breathing and whispered prayers. "A few weeks ago," she continued. "In the, um, ordeal." Lily, her nurse friend at Maple Grove, had taught Circa to use the word *ordeal* in place of just about any big, bad thing.

As expected, Miles looked puzzled.

"In the *storm*," Circa explained, wishing she could have left it as *ordeal*.

"Oh, man," said Miles. "That's awful."

"Mom and me have been up the street at my friend's house," said Circa. "But I came back over here some."

The boy struggled to wipe the bits of sticky pulp from his fingers.

"Hey," said Circa. "Don't mention the breaking-in thing to my mom, okay?" She slid him a napkin, quickly so he wouldn't notice her nonpinkie. "I don't think she'd handle it too well right now."

Circa hoped to goodness the boy had not been lying about being only in the kitchen and bathroom. Surely he'd not been messing around the studio.

"I didn't exactly break in," said Miles. "The back door was unlocked."

He wiped his mouth. "Hey, I remember something about that," he said. "Not about your dad . . . but about a storm."

Mom came back in with an ounce of composure and a phone.

"Sorry," she said, sitting back down and handing the phone to Miles. "I had to find one that still had some charge on it."

"Thanks," said Miles, but he didn't seem eager to dial for help. He held the phone tight in his palm and stared hard at it. He closed his eyes for a second. Then he glared at the little screen again.

"Sorry," he said, giving the phone right back. "I guess I was hoping you all might know the number." He looked searchingly at Mom, who drew in a deep breath and let it out without saying a word. Then he looked to Circa, who shook her head as slightly as possible, like a full-on "no" would crush him.

Mom clapped her hands together and stood up quick, startling both the kids.

"Know what I think?" she said. "I think you just need something more to eat, and then it will all come back to you." She instantly set to searching the cabinets.

"Some protein," she mumbled, knocking around old sardine cans and packets of noodle soup. Mom even searched the drawers, which were stuffed full of all the as-seen-on-TV gadgets Dad used to buy to make food into special shapes or to slice things even thinner.

"I don't get it," said Miles, resting the back of his head on the chair. "Something about this house feels so *same* to me."

"'Same' how?" said Circa, wondering if he was having the same weird déjà-vu that she'd felt on the porch.

"Not sure," he said. "It's like it matches up with a thought I can't find," he said.

"Here we go. Protein," said Mom, grabbing a jar of crunchy peanut butter from the last cabinet.

Circa imagined Miles playing a memory card game, the matching-pairs kind the folks would do up at Maple Grove. Mom held the bread bag upside down and dumped out the very last pieces, the end pieces, and plopped two sandwiches' worth of peanut butter on them.

"Maybe this looks kind of like your house," Mom suggested, spreading the peanut butter so fast and heavy, it tore the bread in half. She patched the sandwich together and put it on a paper plate for Miles. Then she poured the last of the orange juice into his cup. Circa noticed there was only an inch of juice, making the cup start out looking like somebody had already finished it.

Mom held her fingers over her mouth like Circa had only seen her do when she and Dad talked about serious things like overdue taxes and people with cancer. "Miles," she said, "how exactly did you *get* here?"

The boy rotated his sandwich again and again, maybe stalling, or maybe looking for the least globby part.

"It only goes back so far," he said.

"What does?" said Mom.

"How I got here."

Miles finally settled on a decent first bite.

"I came from that way," he said, all globby mouthed and pointing in the general direction of half the country. "I just walked until I couldn't walk anymore, and then this nice old man picked me up and drove me the rest of the way."

Another bite.

"I told him my name was Miles," he said. "Mainly because I saw it on a sign right after he asked me."

The boy took his one sip of juice.

"But I'm pretty sure it's not really my name."

He set down his sandwich, like the next part of his story couldn't be mixed with peanut butter.

"I came from someplace where people were screaming, and stuff was getting thrown around in the wind."

Circa and Mom darted a sidewise look at each other.

"A tornado?" said Mom.

"I think so," said the boy, running his hands through his hair nervously. Mom's jaw clenched tight, the way it had when she'd gotten the phone call about Dad. Her composure was leaking.

"*Ordeal,*" Circa said quietly, thinking it might help them all to switch to that word.

The boy's eyes got glossy with tears, but not enough to spill over.

"I don't—" he said, clearing some hurt from his throat. "I don't remember what came before that."

Silence. Circa stared at the brass knob on the studio door.

"What do you mean?" said Mom.

"I mean I don't remember *anything* before three weeks and four days ago," he said.

Mom looked desperately at the remains of the sandwich as if she was willing it to do some kind of magic on this kid. Comfort him, make him remember, make him go home.

"I don't understand," she said. "How have you gotten by? How have you been surviving out there?"

Circa knew the answer. Miles knew the answer. But the boy just looked at her and shrugged.

"Okay then . . . why did you stay here?" Mom asked. It came out like she was nearing the end of her rope. As much as that question needed answering, Circa knew they couldn't have been the words the boy was counting on.

Suddenly, he sat straight and toughened up a bit.

"Because I've been waiting for you guys to get home," he said. "Because I thought you might know who I am." Miles reached for the backpack on the floor. "All I've got to go on is eight dollars, two T-shirts, a pair of jeans . . . and *this*," he said.

Circa's heart beat faster as Miles unzipped the pack and reached his hand inside. He pulled out a crumpled paper and pressed it out flat against the table before sliding it over for Mom and Circa to see. It was water-smeared and badly creased, but Circa recognized it so immediately and so certainly, it nearly stole her breath.

The Linholt family reunion photo.

The last time she'd laid eyes on the print, it had been safe in a stack and held tight in her dad's arms.

7

The Reunion

Mom gasped. Circa snatched up the photo and took in every smeary inch of it.

"Where did you get this?" she said, no less spellbound than if she held the world's biggest diamond in her hands.

Miles rubbed at his temples. "I woke up in this grassy place near some bricks, under a bunch of leaves," he said. "All around, people were yelling and running and trees had fallen and tables were turned over and junk was everywhere. That picture there was on the ground right next to my face. So I grabbed it, crawled out fast as I could, and got out of there."

"The *reunion*," said Mom, frozen in shock. "You were at the reunion?"

Circa felt a jolt of hope course right through her. What if the boy had come all this way to give them a message from Dad?

"I saw the Studio Monroe address on there," Miles continued. "And hoped that they—*you* all—could maybe help me sort things out. I figured you were my best chance at some answers."

Circa flipped the print over to see the studio info stamped

on the back. Her spirit went limp from the dose of reality. The boy wasn't here with a message from Dad. He'd just followed a lousy address.

"I didn't even know there was a picture on the other side until I stopped for the night," he added.

"So why didn't you just call us?" said Mom.

"I did every chance I could," said Miles. "But you guys didn't answer."

"Oh. Yeah. I guess not," said Mom.

Miles continued. "I wandered from torn-up place to torn-up place, getting food and water from relief stands. I slept on whatever soft something I could find in the shade during the daytime heat and then walked along the highway at night. Then one day when I couldn't hardly stand the walking anymore, this old soldier guy offered me a ride," Miles said.

A tear let loose from Mom's jaw and landed on the table. Circa flipped the picture back over and pressed it out flat on her place mat as she summoned one last ounce of hope.

"Did you see my dad there? At the reunion?"

Miles rested his head on the table for a minute like his thoughts were heavy.

"I don't think so," he said. "It's really all so jumbled."

Mom laid her hand on Circa's. "Then what happened?" she said.

"The man dropped me off at the end of your street and left," said Miles. "He said he lived here in town, but that's all. He'd hardly said anything the whole way, and I couldn't wait to get out of the van because the guy had the heat blowing full blast. I was about to melt in there."

Mom took the picture from Circa. "Do you know any of these people?" she said. "Could the Linholts be your family?"

Circa leaned over Mom's arm to search for a young Miles in the picture.

Miles shook his head. "I don't know them," he said. "I don't know them at all."

Mom gave the picture right back again, as if it had begun to hurt her fingertips. Circa fixed her eyes on the image, wishing she were looking at the Shopt version instead. They could sure use a few pixels' worth of giant grinning potato right now.

Such a silence came over the table that all three of them jumped when the phone rang. Circa picked it up quick. She knew the number well.

"Hey, Nat," she answered quietly. "Um . . . I can't really talk right now.

"Yeah, everyone's sitting right here.

"Yes, we're okay.

"No, Nat.

"Really, Nat."

Circa rolled her eyes.

"Yes, I mean *really*, really.

"Nat, I gotta go."

Circa hung up. Mom had her elbows on the table, her chin resting on her fists. Miles tugged at his dirty ear. They were both looking at her.

"She wanted to know if he . . . if we saw her, um, get pooped on," Circa said.

Mom took the phone and nodded in the direction of the studio.

"Miles, there is a little bathroom over there to the left in that short hallway," she said. "You may go in there and clean yourself up a bit if you want."

"Okay, thanks," said Miles, gathering his backpack and shuffling into the bathroom that Circa knew good and well he was already acquainted with.

Mom touched Circa's arm and leaned in close. "Let's try not to get overupset about this," she whispered. "I'll just call the police and they'll come get the boy and take him to where he needs to be."

"To his home?" asked Circa.

Mom hesitated. "Of course," she said, dialing 911.

Mom then proceeded to tell Miles's story in a nervous, wandering way to the dispatcher. Within seconds, though, Circa noticed that her mother looked far more troubled than relieved.

"I don't see why you won't just send someone here," Mom argued.

"But we're not . . .

"We just . . .

"We can't . . .

"All right."

Mom hung up and swallowed big.

"They said he's got to go to the station for a report, but they can't come pick him up," she said. "They're too busy with storm stuff."

Mom had once told Circa about a technique she used to get through a panic attack. When she felt one washing over her, she'd picture a traffic light changing to red to remind her to stop that thought, and then turning green to tell her to push right through the panic. But right then, judging from the way she jumped up and began searching through the cabinet for her pills, she was ignoring all traffic signals. Circa could count on her fingers the times Mom had left the house to go anywhere but church, and now she was going to have to take a mystery kid to the police station.

"I bet the cops will know just what to do," consoled Circa, joining Mom at the counter. "Maybe his parents will even be there waiting for him."

Mom pushed hard to turn a childproof medicine bottle lid, oblivious to Circa's optimism. The hot water running in the bathroom made the pipes in the wall knock and clang.

"He must have some kind of amnesia," Mom said, tapping out the pink pill onto her palm.

Circa searched for the least mushy apple on the counter, her mind drifting toward that soft swivel chair waiting for her in the studio. If Mom and Miles had to go the police station, then she could finally get some time alone at the computer to practice her skills, without anyone to tell her all the things she wasn't capable of.

"He'll get his wits about him soon," Mom went on.

Mom will be okay, thought Circa. After all, if you can't be okay at a police station, where can you be?

"No big deal, right?" said Mom. She swallowed the pink pill.

It occurred to Circa that Mom never took her medicine before without Dad handing her a mug of milk and a sandwich, bagel, or hunk of cake to have it with. That is, until today. More than once, she'd asked Mom why she'd want to take a pill that made her so tired all the time. Mom would always just say, "Because tired is better than the alternative."

"We'll just drive him to the police station and come back

home," Mom said, scooping herself a sip of water from the faucet.

Circa coughed. *"We?"* she said.

Circa instantly saw the light turn red on her plans once again. She flung the apple hard into the trash can, making the plastic lid spin. Couldn't the boy have found a better place to bring his ordeal? Maybe to a family in need of an ordeal? Didn't he know that they might not have room for his *and* theirs?

"But Mom," she said, "you know, I was really hoping for some alone time at Dad's computer today. You know, to maybe get better and better so that I can maybe do the Memory—"

"All right, listen," Mom interrupted, glancing over at the reunion picture once more. "I don't mind if you mess around with your dad's Photoshop for fun, and we can maybe do for now without selling his equipment, but let's just not mention the Maple Grove project anymore, okay? I just can't—"

Mom's chin began to quiver as Circa realized something for the very first time. Plain and simple, Mom blamed Dad's work for killing him. That's why she couldn't bear to talk about, think about, or even go near it. Circa, on the other hand, believed with every shard of her broken heart that the exact opposite was true. That Dad's photo work was their best way to keep part of him alive. Only, at that moment, feeling unhinged by the raw hurt in her mom's eyes, Circa couldn't find the words to explain herself. So instead, Circa reached out for a big hug, and she made no promises.

"You know what, Mom?" she said. "Nurse, I mean *Miss* Lily at the Res— I mean at the *place*—she always said that Dad and I were like a rainbow up there."

"*You* know what, Circ? You're a rainbow right here," said Mom, mustering a weak smile as she smoothed Circa's hair away from her eyes. All Circa could think was how Mom's color-drained face was in dire need of some pinkening, like Dad had done for all those Linholts lying flat on their kitchen table, when a voice from across the room startled them both.

"Thank you," Miles said.

He stood in the doorway wearing a different, much less stained shirt. His hair was damp and arranged somewhat. His sunburn was even more shocking now, but something else struck Circa more than that. Now that the boy was wiped down, the familiarity she'd felt before was suddenly specific and undeniable. It was something about the way his eyebrows slanted up with the crinkle in between. It was a lot like her own father's.

"I feel a little better," he said. "Thanks."

Circa looked up at Mom, who didn't seem to be moved at all by the brow crinkle. Circa decided to chalk up the familiarity to her own grief.

"Miles, we're going to drive you up to the police station," said Mom.

Miles shot Circa a panicked look, like she'd totally ratted him out for using their house. He looked like he would have bolted out the door if there was any bolt left in him at all.

"To see if they can help you," said Circa.

"Have you gone to the police at all yet?" said Mom.

"No, not yet," said Miles. "I didn't really have much to tell them."

"Well, it seems we've got no choice but to start there," said

Mom, searching her purse for keys that were already in her hand.

"Okay," Miles said, hoisting his backpack. "But before that . . . can I please have an apple?"

"Sure," said Circa. She searched the baskets, finding the second-least-mushy apple as Mom turned away and whispered a silent prayer.

Toots (as in Tootsie) so looked forward to New Year's Day every year, when her three friends from the future (a.k.a. "Future Guys") would appear on the big console TV for a chat. From 1:23 to 1:53 p.m. mountain time, she'd sit down with a big bowl of Jiffy Pop, and the four of them would exchange tales of Hong Kong Phooey vs. Spider-Man, Neil Diamond vs. Coldplay, and Space Invaders vs. Minecraft. Decades later, Toots would have the triple joy of meeting the Future Guys in person. They would, after all, be her very own children.

8

Code 32

Getting Miles to the police station involved three false starts for Mom. Circa waited in the front seat of the car, and Miles sat in the back with his head leaned against the window. During Mom's third trip back into the house to get something she'd claimed to have forgotten, Circa finally spoke up.

"Just so you know, she might not be able to do this," she said to Miles. But then Mom came out for the last time. Without a word, but with a lot of drawn-out breathing and hands clamped tight on the wheel, she drove them straight into town.

The station had two white glass globes that said POLICE, one on either side of the front steps. The building sat directly across the street from the Maple Grove Residence, and Circa felt pulled over there like a magnet as she and Mom and Miles walked up to the big station doors.

"Can I just go to Maple Grove for a minute while you guys are here?" she whispered to Mom, who instantly shot her a look that said *no way*.

"Not by yourself," Mom said.

Well, then who in the world with? thought Circa. She glanced back over her shoulder across the road and saw scrawny Stanley, the teenage custodian, over in the iris garden sneaking a smoke. Stanley immediately locked eyes with Circa and blew her a big, exaggerated kiss. Much as Circa longed to go and visit the non-Stanley parts of Maple Grove, Mom had not been entirely unreasonable in her ruling. Dad had never let Circa go alone either, for the same smoochy reason.

The inside of the police station was nothing like what Circa had expected. She had imagined a swarming mob of criminals in various stages of fingerprinting and mug-shot making. A crowd of scowling people that, upon Miles's entry, would part in the middle to reveal a tearful little couple on a bench who waited hopefully for their boy, whatever his real name might be, to come back to them. But there were no criminals being booked. And worse yet, there were no tearful parents. Just a stumbling man wailing some kind of patriotic song and a whole bunch of people jabbering away on phones. Circa tried to make out what they were saying, but the conversations all merged into one big crazy story about looting, flooding, and fights in surrounding areas.

Mom stepped forward and explained their problem to a man called Sergeant Simms, who was wedged into a metal desk that squeezed him on all sides like it was more suited for a Sergeant Simms Jr. Circa and Miles stood behind quietly as Mom sat in a chair and went round and round with the cop about the police department not having a *Found* Person Report per se, just a *Lost* Person Report. How he figured they would have to classify this as a "Code 32." Most all of his unhelpful sentences came with finger quote marks and a *per se* tacked onto the end. Miles leaned slightly closer to Circa during the Mom-and-cop back-and-forth.

"Wonder what a Code Thirty-two is?" he said.

"I bet it just means special case," Circa said.

"Maybe it stands for 'Can I please just get me a honeybun and start this fail of a day over?'" whispered Miles. It was the first thing she'd heard come out of his mouth that wasn't tragic. He looked at Circa with the most subtle grin she'd ever seen on someone. And there was that Dad crinkle between his eyebrows again.

"Young man," called the desk sergeant. "Yes, you, could you please step around here and answer a few questions for me?"

Mom stood so that Miles could have her chair. Mom shrugged at Circa as if to say she'd tried her best to handle things right. Sergeant Simms began by taking a picture of Miles's face with a cell phone. Then, after asking Miles twenty questions that had little to no answers, the cop removed his cap and wiped the sweat from his bald head.

"Here's the deal," he said. "We're going to have to turn this over to Child Protective Services."

"Okay," said Mom, nodding.

"Only problem is, they are just as deep in the weeds, per se, as we are," said the sergeant. "And frankly, ma'am, I believe this boy needs medical attention, and soon."

"Yes, sir," she said. "I thought as much too."

"I strongly advise you to make the emergency room your next stop," he said.

Mom looked like she'd been splashed in the face.

"Next stop?" she said, wringing her hands. "But I thought you all would help him."

"Ma'am—" the sergeant began.

"Can't you find his family?" she said. "Someone's bound to be looking for him, right?"

"Ma'am," he began again. "All we can do right now is send out an electronic notification that this kid has shown up in Wingate. Beyond that, what would you have me do with him? I'm sure not gonna lock the poor guy up with Uncle Sam over there."

Across the room, the stumbling man was saluting every person who walked past. Mom had wrapped her purse strap so tight around her fingers, the tips were purple.

"Where I'm going with this," said the sergeant, "is that I imagine if you get this boy to the hospital and have him treated . . . by the time he's released, you probably will have heard back from Child Services."

Sergeant Simms shoved Miles's info into a big yellow envelope. "Plain and simple, ma'am, the boy needs a doctor, and now," he said. "Now beyond that, due to the recent storm damage stretching the district's resources so thin, per se, I'm going to rely on your compassion and goodwill until we find out who he belongs with."

Circa made it a point to look for Miles's crinkle every time the man threw out another *per se*, but the crinkling mood seemed to have left him as fast as it had come on.

"Who knows?" said the policeman. "Maybe the hospital will admit the boy, and his mama will show up just in time to pay the bill and whisk him away."

"Yes, who knows," said Mom. She turned to leave with Circa and Miles following behind.

"Just please let us hear something soon," Mom said, without even a look behind her. Circa wondered if she was speaking to the sergeant or to God.

A perfectly good tuba. A perfectly good chair. One could only hope that the perfectly good musician didn't meet the same fate.

9

PTSD

Another short, silent car ride later, Circa, Mom, and Miles arrived at the hospital. The packed-full parking lot made Circa think that the people who weren't at the police station might very well be at the emergency room instead. Inside, the big waiting room was a mint-green, flickery-lit place with cable news playing on TVs high up in every corner. Mom lingered for a minute in the doorway. When she went to pull a paper number from a dispenser, she walked as though every step was an effort. Circa wondered if that was what pushing through a panic looked like.

Mom returned with a number eighty-seven just as Circa and Miles found three empty chairs in a row. After they settled into the hard plastic seats, Circa took in the whole strange scene around her in stolen glances. In every direction, people of all ages were coughing violently, pressing their arms across their tummies, holding bandages over bleeding wounds, or keeping ice on wrapped-up hands or feet. A woman with a screaming baby was demanding to be seen and threatening to go over the check-in person's head. She quieted down only when a security guard approached.

Circa didn't know about Miles, but she had never actually been inside a hospital before. Turns out, it was just as bad as she'd seen on TV. All these bright lights. All these weary faces. Enough visible blood to keep Circa on the edge of woozy. If ever a place needed to be Shopt, it was this room, she thought. An instant garden of giant sunflowers over there, or maybe even a few floating puppies mixed in with these groaning people and their paper numbers.

Every one of the small overhead screens was showing scenes of still-fresh devastation all across the Southeast, flashing up lists of donations needed and where to take them. Circa and Mom had been careful not to watch the news since the ordeal had happened, and hearing about it over and over from four different directions instantly turned Circa into one of the people with her arms pressed across her aching belly. Circa kept looking at Miles to see if any of this bombardment of information sparked a memory in him. But he just sat there, slumped and staring in the direction of a poster that listed all the appropriate times to wear a germ mask. When Miles sank low enough for Circa to see over him, she noticed that Mom was kind of zoned out herself.

"Maple Grove is nothing like this," Circa said to him as she shifted in her seat. "I mean it's kind of medical, but they hide that part to make it homey," she added, but no one was listening.

"I didn't think we'd be gone this long," said Mom, looking at Circa worriedly. She kept opening her eyes big like she was trying to focus them. "I just knew we'd be home by now with it all fixed."

Circa thought about how Mom had always been at home

after taking a pink pill, not having to be in charge of much more than a nap. "Maybe a snack from the machine will help," she whispered to her. "You haven't really eaten today, Mom."

"Okay," Mom said distantly as she rummaged through her purse for some cash. "Circ," she said. "If I'm a little weird, please help me do some of the talking, okay?"

"Sure," said Circa, embarrassed for Miles to hear that. No wonder Mom had told her she couldn't be Dad, she stewed. It was because Circa was going to have to be the mom from now on.

After Mom left for the vending area, Circa dug out some Jolly Ranchers left in her pocket from who knows when. "She's usually at home when she's taken her medicine," she said.

Miles just bounced his leg nervously and closed his eyes, like he was desperately searching for a shred of a something inside his head.

"You awake?" she asked as she handed over a green apple Rancher.

"Yeah. Thanks," he said, straightening himself up in his seat. He popped the candy into his mouth. "So what's Maple Grove?" he said as he slurped. "Why do you want to go there so bad?"

Circa blew a fuzz off her cinnamon Rancher. "It's this place here in town. Kind of like an old-folks' home. And I want to go there because it's real special to me," she said. "My great-aunt Ruby lived there before, and we go—I mean went—all the time. And besides, I just feel like my dad would want me to check on our friends."

A voice called the next three numbers over a loudspeaker.

Miles scratched wildly at a mosquito bite on his thumb.

"You might like to know that these friends I'm talking about have also forgotten a lot of things," said Circa. "But sometimes they do remember, and that's when it's fun."

"Yeah, okay," Miles said skeptically, trying to free the candy from his back teeth.

"So at that reunion spot where you came from," Circa said. "Did you maybe see a man there with a plastic poncho? In an old blue Jeep?"

Miles stopped bouncing. "I really don't know if I did or not. Why? Is that your dad?"

"Never mind," said Circa. "Don't worry about it."

"Why do you keep asking me if I saw him?" he said.

Circa pressed her arms into her tummy again. "Because that's where they said he died," she said. "At the reunion place. He was there to deliver that picture."

"No way," said Miles, squinting his eyes like he was calculating the weirdness of it all.

"Number eighty-seven!" a nurse called out loud enough for a room three times that size. Circa stood and waved Mom over from the snack machine, where she was trying to smooth the creases from an uncooperative dollar bill. A couple minutes later, Mom and her Cheez-Its and Mountain Dew joined Circa and Miles in a small triage area, where a nurse checked Miles's blood pressure and temperature before showing them to their own curtained room.

Then a different nurse came in. "This wraps around and ties in the front," she said, handing Miles a pale blue gown that was frayed at the edges. "Your mom and your sister can help you tie it up."

"Oh, we're not . . . We just . . ." stammered Mom.

"He's not family," said Circa. "He was hurt in the storm, and we're helping him is all."

"Oh, wow, I'm so sorry," said the nurse. "I just saw the resemblance and assumed."

Circa looked curiously at her. What kind of resemblance? she wondered.

"I'll make a note for our billing folks to see if we can write this up as a charity case," the nurse said.

"Thank you so much," said Mom.

Miles turned ten shades of embarrassed as he held up the gown. Circa and Mom turned away. There were all manner of life-support gadgets on the wall before them. Pedals, switches, plastic pans, glove boxes, giant swabs, and five sizes of cloth tape. Circa couldn't begin to imagine what all of them were for.

"It's okay now," Miles said after he'd changed and climbed onto the bed.

Circa and Mom settled onto a couple of folding chairs just as the doctor yanked the curtain open and peeked his head in.

"Everyone decent?" he asked.

"Good thing we are," said Miles. He was still red as could be.

Once inside the room, the doctor seemed to move in fast motion, asking Miles a bunch of questions that overlapped each other while he shined a light into Miles's ears and made him follow the same light with his eyeballs, squeeze his hands hard as he could, touch his fingers to the tip of his own nose, and then balance while standing on one leg at a time. All the while, Circa tried to distract herself, but found it harder and harder to keep from staring at the newly exposed collection of scars on Miles's arms and legs. On just the areas she could see, there were at least a dozen red and purple marks of all shapes and sizes on him. Some scrape-ish ones like you get falling off your bike. Other ones, more like cuts. Some looked older than others, but none were fresh. It wasn't until they took Miles away for a scan of his head that Circa found out Mom had noticed the scars as well.

"Circ, what could have happened to him?" Mom whispered as soon as he was gone. "All those marks—"

"I don't know," said Circa, feeling more than a little relieved that Mom was back from space. She'd begun to wonder how they were going to get home with Mom all hazy eyed like she was.

A few minutes later, the doc wheeled Miles back in. "Well, we can rule out a bleed in the brain or a tumor," he said. "And there are no signs of acute head trauma whatsoever. Which leads me to believe the memory loss may be PTSD-related. Some kind of temporary effect of post-traumatic stress disorder. Has Child Services been called?"

"Yes, the police did that," Mom said.

The doc scribbled across his clipboard. "You may get dressed, son," he said. "On the discharge paperwork, I'll recommend that the state follow up with some sort of psychological workup."

"Discharge paperwork?" said Mom. "You mean you're not going to keep him here?"

"No reason to," said the doctor. "By exam, he checks out fine. I think this kid needs a place to rest his head so that everything in there will settle."

"You mean he can't rest his head *here*?"

"Not this week," said the doc. "We've got three to a room with tornado injuries as it is."

Keeping her head turned as he dressed, Circa asked Miles what the CT scan was like. If it hurt any.

"Nah," he said. "Kind of like being in a big toilet paper tube is all."

"Isn't there a medicine he can take that would help him remember?" Mom asked.

"I'm afraid not," the doctor said. "I can only prescribe time for that."

"Decent again," announced Miles, scrunching up his jeans one leg at a time to yank on his socks, drawing Circa's attention once more to the collection of scars there. Circa instantly got goose bumps just thinking about the pain that must have once meant for him. When her eyes met Mom's, it was clear that both of them had been struck with the same thought. Whatever Miles had been through in his past, it must have been a doozy of an ordeal.

"Miles," said Mom with a sigh, "why don't you come on home with us and stay until we get word about your family? I'm sure it'll only be a day or so until we hear something, and Circa won't mind if you take the room next to hers, will you, Circ?"

Mom looked to Circa for consent as Miles stooped wearily to tie his beat-up tennies. Circa instantly found herself beyond conflicted in that room full of buzzing lightbulbs and sterile smells. Here she was another whole miserable day farther from Dad and the things they had once shared. And yet, strangely enough, that was the very reason she couldn't bear to pile another hurt on this mystery boy who shared her own father's crinkle.

"No, I don't mind," Circa said, adding a quiet *"Code Thirty-two"* under her breath.

Bud and Marla instantly regretted bringing Sleepy along on their drive through Yellowstone. After hours of being stalled by the curious bear family, they ended up trading their friend for a few pieces of licked-on garbage. By winter, the black bears deeply regretted their trade, when Sleepy hogged up all the hibernating space.

10

Nattie and the Nest

It was already night by the time they left the hospital, and Mom, Circa, and Miles were all drained of color and words. Miles dozed all the way from the hospital parking lot to the house, but much to Circa's relief, Mom didn't.

"Circ, you show Miles to his room, and I'll scare up a toothbrush for him," she said as they entered the front door.

Circa led Miles upstairs, to the bedroom right next to hers, just across the hall from Mom and Dad's. The decor was made up of stuff that Dad had brought home from Maple Grove when Aunt Ruby died, great-auntish things like beige circles of lace and dusty, rosy-cheeked cherub figurines. But Miles didn't seem to mind. He set his backpack down on the rocking chair and sat on the edge of the bed.

Mom came in with two bottled waters and a small scattering of pretzels on a paper plate. She had a fresh hand towel and a spare toothbrush pinched under her elbow. "I apologize for the slim pickings," she said. "Mr. Monroe was the executive chef around here."

Circa thought about the bedtime snacks Dad used to make

for her. Tiny faces carved into cubes of cheese. Carefully balanced grape pyramids. Not so chef-like maybe, but perfect.

"Don't you worry, Miles," said Mom. "Now that we've gotten the word out, I'm sure we'll hear something from your family tomorrow."

"Yeah, maybe so," he said, taking a handful of pretzels and a water. "Good night. And I'm sorry for all the trouble."

Mom and Circa turned to leave him for the night and walked to Circa's room, where Mom kissed her on the head and squeezed her tight. "Get you some sleep," she said. "And thanks for the help today. I sure couldn't have handled that without you."

Circa only wished she could disagree with her. It felt weird to have to be ready to speak for your own mother in case she totally flaked out. Mom had always been able to get Dad to fill in those gaps before.

"This will all be cleared up soon," Mom said, "and we'll be back to—well, I'm not sure there is any normal for us, huh?"

Circa shook her head and reached for the remaining pretzels. "Good night, Mom."

"Night, Circ. I love you." Mom gently pulled the door closed on her way out.

Circa licked the salt off a pretzel as she heard Miles settle into the squeaky brass bed on the other side of the wall. Then she sat on the floor and looked around her own room, a sparse tiny space with little else but a dresser and a bed and a reading lamp. Circa had always spent more time awake in Studio Monroe than in her actual room, so she'd never really put much effort into this one. Just weeks ago, Mom and Dad had let her stay down in the studio every night of spring break in a little fort built from Mom's photography light stands and some sheet backdrops thrown over them. Circa went to sleep looking at the shape of Dad's head and shoulders silhouetted on the big, glowy monitor. It was the last time she'd seen him work on one of the Maple Grove pictures, a particularly worn one of Miss Rempy standing next to her crop-dusting plane.

Circa thought about the hours of toil Dad put into that photo. She wondered if she was fooling herself, thinking she was capable of doing his work. Frustrated, she tossed the half-full water into her garbage can so hard that it splattered up the wall. Desperate for something that might offer some comfort, she crept out of her bedroom and down the stairs, tiptoed through the foyer and the kitchen, and creaked open the studio door. Then she fumbled around the studio in the dark for the one thing she knew could make tonight better. Circa grabbed the Shopt folder, tucked it under her arm, and tiptoed back up to her room.

Sitting on the floor, Circa laid the folder open on the carpet in front of her and closed her eyes to pick from the stack randomly. The one she picked was a personal favorite, an old picture of a classroom full of fourth graders. Above their heads, plump green vines grew long and tangled from the ceiling, each branch bearing a different kind of candy. All sorts of sugary things, ripe for the picking, dangled above the students' heads, each and every one a kind that Circa loved. Underneath the photo, written in Dad's scrawly handwriting, the story read:

It was October 23, 1959, and Mrs. Lipman had found it increasingly difficult to teach that day. Hands were raised all morning long, but for harvesting goodies instead of answering questions. By noon, nine bellyaches had already been reported to the nurse's office. And absolutely nobody wanted to say "cheese" for the photographer.

It was like Circa could hear Dad's voice reading the words to her, and gazing at the delightful scene gave her a sweet surge of calm. She fanned out all the Shopt photos in front of her. Then she slid out the bottom-most one, the sight of it making her well up with tears. It was the Linholt Reunion, but not a crumply one laid across a table by a lost boy. Instead, it was full of wonderful Shopt things . . . the golden pocket watch tangled in the branches, the big sneaky potato, the bugle-playing beaver, and that cute little pudgy baby. One by one, she took in all of the crazy, all the happy things that made Circa long for this to be the *real* picture of the park where Dad's accident had happened.

Each Shopt item was a comfort in its own way, but Circa soon found herself aiming her attention at one small detail in particular. One that hadn't seemed important until now. As Miles flopped over noisily on the other side of the wall, Circa drew the picture closer to verify. Yes, indeed, there it was. A tiny crinkle on that baby. Like Dad. Like Miles.

Circa wondered all the more what tale Dad had concocted for this little chubby Monroe-ish Linholt. Her eyes wandered to the big empty white space underneath the photo, where the story would have, *should* have, been written for her. She clutched the picture tight to her chest, leaned back onto her pillow, and thought about the way it was really supposed to be. That if your dad absolutely *has* to die, then it should be his hundred-year-old self lying in a cushy place, where he assures his gathered loved ones that his race has been run and his job here on earth is beyond complete. One thing Circa knew down to the sorest part of her heart was that it's really, really not supposed to be like *this*.

Circa thought about Great-Aunt Ruby and how *she* had run her whole race, and had died so peacefully, despite hardly recognizing her own family. How tenderly Dad cared for Aunt Ruby and all of her friends at Maple Grove. She thought about how there was never a picture that Dad wouldn't at least try to restore, no matter how hopeless it seemed, and she felt the Memory Wall pull at her heart, strong as ever. She decided that she would absolutely go visit Maple Grove tomorrow, even if she had to walk there. She'd assure them that the Memory Wall was still alive and well. And she would take Miles there too, if for no other reason than to maybe distract him from his own blank page.

Circa looked at the Shopt reunion picture again. She'd been gripping it so tightly, and her hands were sweating. She couldn't explain it, but something in that baby's face kept telling her that there were things worth discovering about that boy on the other side of the wall. A crinkly feeling that there was much to be gained in helping him pull his story off the shelf.

Just then, Circa's thoughts were interrupted by the sharp crack of a stick hitting her bedroom window. She jumped up, shuffled the Shopt photos back into the folder, and slid them under the bed. Then she crept toward the window and took a peek down below. There, in the middle of the front yard, bathed in the glow of the streetlight, stood Nattie Boone in her best pajamas and matching slippers, looking around nervously like she might get busted any minute.

Circa opened her window as quiet as possible and whispered as loud as possible.

"Nat, what are you doing out there?"

"I snuck out to check on you," she said, putting her hands on her hips. "I tried to call like ten times. Why didn't you answer?"

"Because we had to go to the police station and the hospital."

"You did? For what?"

"To help Miles find his family. I can't believe you snuck out."

"Is that his name . . . Miles?" said Nattie.

"Sort of."

"What do you mean, sort of?"

"I'll tell you tomorrow."

"Wait," said Nattie. "You mean your *mom* took you guys?"

"Barely," muttered Circa with a nod.

"Is he still there?"

"Yeah, in the guest room. And get this . . . He's been sleeping in our backyard for days. That's the noise I kept hearing."

"No way!" Nattie's whisper came too close to a shout. "So what's up with him? Where's he from? How old is he? How'd he get here?" She stacked the questions all the way up to Circa's window.

Circa cupped both hands to her face to aim some answers directly below. "He's lost," she said. "He doesn't remember anything. Like amnesia or something. And get this, Nat . . . He hitchhiked here from the place where my dad was . . . from that reunion. He came here because of our address on the back of a picture."

Nattie's eyes were huge. "Wild," she said. "Totally wild."

Circa heard Miles flop over again. "We'll talk more tomorrow," she said. "When you guys come over for your dad's work portrait."

"Okay, then," said Nattie. But she stayed put. "Hey. You never told me," she said.

"Told you what?" said Circa.

"Did he see the bird poo on me?"

Circa sighed.

"No, Nat, he didn't see the bird poo on you."

"Good. Night, Circ. See you tomorrow."

"Good night, Nat."

Nattie turned to walk home, but then turned right back.

"Oh, yeah, my mom made me promise I'd apologize to you for talking about poop so much on the phone."

"No big deal, Nat."

Nattie gave another false start.

"You ought to see if it's a brown-headed nuthatch in that nest. They like to live in small pine trees in this area."

"What nest?" said Circa.

"The one outside your window right there," said Nattie, pointing up at Circa's tree. "The one you took a picture of."

"Picture?" said Circa, leaning farther out her window. Sure enough, there was a tangled mess of twigs nestled into the topmost pine tree branch that reached out closest to her room. She'd never noticed it there before, and it sure enough seemed to occupy the very spot she'd photographed that morning.

"Because if it is a brown-headed nuthatch," said Nattie, "she'll lay eggs that look like they have freckles, and we can watch them hatch right outside your window and give the babies names."

Circa could have sworn she'd snapped a picture of a thoroughly naked tree branch. But she also knew enough not to argue bird knowledge with Nattie. So she answered the only way she knew how.

"Nattie, *you're* a brown-headed nuthatch."

Nattie smiled and glided off in her silky jammies as Circa pushed the window shut. Before she could go to bed, though, Circa felt compelled to put the Shopt folder back in its spot on Dad's desk, as if she'd been viewing an important ancient manuscript that needed to be returned to its spot at the museum. So she snagged the folder once more from under her bed and dashed down to the studio and back, stopping only to place the file gently into its spot and to get a good sniff of Dad's chair on her way out.

Upstairs, Circa put her ear to Mom's door and heard the familiar whoosh of the *Soothing Ocean Sounds* CD that Dad had given her for Christmas once. Then she peeked in at Miles, who, by his grizzly-bear snoring, had just added another item to the list of his Todd Monroe–ish characteristics. Miles lay there sprawled atop the covers, all conked out with even his shoes still on. She noticed that, peaceful as the rest of him looked, his legs still twitched and shuffled like he was running away from something.

Bryan struggled once more against the weight. Snoopy was simply not budging, and the pomegranate-throwing orangutan wasn't making things any easier.

11

Crinkle

On Monday, Circa woke up with that *oh no, Dad is gone* feeling that slapped her upside the soul at least a dozen times a day. Her thoughts bounced wildly from Miles and Maple Grove to that mysterious nest; so much so that, before she got dressed, Circa lifted her window and checked to make sure she hadn't imagined the nest. Nope. Still there. And with freckled eggs in it, just like Nattie had said. There was even the mother bird chirping on the next branch over. She wished she could compare it to the real thing. Circa instantly regretted how she'd torn her nest picture to bits after Mom had pointed out the Shopt addition.

Just then, Mom appeared at Circa's door tying a robe around her middle. She pulled her cell phone from the big square front pocket and checked the screen to see if anyone had claimed Miles as their own in the night. No messages.

"The Boones will be here any minute," Mom said. "Mr. Boone will be on his lunch break, so I need to be ready."

Mom ran her fingers through her tangly, black-brown hair. "I'm going to get cleaned up real quick," she said. "You want to wake up our guest?"

"Sure," said Circa, closing her door to throw on a T-shirt and some shorts.

Next door, Circa found Miles in the very same position she'd last left him, and still snoring. She called out to him quietly.

"Miles?"

It occurred to her that he probably wasn't used to anyone calling him by that name, so she resorted to clearing her throat obnoxiously loud, which instantly did the trick. Miles bolted upright and gasped a little.

"Whoa," said Circa. Miles seemed both embarrassed and confused. He looked all around the room, and then back at her.

"*Circa,*" she reminded him. She'd been accustomed to reintroducing herself to her Maple Grove friends on a regular basis. "Do you remember where you are?" she said.

"Yeah," he said with a stretch. "Good morning, Circa."

"Do you remember *who* you are?"

Miles yawned and shook his head no. "And I still don't remember your dad," he said. "Sorry."

"It's okay," said Circa, trying to mask her disappointment. "Come on downstairs. Mom says Nattie and them will be here soon for their portrait, and I bet they'll bring pie."

"You kids sleep okay?" Mom asked as the three of them met up at the top of the steps. They both nodded drowsily as Mom gave Circa a little half hug and patted Miles on the arm. As they descended the stairs, Circa could see the silhouettes of the Boones through the frosted glass of the front door. She opened the door before they could even knock, and was thrilled to find most of the family loaded down with food. The Boones came in like a little parade of kindness, greeting Circa and Mom and Miles warmly. First there was Mrs. Boone with Nattie's little brother, Durret, in tow, then Mr. Boone in the middle, his arms piled high with a small mountain of groceries. Then Nattie at the rear, which was an unusual thing for her. Nattie was looking just as snazzy as ever, and she'd put on her best smile, but Circa sensed that something was wrong.

"Oh, do come on into the kitchen with all that goodness," said Mom. "Just please excuse the mess."

"Friend, you've seen how we live," said Mrs. Boone. "Thanks to our professional mess machine here."

Circa could see three damp spots where they'd already had to wipe things off of Durret's little man suit. They all proceeded to the kitchen, where Mr. Boone set a pie on the counter, along with a loaf of bread and a stack of paper plates. The rest, including a pot roast, some black-eyed peas, and a gallon of milk, went straight into the fridge.

"You shouldn't have gone to all this trouble, but I'm sure glad you did," Mom said.

Circa eyed the peanut butter pie. She was glad too. Most of Mom's customers had postponed their portrait appointments because of the storm, but Nattie's family wanted to keep theirs. Circa knew this was just so they could help. Mom was always so calm with the Boones.

"Oh, everyone, I'd like for you to meet Miles," said Mom. "He's been, well, displaced during the storm and will be with us for a day or so until his family can come get him."

"It's a pleasure to meet you, Miles," said Mrs. Boone. Mr. Boone reached out and shook his hand.

"Well, since you've gone and done all this, I guess I owe you guys a decent family portrait, huh?" Mom said. "But won't you all sit down for a bite first?"

"Oh, certainly not," said Mrs. Boone. "This is all for you."

"We had a big breakfast anyway," said Mr. Boone.

"Well, we're sure grateful," said Mom, cutting a big piece of pie each for Circa and for Miles. Nattie smoothed her skirt and joined Circa and Miles at the table, while the grown-ups and the spoon-chewing Durret went all whispery-whispery on the other side of the kitchen.

Circa hadn't seen Nattie look so bummed since the day Mr. Boone officially told her she couldn't have a dog. She thought of giving Nattie her own slice of pie to help matters, until she remembered that her best friend hated peanut butter as much as she herself hated jelly.

"Hey, Nat, you want to go with me and Miles to visit Maple Grove today?"

Miles stopped midbite.

"Oops. Sorry I didn't run that by you, Miles," said Circa. "Okay with you?"

Miles nodded and went back to his pie.

"I'll be lucky if they allow me to go get the mail this afternoon," Nattie grumbled.

"What do you mean?" said Circa.

"I mean I totally got busted for coming to your window last night."

"Oh no. So sorry," said Circa. "Maybe Miles and I will just run up there real quick while you're getting your picture done then."

"Wait. What about tomorrow?" said Nattie. "Can we all go then?"

"No, Miles might be gone by tomorrow," said Circa.

Miles nodded and shrugged, making Nattie slump in her chair.

"Here's sort of a neat thing," said Circa, grasping for good news. "There really are freckled eggs in that nest, just like you said."

"That's cool," Nattie said halfheartedly. "Hey, when I get ungrounded tomorrow, if Miles is still here, you promise I can hang with you guys?"

"Promise," said Circa.

Once the kids went totally silent, the parents hushed their whispering and made their way toward the studio door, summoning Nattie to join them.

"It was nice to meet you, Miles," she said.

"Yeah. You too," said Miles.

"Mom," said Circa, "while you guys are doing the pictures, can I go to Maple Grove for a little while?"

"Circa—" Mom began, but Circa interrupted before Mom could get out a decent *no*. Circa planned to answer all the questions before Mom could even ask them.

"I'll take Miles with me," she said. "We'll walk. And I'll show him the neighborhood. There's no chance of rain today. It will be good for Miles, right? To get to meet some people up there . . . I mean, like the *un*-Stanley people."

Mr. and Mrs. Boone smiled at the fast-talking. Circa sensed that Mom was about to buckle under the pressure.

"Okay," Mom answered reluctantly. "But do take Miles with you, and just for a little while."

"Just a little while," assured Circa.

"But you keep an eye on him," Mom said. "And really, don't be gone too long, in case somebody calls to come get him."

"Got it," said Circa.

As soon as their pie was done, Circa and Miles were out the door. "Thanks for coming with me," she said. "Even though I didn't really give you a choice."

"What else am I going to do?" Miles kicked a rock across the driveway.

"I think you'll like Maple Grove," she said. "There are real nice people there. *Not* including Smoochy Stanley, of course."

"Yeah, well, your mom sure doesn't seem too keen on the place," said Miles, looking all around him as they walked, like he was on a scavenger hunt for something that rang familiar.

"Yeah, well, she wouldn't know because she's never even been," Circa said indignantly. "Anyway, I was going to say . . . Lily the nurse and Joe the food man are the ones who work in the daytime. Joe's the one who gives me glass-bottle Cokes. And then there are the people who live there. There's pretty much two categories of them, the ones who remember enough to talk to you about it, and the ones who don't."

"Kind of like you and me?"

"Come on." Circa jabbed Miles with her elbow. "The thing is, my dad and me used to go visit there a lot. He was . . . well, *we* were working on this amazing Memory Wall for the residents."

"That's the project?"

"Yeah, it's this really cool collection of old pictures that he was fixing up, so that the people there could visit their lives anytime they want to. Like little sparks of memory. And there's supposed to be a lot of old photos of Wingate history on it too, so Dad was excited that it would make more people notice what a great place Maple Grove is. Like if they knew a person who needed their help . . . or even if a rich guy wanted to donate some money or something."

Circa slowed her walk. "The wall's supposed to be unveiled in August," she said, her voice falling flat. "And I want real bad to try and finish it myself, but my mom won't let me. Even though my dad showed me a lot about restoration, she doesn't think I'm good enough."

"So are you?" said Miles.

"Am I going to finish it?"

"No. I mean are you good enough?"

Circa gave a defeated shrug. "Maybe not yet," she said. "But I'm still going to ask Nurse Lily if she's got any more photos collected to give me."

Miles slapped some of the dust from his pant legs.

"Hey," he said. "I really am sorry about causing you guys all this trouble when you've got your own junk going on. It's just . . . I really thought that picture meant something. That maybe you all would just walk up and know who I was, you know? I guess that was a pretty thick thing to assume."

"I don't know," said Circa. "Maybe not totally thick. The weird thing is, you do seem sort of familiar to me. I mean, there's the crinkle and then I don't know, something about the way you smile kind of lopsided."

"Huh. Okay, lopsided I get," said Miles. "But, um . . . the crinkle?"

"Yeah, you know," said Circa. "That crease there between your eyebrows. My dad had the very same one."

The two of them approached Circa and Nattie's favorite stone bridge, making Circa wonder if Nattie was okay back in the studio fake smiling for the camera. Out of the corner of her eye, she could see Miles feeling his forehead for the crinkle.

"Nattie Boone, my friend you met," she said, "she loves everything nature. She told me once that a termite colony could build a structure three times as strong as this bridge using their own spit."

"Oh, really?" said Miles, grinning.

"Yeah, she's supersmart about stuff like that." Circa searched the clouds once more. "Does it make you feel scared, to not know anyth— Well, you know, to not know?" she said.

"Kind of," said Miles. "More empty than scared, though. You know, like something big was yanked away."

"Yeah, I do know," said Circa, looking down at the sidewalk. She wasn't sure if it was sad or reassuring that another kid was able to put her feelings into words so perfectly.

"Makes me feel really freaky," he said. "As if I'm just going through motions like some kind of robot person or something."

"Yeah, I bet," said Circa, trying briefly to imagine Miles as a robot. "But you know what? My dad used to say something about Great-Aunt Ruby and the other people at Maple Grove. He said that just because the book's too high up on the shelf to reach, it doesn't mean the story's not there."

"Yeah, I get it," said Miles. "I just wish I even knew where the shelf was."

"Maybe something hit you," suggested Circa. "No matter what that doctor said, maybe you really did get bonked in the head, and that's why you don't remember anything. And then when your brain heals, it will all come back."

"Maybe," said Miles, shuffling on quietly alongside her. The silence-laden half block made Circa wish Nattie were along to fill in the blanks with a few nature facts.

"So what's the deal with the Stanley guy?" Miles said as they neared the business part of town.

"Ugh," said Circa. "Don't even ask. He's, like, nineteen, and he's some kind of grand-stepnephew of the lady who donated the land to build the residence on, and so they promised to give him a job."

"You mean they can't fire him?"

"Lily says not until the grand-stepaunt passes away. She told me once she prays every day for him to just up and quit. Unfortunately," Circa added, "Stanley also happens to be the big brother of the meanest kid in my grade, Chad, the guy who calls me *Circus* Monroe."

Circa grabbed a magnolia leaf off the ground and fanned herself with it. "Used to be, my dad would always get between me and Stanley when we'd come up here, so he couldn't aim his yuckiness at me. Kind of like what Nattie does with Chad Betts at school. She's always standing up for me."

"Wait. *Circus?*" said Miles. "Why? Just because of Circa?"

Circa hesitated, then held up her pinkie-less left hand for Miles to see.

"*That?*" he said. "What's the big deal about that?"

"You'd be surprised at what a big deal it is," she said. "Like those scars you've got," she said, wondering if she shouldn't have soon as it came out. "Bet they're probably a big deal to you, right?"

"Well," Miles said, looking at his arms. "I guess they would be if I could remember how they happened."

Circa tried hard to look away from the many scuffs and dents on Miles. She snagged a wildflower from a crack in the sidewalk and changed the subject as smooth as she could. "It sure is going to be hard to start school this year without Nat there," she said. "But at least *she'll* do fine. Nattie can be kind of foo-foo, but she's also tough."

"Where's she going?"

"Science school."

"To study termite spit?"

"Yeah," laughed Circa. "Maybe so."

"Just teasing," said Miles. "But wait. Back up. So why can't you just blow off that Chad guy?"

"I could, maybe. But other kids think I'm a weirdo too."

"Just because of the finger?"

Circa glanced sideways at the many scars that populated Miles's arms. Suddenly, a nonexistent pinkie didn't quite measure up. "Well, there's that . . . and my mom's deal," she said.

"What, the nervous thing?" said Miles, tugging at his sleeves.

"It's just that she doesn't much ever go out, except to church," said Circa. "Since before I was a baby even. She has all these panics." Circa stomped a dirt clod off her shoe. "She and my dad didn't even tell anybody they were having me until the day I was born in the studio. Then when I was in second grade, Chad Betts started joking that I was really bought from the circus or something."

"Were you really born in the—" said Miles.

"So?" interrupted Circa. "What if I was?"

"You didn't even let me finish," he said. "I was going to say, were you born in the mouth of a lion or standing on a horse?

Then it might not be so lame for them to say all that circus junk."

"Oh," said Circa. "Ha. Sorry. I guess I'm kind of touchy about it."

Miles scratched at his neck. "But your mom took us those places yesterday," he said.

"Yeah," said Circa. "And you saw how she was."

Circa pressed the big pedestrian crossing button at the intersection of Third and Broad. "My mom doesn't handle stress very well. It makes her real scatterbrained. You know, she still hasn't even noticed that you broke into our house."

Miles stopped in his tracks. "It was unlocked," he said insistently.

"I know," said Circa waving him on. "Come on. I'm just kidding."

The two of them crossed over into Wingate's business district, where the Maple Grove Residence's greenery-surrounded, dome-shaped design made it look like a cupcake on a bed of lettuce. They turned one last corner and found themselves at the entrance to the side garden path, still strewn with a few of Stanley's cigarette butts.

"Here we are," said Circa.

"So where is the Memory Wall supposed to be?" asked Miles, looking around as they wound their way to the front entrance. Circa tugged at the big iron door handle.

"Right here in the main lob—" Circa began, when she was suddenly interrupted by a greeting that instantly set her skin to crawling.

"S'up, Shrinkie Pinkie?"

12

Maple Grove

Nurse Lily shot Stanley a fierce *shut-up* look and came shuffling out from behind the front desk.

"Circa!" she said, grabbing her up into a hug so big, she almost grabbed up Miles, too. "Sweet little lady, I'm so blessed to get to see you."

"Hi, Lily."

"Who's this you got here, Circa?"

"Oh, um, this is Miles," she said.

Without hesitation, Lily gave Miles his own hug.

"We were hoping to get to visit everyone today," said Circa. "Is that all right?"

"Don't see why not," said Lily.

On the other side of the lobby, Stanley leaned on a broom and watched the whole scene. When no one acknowledged his presence, he picked up the visitor phone and made like he was on a call. "Hey, Rach," he said. "It's you know who. How's about you let a real man buy you a pizza tonight?"

Circa knew better. She'd heard him do this routine before with all manner of different girl names. She always imagined he was calling his home number over and over and filling up his own answering machine. She might very well have felt sorry for the guy, if it weren't his utter meanness that made him that lonely.

Ignoring Stanley, Circa and Lily pointed out a few key features of the lobby to Miles. The sign-in book with the pen made from a feather from the peacock Miss Lily kept in her yard, the big brass chandelier above that reflected a dozen distorted you-faces, and the shiny black player piano that Lily would let Great-Aunt Ruby sit at and perform pretend concerts. Unfortunately though, Stanley, with his broom and his imaginary girlfriends, filled the spot directly in front of where the Memory Wall was to be.

"Is that the place for the pictures?" asked Miles, pointing right over Stanley's head and paying no attention to his act.

"Yes, that's it," Circa said timidly.

"Yo, stud," Stanley called out to Miles. "She your girl or what?"

Miles reddened. "No. She's not," he said. "I believe she's just Circa."

It reassured Circa that Miles had gotten riled in her defense. "He's my friend," she said. "And that's all you need to know."

"What's your name again, man?" Miles said to Stanley. "I forgot it already."

"Well, then, welcome home, stud," Stanley said. "We got thirty-one flavors of forget in this place."

"And what we'd all most like to forget is *him*," said Nurse Lily crossly, provoking Stanley to wink and make smoochy lips at her.

"The name's Stanley. Stanley Betts," he said to Miles. Stanley held out his hand, and then pulled it back again with a smirk. "But you can just call me *sir*."

"Never mind him, Miles," said Lily. "And Circa, baby, I'm still aching so about your sweet daddy. How are you and your momma doing?"

Stanley made an immediate cringey *oops* face. Like his forgetting about Todd Monroe's death was the thirty-second and most sour flavor of forget.

"We're doing okay," said Circa. "I guess."

"Mmm, mmm, mmm." Lily shook her head. "Way too young for such an ordeal. Way too young," Lily mumbled her own echo.

"Can we go in?" said Circa.

"You bet," said Lily. "You've got some folks up here who've been wanting to see you something awful."

"All right," said Circa, deciding she'd share more about the Memory Wall plans with Miles on their way out. She pressed her palm to a green button on the wall to open up a set of glass double doors, and she and Miles both stepped inside the big, bright sunlit atrium.

"This is where the residents' rooms are," she said. "And they are always *residents*. Lily never calls them *patients*."

"Nice," said Miles, marveling at the space before them. "This is really something."

The living area at Maple Grove was a spacious, round place lit up through an impressive dome of windows at the top. In the middle of the atrium was a magnificent, colorful garden of flowers and plants that didn't seem to care what season it was, and a pond full of bug-eyed, speckled koi fish bubbling at every turn. There was a brick walking path just wide enough for a wheelchair winding through the greenery, and the path began and ended at a carpeted circle that ran around the outer edge of the garden, all the way to the entrances of the residents' rooms. Each room had a different colored door to help a person know which place was home when he or she went for a stroll around the atrium.

Surrounding Circa were so many of the things she had been missing for the weeks she'd been away from the residence. The sun's rays beaming through the skylight as if they might shatter it, that smell of rosebushes and fried cafeteria food, the splashing sounds of the chubby fish. To Circa and Dad, this place had been like a little Garden of Eden. Only now that a key ingredient was gone, the sights and smells suddenly made her a little unsteady. As she and Miles stood at the edge of this big terrarium of memories, Circa began to wonder if she could handle any of this without her dad beside her. What in the world would Dad have done right now if he'd felt like this?

"So where are the people?" said Miles, unwittingly fanning her fog away.

The people. Those two words alone gave Circa the strength she needed. She took in a deep breath and stepped onto the path.

"This way," she said. "We'll start over here."

They made their way counterclockwise around the big circle of carpet, where Circa launched into tour guide mode.

"Good thing is, Stanley's not allowed in the atrium ever since Lily saw him spit in the pond to watch the fish eat it," she said. "So now all he really does is clean the lobby, cut the grass, and take care of the van."

"And be a jackola," said Miles.

Jackola. Circa laughed inside at hearing Miles's version of *shmoo*. She and Miles approached the first door on the path. It was a green one with a wreath of fake cherry blossoms hanging on it.

"This is Miss Rempy's room," Circa whispered. "She was the first ever female crop duster in Georgia. She starts a lot of her stories with 'And another funny thing is . . .'" Circa said as she knocked softly.

"Yes?" drawled out a sweet, Southern old-lady voice.

Circa opened the door and peeked in.

"Come on in, love," Miss Rempy said.

"*Two* loves," said Circa. "I have a friend with me."

"Come on in, *loves*," Miss Rempy said again.

The two of them stepped into the little room, where Circa introduced Miles and also introduced herself, as a courtesy. She was never certain when a Maple Grove friend would recognize her from one visit to the next. But this time, Miss Rempy remembered her. *Maybe.* They began their visit by sitting around a card table for a few minutes' worth of an odd, yet humorous, conversation about how Circa and Miles were the most loving brother and sister pair she'd ever known, and how proud their mother Ruby, God rest her soul, would be. Then Miss Rempy suddenly got distracted by a toy parrot on the shelf and had Miles switch it on, after which the parrot repeated the last thing each person would say, but in a slurred, dying battery kind of way. After numerous tales of plane crash rescues and diamond mines, any of which could have been fact or fiction, Miss Rempy insisted on teaching them how to play a dominoes game called Chicken Foot, with the plastic bird repeating every instruction she gave.

When the kids got up to leave, Miles switched the bird back off for Miss Rempy, who called out after them as she shuffled the dominoes, "And another funny thing is . . . I've never even had to change those batteries in all these years."

As they shut Miss Rempy's room behind them, Miles repeated her words in his best dying parrot voice until Circa shushed him when they arrived at the next door, a blue one.

"This is where Hank-not-the-Mayor lives," she said. "We call him that because we actually have a Hank-the-Mayor in Wingate."

"I figured," said Miles.

"Don't be alarmed when you see him," she warned. "Sometimes he soaks his false teeth in Kool-Aid just for fun."

"What?"

"He also talks about his digestion problems all the time, real loud because he can't hear well. 'Have some couth' is what Nurse Lily always tells him."

Circa knocked hard. "We're restoring a photo of him rescuing a dog from a well," she said.

"You know what to do!" the man inside shouted.

When they walked in, Hank-not-the-Mayor was cutting his toenails and letting the trimmings fly. Miles took the seat farthest from Hank's recliner, and Circa took the next farthest. Circa reintroduced herself to Hank, which did prove necessary this time, and then she introduced Miles. Hank promptly put away his toenail clippers and installed his teeth, like he had a little Nurse Lily on his shoulder reminding him to *have some couth.*

The teeth were purple as ever, and Circa could tell Miles was trying not to laugh as the man told story after story of ailments past and present and future. They ended up visiting with Hank longer than with anyone else that day, mainly because he insisted on sharing his lunch with them, dividing french fries and green beans and corn fritters up slowly with a one-for-me, one-for-you, one-for-you precision. By then, Circa and Miles were both so hungry, they weren't even squeamish about the toenails.

Hank took such a liking to Miles, he made a great effort to stand up and shake his hand as they left, even if he did accidentally call him Mr. Monroe. And then he urged Mr. Monroe to be nice to his intestines while he still could.

Miles shook his head as he and Circa continued on the path.

"Sure is a crazy place," he said. "These folks have so many stories, it makes it hard to remember that they forget. Wait. Did that even make sense?"

"Totally," said Circa, passing up a white door and moving along toward the red one.

"Why did we skip that one?" said Miles.

"Because the ones with the *V* sticker on the knob are the vacant rooms," said Circa.

"Beautiful girl," called out a voice from behind Circa and Miles. It was Maki Lee, exiting the garden path on her way back to her red-door room with a fistful of small twigs. Maki was herself a beautiful, seemingly ageless Japanese lady who wore bright red tennis shoes and loved to walk the circle.

"Beauty," she said, cupping her soft hand on Circa's cheek. "I've cried many tears for your father."

"Thank you," said Circa, feeling Maki's comfort encircle her. "It's great to see you, Mrs. Lee."

"Now I'll go make a blessing for you," said Maki, touching Miles on the cheek before she disappeared into the room beyond the red door. "See you at the wall, my beauty," she called out, filling Circa with warmth.

"Maki Lee remembers better than any of the others," Circa said. "She likes to gather those twigs and wrap them up tight in colored tissue paper. Sometimes when she runs out of colored stuff, Hank-not-the-Mayor lets her dip some white paper into his Kool-Aid."

Miles cringed. "In with his teeth?"

"No, the *spare* Kool-Aid," laughed Circa as they walked on, skipping another couple of doors.

They neared an orange door that was already mostly open, but Circa stopped shy of the room. "This is one of the others I was telling you about," she explained softly.

Through the open door, Miles and Circa could see a red-headed lady in a wheelchair. Joe the food man was gently placing a napkin in her lap in preparation for the soup and crackers he'd brought in on a tray. Circa waved big, and the lady smiled sweetly back at her.

"Glad to see your face, Circ," said Joe. "Don't you be a stranger, now."

"I won't, Joe," she answered, and Miles gave him a friendly nod.

"He's the one who gives me glass-bottle Cokes," said Circa, moving on to a mostly closed brown door.

"Now this room here is the Nelsons, who mostly stay in bed all day. Nurse Lily plays music from the forties on a record player for them sometimes, because she says they probably dance in their dreams. One time, my dad and I heard them singing a song called 'Don't Sit Under the Apple Tree' in there. We stood out here and listened to them sing the whole thing to each other."

Circa turned to cut through the garden. "Let's go on around to the other side of the circle, and I'll show you the inside of my very favorite room. It's the one Aunt Ruby stayed in. My favorite days were when me and Ruby folded ourselves up in her adjustable bed. The room's even still got her old dresser in it, where we used to sit and do our hair all crazy. Taped to the mirror, there's a drawing of a chicken on a bicycle that I made for her when I was little. Nobody's stayed in the room ever since Aunt Ruby died last year, but Lily still lets me play with the remote on the bed."

Circa and Miles took the scenic route all the way around the circle to a purple door.

"Huh. No *V* sticker," said Circa. "We better check with Lily before we go in."

She raised her arm high to wave Lily over from the lobby, but there was no need for flagging. Lily was already halfway to Circa and Miles.

"Oh me," said Lily upon arriving at the purple door. "I nearly forgot to warn you two about this one."

Text on chalkboard:
HOW TO DRAW A CHICKEN ON A BICYCLE

CHICKEN MUST HAVE ARMS

HORN IS OPTIONAL

CHAINS NEED TO BE ...

There isn't a corporation on earth that doesn't value an employee who can successfully draw a chicken on a bicycle. That's why Professor Lo is on a mission to teach you how. His motto: You might get frustrated by the arm part, but stick with it. Your efforts will pay off tenfold.

13

Captain Mann

"Oh, children, do be praying for this man," Lily said.

"Somebody's moved in?" asked Circa.

"Yes. He arrived here the day of the storms," Lily said. "He just showed up shivering like January with a sack full of stuff and wouldn't tell us the first thing about himself, so we assume he's got some kind of dementia. I figure as long as we got the room, how could we turn him out on the street?"

"What's his name?" asked Circa.

"Wish I knew," said Lily. "The man came in wearing an old army captain's hat with some patches on it, so we all just came up with Captain Mann."

Circa grew more curious, but Miles got a sudden sickly look, like he'd had a delayed reaction to the flying toenails.

"We've contacted the police about him, but they haven't done much to turn up any information yet," said Lily.

"We know," said Circa. "There's no such thing as a Found Person Report, *per se*, right?"

"Yeah, that was something like it," said Lily with a grin. "No one's even come by to evaluate him yet," she added. "But

I figure it's just as well, 'cause he hasn't even come out of that room hardly at all."

Lily held up her hand to shield a whisper. "Except of course when the sly fella snuck out and took a joyride in the van last Sunday, while the rest of us were singing in the chapel."

"Nuh-uh!" said Circa.

"True as truth," said Lily. "We didn't write it up, so don't you go telling anybody and get me in trouble, okay?"

"Promise," said Circa.

"Okay?" said Lily to Miles. He solemnly nodded his promise too.

"Imagine that," Lily said. "A man old as him, driving that van who knows where. It's a wonder he made it back in one piece."

"Did he get pulled over?" asked Circa.

"Nope. Just came on back when he got low on gas," said Lily. "But there'll be no more of those antics," she said, pointing to a bell hung strategically at the top of the purple doorway. "Now we've got a homemade alarm rigged up for his own safety."

Circa eyed the little brass bell. Then, without hesitation, she approached the door and knocked gently.

"Hello, Captain," she said. "My name is Circa, and I've brought my friend Miles. It's very nice to meet you."

There wasn't a speck of noise from the other side.

"See on your mirror there," said Circa. "I drew that bicycle chicken when I was little, for my great-aunt Ruby. She used to live in this room."

More silence.

114

"I figure he's got him some kind of unspeakable ordeal he's been through," whispered Lily, shaking her head. "Imagine being a misplaced person."

"Wow," Circa marveled, but Miles remained unresponsive, like the foggy funk he'd waved off for Circa earlier had now settled over him.

The three of them walked the rest of the way around the circle to the lobby doors, where Circa peered around for Stanley.

"Don't worry," Lily said. "I made him go out back and clean the van windows to get him out of our hair." She settled herself back at the desk. "Boy, those van windows sure have been sparkly lately," she added.

Circa and Miles stopped and faced the blank, gray wall opposite Lily's desk.

"Dad said the pictures were going to fill up the whole wall," Circa said. "With bunches for each resident all mixed in with the historical Wingate pictures."

"Stories they can reach," said Miles.

"Exactly," said Circa. She gazed at the vast empty space and felt intimidated by the sheer volume of the work left to be done to make the Memory Wall happen. But then those two words popped into her head again. *The people.* She thought about all those people behind their colored doors and her compassion flickered inside.

"My dad always said the thing that he most loved about photographs was how a good one could make one single *now* speak for a million *thens*," she said.

Miles just stood there frozen, still focused on the center of the empty wall.

"Lily," Circa turned and said. "Do you have any fresh old pictures for me to take back to the studio?"

Lily stopped her paperwork and puzzled at Circa.

"To restore," said Circa. "Dad taught me how."

"Oh my," Lily said. "I guess I just assumed we weren't—" Lily gave Circa a worried look. "I mean, I thought you had enough pictures to work on already," she said. "But let me check here."

Lily did some quick rustling around behind the desk. "Nope, no more pictures."

"So Captain Mann didn't have any with him?" said Circa.

"Well, come to think of it," said Lily, "he did bring one picture with him. It appears to be from way back, but I get the feeling he wouldn't be willing to part with it."

"Okay," said Circa. "But will you please let me know if you collect any more for me to work on?"

Lily hesitated, looking fretfully from Circa to the empty wall. "All right, precious," she said. "But you just take care of Circa for a while, though, you hear me?"

"I hear," said Circa.

As she and Miles walked out the front door, Circa noted that even her step was made lighter from the time there, but her friend's gait was markedly heavy.

"Hey, thanks for sticking up for me with Stanley before," said Circa, but Miles walked on with no response.

"Miles? You okay?" she said, trying to catch up.

Miles stopped. "What do *you* think?" he said abruptly.

"What do you mean?" asked Circa. "Didn't you have fun?"

"At first, maybe," he said. "But tell me, Circa. Do I remind you of somebody?"

"Sure," she said. "I told you before, you kind of remind me of my dad a little."

"No, I mean, from back there at Maple Grove. Who do I most remind you of?"

Circa knew the answer he was driving at, but she couldn't bring herself to say it out loud. *Captain Mann.*

"You know who I'm talking about," Miles said sharply.

Circa nodded.

"So how am I supposed to feel about that?" he said. "Is that what's next for misplaced Miles? What color door will I live behind for the rest of *my* life?"

"But that man probably has dementia," she said. "That's a whole other thing. He's got something that won't go away."

"Yeah, well how come it's been weeks and I haven't gotten any better?" argued Miles. "I mean, what if I never snap out of this?"

Circa's insides began to churn. She felt like such an idiot for not thinking about how going up there might affect Miles that way. So much so, she wished she could erase that part of his memory, too.

"I'm sorry, Circa, I'm not trying to be a big jerk," said Miles. "I know you were trying to help. And that's real nice, especially with all you've just been through. But it's just I can't help thinking . . . Where's my wall full of *thens*? You know?"

Miles picked up a rock and skipped it across the street. "Sorry," he said. "Sort of."

Circa couldn't find the right words to say. Somehow, suddenly, her own ordeal didn't seem to tower over Miles's ordeal quite as much. Even so, she considered how Miles probably had a family right around the corner just waiting to swoop him up and celebrate his memories all flooding back. But Dad would never be around the corner for her. No swooping. No celebrating. Still though, she couldn't shake the sensation that she and Miles had something, maybe even something big and heavy, in common.

As the two of them silently continued their walk, Circa trailed a few feet behind Miles and felt the weight of so many big questions. Who was this boy really, and why had he come to them? Why did she feel so connected to him, so comforted by a crinkle and a crooked smile? She grew angry at herself for asking Miles if he was scared. Of course he was. It must be completely terrifying to walk around in all that blankness, even if it was temporary. She did, after all, have Mom and Nattie and a home, and memories. All he had was a dirty backpack and a sunburn.

"Aren't you coming?" called Miles wearily over his shoulder.

Circa was surprised to see he was so far ahead, sitting on a stump waiting for her. She'd stood absolutely still right under the Wingate town-square clock without even realizing it. "Um, yeah," she said, shaking off her trance. She looked at him as he sat there in the distance with his face in his hands and considered the mystery that was Miles. There were countless unknowns about the boy, but one truth now tugging hard at Circa: that Dad would have absolutely *hated* this boy's suffering. But what would Dad have done about it? That seemed to be the most urgent question.

Then as the clock sounded the half hour loudly above her, Circa had a flash of inspiration.

"Come on," she said, running to catch up to Miles. "I've got something to show you."

Pappy Joe wasn't fond of letting his wife's wings hang on
the clothesline for the whole neighborhood to gawk at.
And little Jamie always pitched such a fit to try them on.
For these two reasons, sometimes Pappy Joe would take the
wings down early, while they were still damp around the
edges. And every time, he would gently assure Jamie that
she too would have her own pair someday.

14

The Wart Scenario

Mom was waiting at the entrance to Studio Monroe when Circa and Miles returned. Circa knew this eagerness had to mean Mom had either gotten a call about Miles or had gotten herself in a tizzy of worry.

"I was getting concerned about you guys," Mom said with her brow pinched tightly as they walked into the studio. "Circa, you promised a short visit."

"Did they call?" said Miles.

Mom shook her head. "Not yet," she said.

Circa felt a small sensation of relief about no one claiming Miles. "Sorry it took us so long, Mom," she said. "Please don't be mad. It's because Hank-not-the-Mayor counted out lunch for us."

"All right, then," said Mom. "So Hank. Is that the Kool-Aid teeth guy?"

"Yep. Grape today," Circa said as Mom wiped her camera lens with a dust cloth.

Miles had already begun his own wandering tour of the studio and its gallery of images.

"Oh, yeah," said Circa. She'd forgotten he hadn't seen it. "Miles, this is Studio Monroe."

Circa's eyes took a minute to adjust from the outside sun to the dimly lit room. So much so, she almost didn't see her own best friend seated neatly on the beanbag in the corner, tinkering with one of the old-timey cameras in Mom's part of the studio.

"Nat! What are you still doing here?" said Circa.

"Mom said I could wait around for you guys after the portrait," said Nattie. "Since I explained to her I was mainly just checking on you last night."

"Checking on *me*?" said Circa.

"Well, yeah, something like that." Nattie smiled. "So how was Maple Grove?"

Circa looked to make sure Miles couldn't hear her answer. "It was so great, Nat," she said. "We all need to go back sometime."

Circa put an extra emphasis on the word *all*, so that Mom would catch on that she was invited too. She so wanted for Mom to ask about their visit to Maple Grove and the people and the wall, but Mom never did. Instead she just pulled down a plain blue backdrop and said, "We should probably go ahead and take a good picture of Miles like the police recommended, in case we need to put out some posters or something."

But Miles didn't even hear Mom's suggestion, he was so mesmerized by the work displayed at the other end of the room. "Circa, is this your father's stuff?" he asked as he drifted to the Dad half of the studio.

"Yep," Circa said proudly. "Those are the befores and afters of his restorations."

"Wow," said Miles. "He was good."

Circa picked up a printout of the Boone family photo from Mom's little printer. "Hey, Nat, is this the one you guys chose as your favorite?" she asked, prompting Nattie to get all weird and squirm up out of the beanbag as fast and ladylike as she could. Nattie snatched the print from Circa's hand and rolled it up in her fist.

"What gives?" said Circa.

Across the room, Mom smoothed out the backdrop and placed a tall stool in the middle of it. Then she asked Miles to come over and have a seat. As soon as he was over there, Nattie grabbed Circa by the elbow.

"Quick, Circ," she whispered as she unrolled the photo. "Take that wart off my face and print a fresh one."

"What in the world?" said Circa.

"Right *there*, on the picture, on my right temple," said Nattie. "It's awful."

"Come on, Nat."

"Circa, for real, Mom made us use this picture because Durret was actually sitting still in it, but my hair is flipped back in this one. And I don't want Miles to see the wart on there."

"Is this why you stuck around?" said Circa, but Nattie just shrugged.

"You think he's kinda cute, don't you?" teased Circa.

Nattie put her hands on her hips. "Well, what's so weird about that?" she said. "There is something kind of special cool about him, right? I mean like in an endangered species kind of way."

"Yeah, whatever, Nat," said Circa, agreeing way more than she let on.

"Quick," Nattie said, glancing over at Miles situating himself on the stool. "Go on and do it, while he's over there."

Circa sat herself down into the dents of Dad's chair. It felt so good to sink back in. Over to the side of her, Mom was asking Miles to turn this way and that way. To smile and then not to smile. The not smiling seemed to come the easiest to him, but Circa still had a plan for that, just as soon as they could coax Nattie home without hurting her feelings.

She wiggled the mouse to wake the computer up and placed the Boone photo on the scanner.

"What did you do to catch warts? Smooch a frog?" she snickered.

"Ha, ha, very funny," said Nattie. "Besides, that's a myth."

Circa opened Photoshop and then quickly clicked on a tool that would let her sample and match Nattie's skin color. Then, with just one swift click, she blotted out the wart on Nattie's face.

"Poof, done deal," she said. "Are you happy?"

"I don't know," said Nattie skeptically. "Can you print it, so I can see for sure?"

"Come on, Nat."

"*Plllllllease*, Circ."

Circa clicked PRINT, and as they waited for the printer to spit out a copy, Nattie nervously chewed on her braid again. When Circa handed the picture over, she took a good look at Nattie's real right temple.

"Nattie Boone," she fussed, "you didn't even have a wart in the first place."

"What do you mean?" Nattie said, feeling her perfectly flawless skin.

"It must have just been a camera speck or something," Circa said.

"But it was there during the photo shoot," said Nattie.

"I didn't notice it this morning," said Circa.

"That's because my hair usually covers it," said Nattie. "I'm telling you, I've had it for days. My mom's been putting gunk on it all weekend."

"Maybe it just fell off then," said Circa.

"Ewww, what if it fell off in *here*?" said Nattie, totally grossing herself out and mildly grossing out Circa too.

Miles came over to Dad's desk as Mom cycled through the shots on her little camera screen.

"Didn't you have something you wanted to show me?" he said.

"Me?" said Nattie, looking beyond mortified.

"No," he said. "Circa."

"Oh," said Nattie, rolling up her portrait diploma-style.

"Um . . . yeah," Circa said sheepishly. "I think I did say that.

"Hmmm," she continued. "What *was* that I wanted to show you?" Circa twisted her mouth and looked to the air in a fake-thinking kind of way.

Miles gazed around at more of Dad's pictures as Circa worked herself into such a restless fit, if she wore braids, she would have chewed on one. Thankfully, Nattie had been so flustered by the wart scenario, she hardly noticed Circa's impatience.

"Bye, Nat. We'll hang later, okay?" Circa blurted out, surprised at how dismissive she sounded to her best friend. It was the first time she'd ever felt something invisible-thick like a secret hanging in the space between them.

Nattie gave Circa a puzzled look and turned to leave.

"Hey," Miles called out after her. "Good picture of your family, Nattie."

After that, Circa thought Nattie might very well skip out of the studio. She was so relieved Miles had killed the awkwardness with his compliment.

"Pull up a chair," she said to him. "*This* is what I wanted to show you."

She'd only just popped up that morning, but the bird
in glasses had already quoted every nursery rhyme six
times over. In the midst of "Hickory Dickory Dock," the
lone photographer wondered if there could indeed
be a "Mother Emu" that he'd never been told about. He
wondered if anyone would ever believe this wild story. But
mostly he wondered . . . Was her bottom half in Mongolia?

15

Something to Smile About

Miles dragged over a portrait stool for himself, as Mom excused herself to the other part of the house to take care of a few things. Circa felt sure that meant another long nap lying between heaps of laundry.

"Sorry to be so weird when Nat was here," said Circa as Miles settled in beside her at the desk. "But this is something nobody has seen except for me and Dad and Mom, because Dad made me promise to keep it just an *us* thing. And the thing is, even though you're not family, well, you sure do—"

Circa paused. "I guess after all that yucky feeling from our visit," she said, "I thought you might need at least a little something to smile about."

Circa leaned across the desk and slid out an old, familiar folder. Then she laid it on top of her crisscrossed legs and slowly opened it up. For a second, it felt as though she was handing over the key to the Monroe family treasure chest, so much so that Circa considered making an excuse and stuffing the folder right back into its spot. She started to close the folder up, but Miles quickly threw his hand out to stop her.

"Whoa. What's that?" he said.

Circa let the folder fall back open across her lap and revealed the topmost picture in the stack.

"This . . ." she said, taking a delighted glance at the photo before gently handing it over to Miles. "This is one of my favorites."

Miles studied the photo for a moment. It was an old gray image of a rickety porch, with a little girl sitting there, smiling peacefully at her own feet. Watching from every available hiding place in the house behind her were three furry koala bears. Miles read aloud the words scribbled beneath.

"'Meet Little Tish, who was carefully looked after by a skilled, if smelly, trio of nannies. There was Audrey to sing her to sleep at night, Reuben to make her toast, and Gus to keep her from falling into the lobster pit. All three would work tirelessly for years to make sure Tish was completely koala-fied for the challenges of adulthood, and one day she would greatly appreciate their efforts. (But on this particular Wednesday, she was far too captivated by her new chunky white shoes to notice.)'"

Miles just sat there for a moment studying the piece of paper in his hands. Circa couldn't stand the suspense.

"Sorry," she said, "I guess it was silly of me to think this would help. It's just that these always seem to make me feel better, no matter what."

Circa reached out to take the picture back from him, but Miles wouldn't let her. Instead, he tightened his grip on the page. And he smiled.

"What *is* this?" he said.

"They're called the Shopt," Circa explained timidly. "Like as in, Photoshopped, on my dad's photo editing program."

"You mean this is all fake?"

"Only some of it," said Circa. "The good parts. He took them from his other photos, or sometimes he just drew them right in. You can't even tell what's not real, can you?" she said proudly. "My dad was the best at that."

"Cool," said Miles, inspecting the photo superclose. "And he made up the story too?"

Circa nodded and picked up the next Shopt picture. Miles grabbed it and studied it intently. It was actually a strip of pictures from a photo booth. Each shot showed a snaggletoothed girl and a disturbingly huge plastic doll with pigtails crowding the frame.

Miles read its story aloud too.

"'Eager to show off her new shirt, Potty Doll pitched an absolute fit to be allowed into the photo booth. She'd never been good at personal space, and this was beginning to wear thin on her school friends. Especially when she'd shout 'I a big kid! I go pee pee!' at the most inopportune times.'"

Miles peered over the top of the page at Circa for a moment. And then, just like that, he began to laugh. Circa felt a tremendous satisfaction at the sun she'd coaxed from behind his clouds. She started to shuffle through the stack of Shopt photos to pick out other personal favorites for Miles, but he stopped her from it, insisting on seeing them all in order so that he wouldn't miss any. One by one, they studied each of the Shopt pictures, taking turns reading the stories out loud. Before they knew it, they'd moved to the studio floor and shuffled through so many Shopt pics, dozens of images were spread out in front of them in a black-and-white, sepia, and full-color display of imagination across the carpet.

"My dad said that some of these had some hints of truth to them," Circa said. "Like this one here, with the tuba going over the waterfall. He told me that once, someone found a chunk of brass at the water's edge. Or this one that has the classroom with all the candy vines growing, he said that he remembered once hearing about a town in Alabama where the kids got to stay home from school while they pruned the walls."

"No way," said Miles. "Was he being serious?"

Circa shrugged. "I thought so," she said.

"Crazy," said Miles as they hit the halfway point in the collection. "I kind of wish this stack would go on and on."

Time seemed to fly by as the two of them read on about the octopus that crashed a wedding, the fisherman who caught a disco ball, a racehorse that wore roller skates, and much more. As they did, Circa noticed that the Shopt seemed to have the very same effect on Miles that it did on her. Like at the end of the afternoon, they'd both choose to be tucked back into the folder with the pictures if they could.

"Check this out," said Circa, pulling a fresh one from the dwindling stack. The photo was of a gardener posing proudly next to a bush blooming with cartoon talk bubbles that said *Kapow!* The story under it was about how she'd snuck her husband's old comic books into the compost pile.

"This one's always been my mom's favorite," said Circa. "She says she wishes she had a *Kapow!* plant to pluck some bravery off of every now and then."

"And speaking of that brave lady," Mom interrupted from behind, spooking Circa and Miles from their trance. Not only was Mom awake, but she carried a tray full of supper, and boy did it look good. She set the tray on the floor and off-loaded two glasses of milk, two not-paper plates full of steaming pot roast and black-eyed peas, and two oatmeal cream pies already out of the plastic.

"Thanks, Mom," said Circa.

"Yeah, thanks," said Miles.

"Thank the Boones," said Mom. "I'm just handy with the microwave is all."

But Circa knew that just being able to assemble a meal was a small victory for her mother. As Mom got up to leave with the empty tray, Circa could see her smiling at the gardener and the prized *Kapow!* bush. And it didn't even look like a fake "Sunny Backdrop" smile.

"Be sure not to spill milk on that one," Mom said as she left the studio.

The kids wolfed down their supper in no time and resumed the storytelling. As they neared the bottom of the stack, Circa recognized the jutted-out corner of a very familiar picture. It was the Shopt version of the Linholt Reunion photo, and it set off alarm bells in Circa's head. She didn't want Miles to see that one, knowing that it would be such a bummer for him. And she certainly didn't want to have to tell Miles about how Dad never got to put a story to it. So, while Miles was reading the next-to-the-next-to-the-last story, Circa slid out the Linholt one and twisted around to tuck it away somewhere. As she did, she snuck another good look at that baby.

And that's when a notion so impossible, yet so suddenly inescapable, began to take shape in Circa's brain. Her mind raced in a dozen directions as she assembled the growing pile of clues. Miles's crinkle, his snoring, the way he had defended her, his crooked smile, the déjà-vu feeling she'd had the first moment she laid eyes on him. The Linholt Reunion, Miles's blank, start-fresh memory. The Shopt photo of a reunion that happened thirteen years ago. That *baby*.

"This one's hilarious," said Miles from what seemed like the other end of a tunnel.

"I know," said Circa, in that slow-motion way a person does when an idea flattens her good. No way, she thought. No way. She looked at Miles. Then she snuck another look at the picture behind her.

"You didn't even see which one I was talking about," said Miles, but Circa was oblivious.

Could that baby . . . No. It can't be.

No, of course he couldn't. It was, after all, an impossible thing. Yet for some reason, she couldn't seem to shake the thought. The *what if* simply wouldn't leave her alone.

Circa reached out, pretending to stretch, and slid the reunion photo under the desk.

"So what was up with that one?" asked Miles. "Why didn't your dad write a story for it?"

Circa cringed at the thought of Miles finding the reunion photo. There was simply no way she could possibly explain the ideas in her head to him right now. Unfortunately, when she scooted closer to him, she realized that he'd discovered something nearly as bad. She'd been so busy trying to hide the reunion picture, she hadn't even taken notice of the very last picture waiting inside the Shopt file . . . a folded-up one that Miles had already smoothed open onto the floor in front of him. It was the old World War II soldier picture she'd tried her hand at editing days before. The one she'd added the poor incomplete baby into. Mom must have found it on the floor and put it in the folder.

"My dad didn't write a story for it because *I* did that one," Circa said, both relieved and disgusted. "And I hate it."

"You hate it? Why?" said Miles.

"Because it's terrible," she said. "Look how bad I did that baby, all lumpy and pixelated. I forgot to even put his other arm on."

Miles laughed. "Well, I agree it's not as good as the rest," he said. "But it's not as bad as you think."

There he went with that Dad way of encouraging, thought Circa. "Thanks," she said. "Even though you're wrong."

Miles looked at the picture again. "So then did *you* give this one a story?" he said.

"Of course not," said Circa.

"Don't you think you're being unfair?" said Miles. He looked Circa right in the eye, so serious it made her squirm. "I mean, come on, Circa. Doesn't that lumpy, pixelated baby soldier deserve a story as much as Potty Doll?"

Miles put on that mischievous brow crinkle again, leaving Circa unsure whether to punch him in the arm or laugh. Since his scarred arms had seen enough trouble, she laughed.

"I got you," he said.

"No, no. You're exactly right," said Circa, feeling a rush of silly mischief herself. She picked up the picture and wondered what in the world Dad would have concocted out of the black-and-white disaster before her.

"As a matter of fact," she began. "I do happen to know this baby's story."

"Tell me more," said Miles.

"You see," said Circa. "This baby here is one of your ancestors."

"Really?"

"Yep. He's your great-uncle Mileage."

"Great-Uncle Mileage?"

"That's him."

For quick inspiration, Circa looked to the snapshot of Dad and Mom and her as a newborn that was taped to the edge of Dad's monitor. She thought of the kind of adventure Dad might scare up for a pixelated baby in the midst of all those army men.

"Your great-uncle Mileage was the only baby soldier to be in the war," she continued.

"Oh, yeah?" said Miles. "Seems kind of cruel to let a baby fight in a war."

"Of course it does," said Circa. "What I mean is that he was a soldier who *spied* during the war."

"Great-Uncle Mileage, the baby spy," said Miles.

"That's right," she said. "The good guys would place him all bundled up on the enemy's doorstep so that they'd take him in. Then he'd fake being asleep while listening in on their plans and crawl out in the middle of the night to be picked up and debriefed."

"Debriefed. Ha. Good one," said Miles. "Meaning he'd have

his diaper changed *and* share the info, right? I'm guessing he could talk too?"

"Nope," said Circa. "He tapped out messages in Morse code. With his nonmissing arm, of course."

"Of course," Miles said. "Great-Uncle Mileage, the one-armed, code-tapping, escape-artist baby spy."

"I was worried you might not be able to handle it," said Circa.

"Handle it?" said Miles. "I wish I could meet him. This is the best thing I've heard about my past in days."

"It's the *only* thing," said Circa.

"Exactly," Miles said.

Circa felt pleased and energized. She'd surprised herself with the ability to make up her own Shopt story. Together, she and Miles gathered up the photos and stacked them back into the Shopt folder. As soon as Miles looked away, Circa snuck the hidden reunion picture from under Dad's desk and slid it back in as well.

Miles muttered *Potty Doll* under his breath and laughed.

"Really," he said. "Thanks for showing me all that stuff. It sounds dumb, I guess, but it kind of helped me to forget."

"Forget the forgetting?" said Circa.

Miles crinkled again, making Circa's mind reignite with thoughts of Shopt magic. "Hey, Miles," she said. "This might be a weird question, but do you remember seeing any crazy stuff that day at the reunion? Like a really giant potato? Or, um, a beaver with a bugle?"

Miles nodded an emphatic *yes*. Circa's heart raced. "Yes? You did?"

"No," said Miles. "I meant yes, that was a weird question."

"Oh," said Circa. "Sorry. Never mind then. But, um, did you?"

Miles shook his head.

"You know," he said, handing Circa the soldier photo, "you really should do some more of that photo work. I think you're actually pretty decent at it."

"I don't know," said Circa. "I want to, but—"

"But what?" said Miles. "You said he taught you how, right?"

"Yes. He did," she said, looking to the family photo once more.

Miles looked to see what it was that kept stealing her attention. "So," he said with a laugh. "Did your dad Photoshop that lumpy baby?"

"No." Circa laughed and slapped him on the shoulder. "That one's *me*, you jackola."

Meet Little Tish, who was carefully looked after by a
skilled, if smelly, trio of nannies. There was Audrey to sing
her to sleep at night, Reuben to make her toast, and Gus to
keep her from falling into the lobster pit. All three would
work tirelessly for years to make sure Tish was completely
koala-fied for the challenges of adulthood, and one day
she would greatly appreciate their efforts. (But on this
particular Wednesday, she was far too captivated by her
new chunky white shoes to notice.)

16

Shopping for Miles

Circa slid the Shopt folder back in its spot as Mom peeked into the studio.

"Miles," Mom said. "Why don't you come upstairs and pick out some clothes that'll fit you. I figure if you're going to be with us a little longer than we thought, you'll need something more than two shirts and a pair of jeans. And I've found an old box of things Mr. Monroe hasn't worn in years."

Miles looked at Circa as if to ask her whether she was okay with that plan. She did feel a little funny about it, but gave him a nod anyway. She was itching for some alone time at Dad's computer.

"Sorry we can't afford to get you something new," Mom called from the kitchen, but Circa knew that even if she found five hundred dollars in her pocket, Mom wouldn't go out shopping.

"I thought you said she couldn't handle anything?" whispered Miles as he stood and stretched. "She seems like she's doing pretty okay tonight."

Mom and Miles went on upstairs, but Circa stayed behind in

the studio. She sunk into Dad's chair and woke the computer, gazing at the screen so intently, the icons started to blur into little glowing shapes, one for each of the new questions in her mind. She wondered what it was about Miles being around that seemed to be making Mom able to do things that were impossible for her before. Could it be that Mom sensed the same weird connection to the boy that Circa had? Circa thought about the appearance of that nest and the disappearance of Nattie's wart and wondered if her own Shopt bits had just been pointing her toward the real answer to the Miles mystery. But *how*? And *why*? Could someone just appear?

Then in an instant, Circa considered the insanity of it all. That she'd completely flipped out, just over a nest, a wart, and a stranger. How she was missing Dad so bad, her mind could very well be playing tricks on her. The evidence seemed like so little and yet somehow just enough to build a dream on. She wondered what Dad would have said about all this. Whether he'd have told her to calm down or, even better, been just as caught up in the possibilities. Or what if all this was because Miles really did have a message for her and just hadn't remembered that part yet?

As Mom and Miles banged around moving boxes upstairs, Circa wondered if she should reveal her suspicions to Miles. Then she considered how she would feel if someone said to her, "Hey, so I've got this crazy idea that you may have magically appeared out of nowhere because of this goof my dad did." And there she found her answer. There was simply no way it would help Miles to know that either Circa was crazy or that he was Shopt.

Circa was tempted to take a new picture with Mom's camera and do a Shopt test on it, but she knew that Mom and Miles would be back down any minute. So instead, she decided to just practice her skills on whatever inspired her. She turned on the iPod and swiped to Dad's favorite song, turning the volume down just low enough to be background music. Then Circa launched Photoshop and clicked on the folder where Dad had stored their own family snapshots. There, she opened the first picture in the list, one taken just a few weeks ago of her and Nattie sitting in the Boones' front yard. They were right next to the empty doghouse that Nattie had built two years before in hopes of getting a dog that she would name Ernie Brown. In the picture, Circa and Nattie were playing "rock-paper-karate chop" with each other like they had when they were younger, and Mom had captured them in a fit of laughter. Just looking at the picture made Circa feel bad about blowing Nattie off earlier. Inspired by the words of the song, she set to work adding a cloud shaped like an angel into the vast blue sky above them. As she worked, she repeated in her head her dad's special techniques that he'd shared with her over the years.

Once the fluffy angel was complete, Circa rolled the chair back and took a good look. Even if clouds were among the simplest Shopt things to do, still, she was delighted by the result. So much so, it was just as if Dad were sitting on the stool right next to her, egging her on. She considered the sad fact that Miles being Shopt would mean that there was no story for him to even pull off the shelf. No matter how hard he searched, it would go back only so far. This thought alone let her know what to do with that angel. "Let's give it a story," she could almost hear Dad saying. Something else about that soldier baby. So she did.

While the photo printed, Circa found the very same pen that Dad had used for Shopt stories, the kind that would write on glossy photo paper without smudging. She wrote underneath the picture:

Great-Uncle Mileage, as it turns out, loved the sky and always wanted to be a pilot, but had to of course wait until he was no longer a baby to become one. As a grown-up spy, he got real good at being a skywriter and sending his spy messages in the air. And many years later, when he retired from spy work, he still used his skills to make smoke drawings for fun. Smoke donuts, smoke hearts, and smoke shamrocks that lingered like clouds in the sky. Once, he did his stealthiest mission yet, puffing out an angel far above two unsuspecting Georgia girls' heads. He was hovering above Georgia, though, for a mission a lot more important. He was on the hunt for his long-lost nephew . . . code name Miles.

Just as she finished writing the last line, Miles poked his head into the studio and said, "Well? Is it me?"

Circa turned to look. Miles stood in the doorway wearing one of Dad's outfits from way back when Circa was little and when Dad was skinny. An Oscar Mayer Wienermobile T-shirt and gray sweatpants from so long ago, Circa was surprised that they even still had them. She knew in her gut that she should be saddened by this scene, but it felt all right to her. So much so, she struggled to hide her perplexed look from Miles.

"Hang on," he said. "I forgot the best part."

Miles looked away for a second and turned back around wearing something that made Circa have to do a double take. It was a pair of purple, star-shaped glasses. Glasses just like the ones she had added to Dad's picture the other night. Circa couldn't believe her eyes.

"Where in the world did you get those?" she asked.

"In the same box as the old clothes," said Miles. "Why? You want to look this cool too?"

"Let me see them," she said.

Miles walked over and handed her the glasses. Circa turned them over half a dozen times, gawking at and feeling every inch of them.

"Bad move, I guess," said Miles. "Did I just make you sad?"

"No, no," she said, inspecting every scratch and scuff. "Definitely not sad."

She set the glasses carefully on Dad's desk, planning to follow up on this mystery as soon as possible. "Look," she said to Miles. "I did something while you were upstairs."

Circa handed him the freshly edited pic. "It's not much," she said. "But I think you'll like it."

"You Shopt," he said with a hint of delight in his voice. "And fast."

"Look," she said. "I did a story too."

Miles mumbled the story to himself, enjoying every bit of it. "You've definitely inherited your dad's weird imagination," he said. "I dig it. Great-Uncle Mileage makes me proud again. I can't wait to hear about what he does next."

Miles handed the picture back to Circa, but when she moved to set it on top of one of the messy stacks of business on the desk, he stopped her.

"Why aren't you putting it in the Shopt folder?" he asked.

"I don't know," said Circa. "Didn't seem good enough, I guess."

"Of course it is," said Miles, grabbing it from her and putting it into the folder himself. "Great-Uncle Mileage will not be denied his proper place!"

"Thanks," said Circa.

"I gotta go," said Miles. "Your mom told me to pick out a couple of dress shirts before she puts the box away. I'll see you later."

"And don't worry," he said on the way out. "I won't take the Wienermobile shirt with me when I go home . . . or the purple glasses."

"So glad," said Circa, wearing a grin, but feeling a twinge of sadness at the thought of him leaving. "Good night."

Mom and Miles passed each other in the doorway.

"Circ," Mom said, coming over and giving Circa a big hug from behind the chair. "Don't linger too long in the studio tonight, okay?"

"Okay, Mom. I won't."

"Oh, I just love that shot of you and Nat," Mom said, coming closer to Dad's desk than she had in weeks. She stopped halfway there and gazed at the screen. "And would you look at that? I never noticed that cloud looks just like an angel. How sweet."

Circa puffed up inside. But she was far too distracted by a purple plastic mystery to revel in her Shopt success for too long.

This felt big. This felt like proof. Yet even Miles had mentioned that she had her dad's weird imagination. So could that be what this Shopt theory of hers was? Just imagination?

"Mom," she said, feeling chills run up both arms. "Didn't you say you'd never known Dad to wear star glasses?"

It was a really big deal, the first time Lady Liberty sneezed.

17

Platypi

Circa swiveled around and handed Mom the glasses.

"I did say I'd never known your dad to wear these," Mom said, looking them over thoroughly. "He must have picked them up as a joke way back when," she said. "I'm surprised you remember them from when you were so little. I don't even remember them."

Mom left for bed with a last reminder for Circa not to linger too late. But Circa wasn't so content. She shuffled around the desk until she found the edited version of the picture of Dad. Then she held it up and compared the real glasses to it. The ones in the picture looked new and bright, but the real deal glasses were warped and faded like they'd been in an attic for years. Still, Circa couldn't help wondering if the glasses were yet another in a series of extraordinary events, perhaps the most extraordinary being Miles. But who in the world could she talk to about it? Certain that she had no one in the house who could handle her going loopy, Circa picked up the phone and dialed.

Thankfully, Nattie answered.

"First of all," Circa said, "no, I didn't tell Miles about the wart."

"Phew, good," said Nattie. "If you find it, you can keep it."

"Yuck."

"Sorry," said Nattie. "Watching your little brother slob all over a hunk of cheese kind of puts you in gross mode."

"Double yuck," said Circa.

"So what's going on?" said Nattie. "You sound spacey. You all right? Did Miles remember anything yet?"

"I'm okay, and no," said Circa. "But I have to ask you something, and I know it might sound crazy, but just hear me out."

Circa wondered how in the world she could phrase her question without sounding totally nuts.

"Nat, do you think that things can just appear out of nowhere?"

"What kind of things?"

"Like anything."

Nattie was silent for a few seconds. "Sure," she said. "I guess anything's possible."

"Yeah, but I mean, you think that still happens nowadays?" said Circa. "Things appearing out of nowhere? And not just that, but maybe even with the help of a person?"

"You mean like a miracle?"

"Sort of," said Circa. "It's kind of hard for me to explain right now without you thinking I'm nutso."

"Hmmm," said Nattie. "Maybe you're just having a platypus moment, Circa."

"A what?"

"You know," Nattie said. "Like the way the first person

147

to ever see a platypus must have felt. Like it's such a bizarre thing that it's hard to describe to anyone without them thinking you're Looney Tunes. And yet, there's that platypus right there in front of you, real as it can be."

Circa thought about the nest, the wart, and the glasses. And then she considered the really big platypus . . . Miles. "But what if it's several bizarre things?" she said. "Would a few platypuses wander up to you in the very same week?"

"Platy*pi*," said Nattie.

"Whatever," said Circa. "Wait. I have an idea. Stay up a little while, Nattie. I'll call you back."

Powered by the confidence that came with her successful cloud angel, Circa rolled up to Dad's computer again and took another look at the pic of her and Nattie in the Boones' front yard, wondering what she could edit fast and simply as a test. She was immediately inspired by the little empty doghouse in the background and searched up a photo of the perfect dog for Nattie, the dog who never quite happened because Durret was born and brought with him three dogs' worth of mess.

After finding a shaggy brown-and-white dog just like the one Nattie had always wanted, Circa set out to do the work quickly. She used a basic Photoshop technique that Dad did all the time, carefully tracing around the dog, copying him from the one pic and pasting him onto the yard. She blended and tinkered with the coloring and such to make him look like an actual part of the scene. Like a real deal Ernie Brown Boone. After that, she saved her work, just in case that made a difference when it came to Shopt magic. Then she went to the front studio window to check. It was a too shadowy for her to see that side of Nattie's yard in the distance, and she sure didn't want to scare the maybe-dog off by running out there, so she called Nattie back for a bird's-eye view.

"Hey," Circa said. "Look out your bedroom window at your yard, and tell me what you see."

"Okay . . ." Nattie said all drawn out. "Hang on. All right, I see a mailbox, a light that needs changing, some bushes, some grass. What exactly—"

"Look all over the yard."

"I'm looking."

"Near the doghouse."

"Okay . . ."

"Anything moving around?"

"Yeah."

"*Yeah?*" Circa felt a flood of exhilaration.

"Yeah," said Nattie. "I see my dad sneaking from the car with a stack of presents in his arms. Is this a trick? Have you done something goofy for my birthday?"

Circa was jarred back into reality. Oh no, she thought. She'd totally forgotten Nattie's birthday was this week. "Never mind, Nat," she said, her excitement drying up as fast as it had come. "I was just being dumb is all. And um, happy early birthday."

Circa hung up and shut down the computer. In a muddled haze of potential, disappointment, guilt, hunger, and exhaustion, she left the studio for the night. On the way upstairs, she stopped in the kitchen for a snack and noticed that Mom had neatly sliced a bad-day pill in two, leaving one of the halves on the edge of the sink. That small win for Mom seemed like reason enough for Circa to have dessert at bedtime, so she cut herself a giant wedge of peanut butter pie and whisked it up to her room. There, she perched at her open window and savored every bite, pausing in between to look at only one thing. That nest. That big, goofy, lopsided nest. All the while, as if they were mocking her, a bevy of neighborhood dogs barked in the distance.

When you're hired to lead all the inflatable weirdos out of a town, the problem arises where to house said weirdos. You can't just deflate them all, because that would be cruel. And you can't very well open a bouncy playground, because after all, it is only 1903. So, instead, you let them stay with you. . . . Then you scatter some nails around your yard and hope for the best.

18

No News

For three days they ran Miles's picture on the local news, but still, no word. And for three days, Circa began every morning and ended every night at her window, studying the freckled eggs in that nest and still wondering about it, the wart, the glasses, the dog, and the boy. Mom was doing more and more portrait appointments, sometimes as Sunny Backdrop, but mostly as her real self, with the occasional need to be excused to secretly compose her thoughts. Miles was eating better, sleeping better, and looking surprisingly less lost by the hour. Nattie popped in as often as she could for lessons on how to play Chicken Foot, when she wasn't busy watching little Durret eat cheese. All of this made life at the Monroe house feel like it had been sprinkled with a dash of normal across the top. Circa felt glad that Miles had not been claimed yet, comforted by his company and convinced that his presence alone meant that there must be some kind of message from Dad inside him. After all, she thought, why else would this sort of thing even be allowed to happen?

During her rare alone moments, Circa brainstormed possible

ways to further verify her Shopt ideas. She couldn't ask Miles too many questions without him being suspicious. She knew that it might crush him for her to blurt out her thoughts, like she was telling him he wasn't human, or worse yet, not even real. She tried secretly searching up some of Dad's past Shopt work to see if any of it had come true, but had found that near impossible with the Internet still knocked out from the storms. Not to mention the fact that most of the Shopt pictures were so old that most of the stories would be unverifiable anyway. Besides, Circa thought, maybe not *all* the stuff became real? Maybe the only Shopt details that came true were the ones that would help deliver Dad's special message from heaven to her. Either way, it was clear that the only way to gather more evidence was to put her own Shopt powers to the test as soon as she could.

Thankfully, she and Miles were spending as much time as they could at Dad's computer getting in some good practice on some Dad-style Shopt work. Together, the two of them came up with crazy photo concoctions for Circa to copy and paste Great-Uncle Mileage into. And together, they made up even crazier stories to go with them. Tales of the continuing saga of the spy baby and his exploits throughout the decades. How he grew up to travel the world, obsessed with the ongoing mission to find his great-nephew Miles. How he never stopped searching, even after being injured when his plane grazed a towering twenty-story pretzel and had to make an emergency landing.

Every time she sat in that swivel chair and worked, Circa wondered if Dad had felt such satisfaction when he created the Shopt stories for her. She wondered if he would have done things differently had he known that they just might come true. Most of all, she loved the sparkly, hopeful feeling it gave her inside. Made up as everything was, Miles also loved discovering a possible version of his history and seeing a Shopt photo to document it, so much so he'd cut a meal short to join Circa at the computer. Even when she was only half done, he'd nag her to give him hints about the story.

One particularly sparkly afternoon, Circa and Miles had just wrapped up an image of the Great Sphinx covered in orange sherbet. In its story, Great-Uncle Mileage had hijacked an ice cream delivery truck and cooled down the monument just before record high temperatures could destroy it. When he finished reading the tale, Miles paused.

"So you think Captain Mann has tried to sneak out of Maple Grove any more this week?"

Circa couldn't believe Miles had mentioned the captain, after all that misery before.

"Did the hijacked truck remind you of him?" said Circa.

"No, the Egyptian heat he was blasting in that van," he said. "But honestly, I haven't been able to get him out of my head ever since Monday."

"Oh, man. Sorry," said Circa. "I told you. You're *not* going to end up at Maple Grove, Miles."

"No, it's okay," said Miles. "I didn't mean that. It's just I've been feeling sorry for him, sitting there all day long in a room by himself."

"Yeah," said Circa. "Me, too. I just don't know how to make it better, though, if he won't even let us see him."

Miles's face lit up. "This might be dumb," he said, "but maybe we could do a Shopt story for him. You know, just for fun. You could put it under his door or something."

Circa got all twitchy inside. "I don't think so," she said.

"How come?"

"I told you before," she said. "We've just kind of always thought of the Shopt as a Monroe thing, you know? My dad took his work very seriously. He didn't want this to mess up his reputation. I mean, I've never even told Nat about the Shopt stuff."

Miles gave her a baffled look. "Circa, are you forgetting something?" he said.

"What?"

"That *I'm* not a Monroe," he said.

"Yeah but you might—" Circa began. "Well, you live here. So that counts," she said. "Besides, the Maple Grove people will have the Memory Wall someday."

"But what if Captain Mann doesn't have anything to put on the wall?" said Miles.

"Nurse Lily said he's got that one picture," said Circa, feeling a twinge of guilt for keeping the Shopt a secret from a man who could probably really use it. "Hey, you want to see some of the Maple Grove pictures?" she said, changing the subject fast.

"Sure," said Miles. "But aren't they, like, protected by a mom alarm or something?"

"Yeah. Probably," said Circa. "But she still doesn't come near this desk, so maybe she won't notice."

She double-clicked open a file called MEMORY WALL on the

155

computer. Then she dragged to select thirty or so scanned pictures and launched an automatic slideshow.

"My dad had finished restoring a few of them," she said. "He'd begun to restore a few others, but most of them are still damaged or faded."

Circa narrated the photos as they appeared on the screen as if she were telling of lifelong friends. Miss Rempy next to her plane. Hank-not-the-Mayor as a little boy in his family's pecan orchard. The Nelsons with a shiny silver cup they'd won in a dance contest. Even one of Joe the food man with a huge catfish caught when he was Circa's age. Then there were photos of things the way they used to be in Wingate. People riding horses and driving tractors. A drive-in restaurant with a giant onion ring—or was it a skinny doughnut?—on top. A myriad of storefronts that had changed hands a dozen times.

"See?" Circa sighed. "It's a ton of work still to be done."

"So when are you going to start?" said Miles.

Circa's shoulders went heavy. "I don't know," she said. "It's kind of overwhelming to think about, the big pile of work and my mom not wanting me to even try it."

Miles grinned. "Hey, it can't be any more overwhelming than covering the Great Sphinx in sherbet, right?"

"I guess not," laughed Circa, a new confidence awakening in her.

Mom wandered into the studio to set up for her next portrait appointment. Circa stopped the slideshow and closed out of the Maple Grove folder with a swiftness that made Miles snicker.

"Guys, I've been thinking we might need to go ahead and make a poster with Miles's picture on it to post on a few bulletin boards around the area," Mom said. "Like the post office and grocery stores and such. For people who've quit watching all the coverage about the . . . what do you call it, Circa?"

"Ordeal."

"Yeah, for those who've quit watching about the ordeal on the news. Plus there are still tons of people like us without Internet connection. One of those people might just belong to Miles."

Mom loaded a big stack of paper into her printer. "I've put together a simple poster on my laptop, Circa. Would you guys mind printing fifty or so off?"

"Sure, Mom."

"And maybe you can go hang them around after church tomorrow?"

"Me and Miles?"

"That's fine."

"Will you go with us?" Miles asked Mom.

"No, I trust you two to handle it," she said without hesitation.

Circa shot an *I knew she wouldn't* look at Miles.

"How about Nat?" Circa asked.

"If it's okay with the Boones."

"If *what's* okay with the Boones?" came a cheerful voice from the front studio entrance.

Nattie came bouncing in wearing stiff new jeans and a tie-dyed tank. "Hey, guys. We playing dominoes?" she said.

"Printing posters," said Circa. "Want to help?"

"Sure," said Nattie, gliding gladly into the mix.

Per Mom's instruction, Circa printed fifty of the Miles posters. The poster was a simple one, with the picture Mom had taken of him, and underneath in big letters it said, DO YOU HAVE INFORMATION ABOUT THIS BOY?

Once the printing was done, Miles laid the posters out next to each other ten at a time on the available desk space while Circa set to stamping the Studio Monroe info on the bottom of each one. Ever since Circa was old enough not to make a total mess of it, Dad had always let her be the one to stamp the Studio Monroe logo on the backs of restored pictures. The smell of the inkpad gave her a lump of sadness in her throat. On the other end of the desk, Nattie found herself a yellow highlighter pen and drew borders around the edges of the posters for extra effect. Circa laughed inside when she saw her friend sneak one of the posters, fold it twice, and cram it into her back pocket.

Once the flyers were complete, Circa stacked them up neatly and Miles rested on his stool near Dad's computer. Mom had already ushered in her next portrait family and was arranging two parents and twin five-year-old kids on a velvety bench.

"Dominoes?" said Nattie, trying to wipe the yellow from her fingertips. But Circa had found herself itching to do some more Shopt work with Miles, especially since she'd found out they'd be busy hanging posters all day tomorrow. She could even maybe sneak some kind of a secret Shopt test into the work they did together.

"Nah," said Circa. "I'm kind of tired of playing Chicken Foot."

"How about another game, then?" said Nattie. "We could do just regular dominoes."

"I'm not really in the mood," said Circa.

"Me, either," Miles chimed in.

"Hey, Nat, how about this?" said Circa. "Mom said me and you and Miles can all go hang the posters tomorrow after church. You want to?"

"Sure," said Nattie, with a hint of huffiness. "But you can still play a game even if you're not in the mood, you know. Especially on somebody's *birthday*."

Birthday. Oh, man, Circa thought. No wonder Nattie had the new outfit on. How could she have forgotten her best friend's birthday not just one time, but *twice*? She'd made a mental note, but somehow her crowded brain had crumpled it right up.

"Um, surprise!" said Circa with awkward overenthusiasm. "Happy birthday, Nat! Look here." Circa started clicking like crazy on the computer, making the printer spit out a picture in record time. "I made you a present this year."

Circa handed over the still-wet photo of the brown-and-white dog. "See?" she said. "I did you an Ernie Brown."

Nattie took the picture by the corners. "Thanks a lot," she forced out under her breath. Mom's camera flash-lit the whole room, as Circa flashed a nervous grin.

Nattie turned dramatically on her heel to leave the studio, but not without first leaning in close to Circa's ear. "You and your new favorite friend have fun today," she whispered sharply.

Circa felt her face go hot. "Nattie Boone, I'm going to pretend you didn't even say that," she said. "See you tomorrow."

In a swirl of air, Nattie was out the door.

"Happy birthday," said Miles to no one.

Cousin Octibald had never RSVP'd to the wedding, so
no one really expected him to show. Yet there he was,
sopping up the dance floor, hogging the punch bowl, and
wriggling his way into every single picture. Someone heard
the preacher nearly curse. Two of the in-laws fainted.
All Aunt Floreen would say was that the big sucker could
have at least had the decency to wear a suit. Fortunately,
the bride and groom were unfazed. After all, hitched is
hitched, whether it's squishy or not.

19

Stanley Gets Flattened

Before the Monroes even got past the church welcome mat on Sunday morning, a dozen people had swarmed around to meet their young guest like he was some kind of celebrity. Word had spread about Miles's plight, and as a result, the amount of food brought into the church kitchen for the family had doubled. Circa made a special point of apologizing to the secretary for wrestling the photo of the building out of her hands the week before, but immediately followed her apology with a quiet request to get the pic later for use on the Memory Wall. Then Circa, Miles, and Mom sat in the little room with the one-way window at the back of the auditorium, just in case Mom was overcome with a panic that was difficult to push through. There were three short pews in there full of young mothers and their newborns, old people and their walkers, and the Monroes.

After church let out, Circa and Miles met up with Nattie in the parking lot, where they grabbed up some foil-wrapped sandwiches from the big tray in Mom's arms and retrieved the stack of posters and two rolls of tape from the car.

"Thanks for coming with us today, Nat," said Circa.

"Sure thing," said Nattie quietly. "And sorry about that friend thing I said yesterday."

"That's all right," said Circa. "I'm sorry I forgot your birthday."

"No sweat, marmoset," said Nattie. "That's the thing about birthdays. There'll always be another one."

Nattie looked sheepishly at Circa, like she hoped Circa hadn't heard that last part.

"Be safe and be sweet," called out Mrs. Boone.

"Take care of each other," said Mom, searching for her keys.

"Bye," said Circa and Nattie in unison, accompanied by a quick wave from Miles. Then they set off to go hang forty-nine posters, planning first to hit the church side of town, and then work their way toward the business side. With each poster, Circa considered saying a little prayer that no one would respond, but then felt guilty for it.

By the time they turned onto Third Street, most of the posters had been successfully taped to bulletin boards all over town. Circa rolled up the last few in the stack in her sweaty fist as the three friends neared the Maple Grove Residence, where she conveniently suggested they stop and rest their feet out front.

"Hey, how about we go in for a visit?" she suggested as if it had just popped into her head.

"No, Circa. Not today," said Miles, already sweating through Dad's old dress shirt. "I'm not in the mood for Stanley today."

"Yeah, Circ, come on. We're all kind of pooped out anyway, right?" said Nattie.

"Stanley, schmanley," said Circa. "He's probably off on

Sunday anyway." Circa nudged Nattie with her elbow. "And you'll get to meet my friends," she said.

"Well . . . okay," said Nattie.

"Come on, Miles," said Circa. "We can check on Captain Mann."

At the mention of the Captain, Miles seemed to briefly consider her offer, but then declined.

"You guys go . . . and tell him I said hello," he said. "I just want to hang back this time."

"You sure?" said Circa, but inside, she really couldn't blame him after how the last visit had made him feel.

Miles nodded. "Wait," he said as they walked toward the door. "You sure that creep won't be in there to bother you today?"

"Sure as I can be," she said. "You just wait here and don't go anywhere."

"I'll be on that bench over on the side," he said. "And you all don't make me sit in this hot sun forever."

"Got it," said Circa as they walked toward the front door, hope-hope-hoping she'd been right about Stanley being off on Sunday. Then sure enough, *hallelujah*, he wasn't in the lobby.

"See, I told you guys," she said to Nattie. "No Stanley."

"Hey, Lily," said Circa as they entered the cool lobby.

"Circa. What a treat," said Lily.

"And this is Nattie," said Circa.

Nattie smiled and waved as she looked around the lobby.

"Pleased to meet you, Nattie," said Lily. "Where's your other friend, Circa?"

"Oh, Miles?" said Circa. "He couldn't come in today." Circa

rolled and rerolled the posters in her hand. "We just want to say a quick hey to everybody," she said.

"Well, you go right on, then," said Lily. "Most of them are napping right now, but you might catch one or two awake."

"What about Captain Mann?" said Circa. "Can we see him?"

Lily sighed and shook her head. "Still not talking to anybody," she said. "He hasn't even come out of that room in days. And the only thing he'll let inside is a food tray."

"All right," said Circa. "Come on, Nat."

When the two of them entered the atrium, Nattie gasped. "Ooowee, Circ, you never told me it was this beautiful," she said.

"Yes, I did," said Circa.

Keeping Miles in mind, Circa began a fast-talking tour of the circle for Nattie. Sure enough, Lily had been right. Most all of the residents were asleep. All but Hank-not-the-Mayor, who managed to tell Nattie all about his colon polyps before Circa pulled her away.

Within a matter of minutes, they made it around to the purple door.

"This is the room where my great-aunt used to live, and where Captain Mann lives now," whispered Circa. "Only that's not really his name. He got here last week, and he won't much talk to anybody. Lily says they think it's dementia. And you can't tell another soul this, but—"

Nattie leaned in close.

"He escaped in the van the other week," said Circa.

"No way," Nattie said. "Where'd he go?"

"Don't know," said Circa. "Lily said he just up and came back when the gas got low."

Circa stepped up and knocked softly. "Hello in there, Captain," she said. "It's me, Circa, again. I've got my friend Nattie here with me. Our other friend Miles couldn't make it today, but I wanted to tell you that he sure has been wondering about you a lot this week."

Circa and Nattie stood with their ears pressed to the purple door.

"Sad," said Nattie. "I wish there was something we could do for him."

Circa thought about what Miles had said yesterday and suddenly got an idea.

"You know, you and my friend Miles have a lot in common, Captain," she said.

There wasn't a peep from the other side.

"Anyway, I thought maybe you'd like to at least see a picture of him," said Circa, unrolling one of Miles's posters and gently sliding it through the gap underneath the door. It wasn't as good as a Shopt story, but at least it was something.

"Let's wait a minute," said Circa. "Maybe he'll let us in."

While they waited, Nattie gazed through the kaleidoscope of windows in the ceiling of the atrium.

"You know, I've been thinking," Nattie whispered. "There hasn't been a full moon yet this month. And you know how weird things happen during a full moon. Who knows?" she said. "Maybe Miles will get his memory back then."

Circa shushed Nattie when she heard some slow shuffling followed by what sounded like a piece of paper being picked up.

"Um. Anyway . . ." Circa spoke softly to the door again, her heart beating fast. "There's going to be a big surprise in the lobby here one of these days soon, and you sure don't want to miss it. It's a big wall full of pictures, and if you have a photo you want on there, I can scan it and fix it up real good for you."

Circa pressed her hand to the door. "I'm in charge of it," she said. "It's called the Memory Wall."

Still there was no response.

"Come on, Nat," Circa said. "We'll come back another time."

Just then there came another sound. Circa and Nattie stood still. There was more shuffling, which moved farther away and then back to the door again. Circa held her breath as she saw something being pushed out from under the door. The photo, she thought. He's sending out his photo. Circa felt a thrill inside at getting through to the mysterious Captain Mann. As soon as the facedown piece of paper made it all the way out, Circa picked it up and flipped it over as quick as she could to marvel at the photo. However, to her dismay, it was not a photo at all. Instead, it was a sketch of a chicken on a bicycle drawn for Great-Aunt Ruby by none other than Circa, age eight. Circa wondered, could this be Captain Mann's subtle way of telling her to take a hike? It sure did feel like that.

The girls walked the short remainder of the circle path to the front of the atrium. Circa tried to shake off the disappointment. "So a full moon, huh?" she said with a doubtful grin.

"Stranger things have happened," said Nattie. "Remember the platypus."

Nattie dragged her hand across an azalea bush. "And hey, speaking of platypus," she said. "What were you talking about the other day with all that miracle stuff?"

Circa floundered for an answer.

"It was nothing. Just me being—" she began as they returned to the lobby, where Nattie made a beeline for the player piano, which was slow-tinkling a familiar hymn. Circa smiled inside. She'd been saved by "Amazing Grace."

"Are there any pictures for me to pick up today, Lily?" she asked.

"No, ma'am," sighed Lily. "Still no pictures."

"Okay," said Circa. "I'll check back next time."

As the front door was shutting on the girls, Circa spotted a twisted cluster of wires poking out of a freshly cut hole at the bottom of the big empty wall. Underneath the holes, there was a plastic electrical outlet cover sitting on the floor next to some tools. It gave her a little jolt of excitement to think that maybe someone had begun making preparations for the Memory Wall. For some fancy lights, maybe? she thought as the door came to a close.

Circa and Nattie rounded the front corner of the building to pick up Miles in the garden, where the sight of an empty park bench made them both panic a little. They'd just begun to look around when they heard a scuffle in the bushes. The girls dashed over to the area just beyond the iris garden, where Miles and Stanley were on the ground, wrestling around in a total dust ball. Miles had scrawny Stanley pinned hard, while Stanley flopped and flailed and cussed.

Nattie covered her face with her hands.

"Lily!" yelled Circa.

Lily was outside in a flash, pulling the boys apart and fussing all the while.

"Mercy! What is wrong with you two?" she said, almost

tipping over onto the ground herself, when Miles caught and steadied her.

"Sorry, Miss Lily," he said, taking his place by Circa and Nattie on the sidewalk.

Stanley peeled himself off the ground and stood up all wobbly and spitty. "All I did was flick my cig—my *gum*, in his direction," he said. "And then the psycho totally flipped out."

Lily's mouth squenched up tiny. She wasn't buying it.

"Don't be crying to me, you ol' so-and-so," she said as she straightened her nurse jacket. "You get what you get. Circa, you all go on now."

Miles pressed his sleeve to his face to stop the blood from dripping off his lip.

"Yes, ma'am," said Circa.

Miles dusted himself off as best he could, and the three of them headed for home, and fast. Lily walked back to the entrance with Stanley stumbling slow behind her. As soon as Lily disappeared inside, Stanley turned back to holler a bunch of junk that moved Nattie to cover her ears with her hands. Then he said one last thing that made Circa wish she had done the same.

"Hey!" he yelled so loud the whole block could hear. "Did Lily tell you about the wall fountain they're putting in the lobby? It's going to be sweet."

"Quit it!" snapped Nattie over her shoulder. "Circ, you know he's just making all that up."

Circa thought about that electrical outlet, and hoped to goodness Stanley was making all that up. She instantly developed a sickening lump in her throat, and considered running back and asking Nurse Lily about it all. Unfortunately, right then, a policeman stepped out of the station across the street. It was Sergeant Simms, and he was peering across curiously.

"He must have heard the hollering," said Miles. "Come on. Let's go."

"Oh me," said a flustered Nattie. "Oh me."

Circa agreed they should probably get bloody Miles out of there before Stanley could twist it all up and get him arrested as the violent stranger who lost it on an angelic local kid, but she still felt torn about whether to go back to Maple Grove for answers or to go home straightaway for Miles. Until she suddenly remembered the words Dad had said to her so often . . . *Sometimes doing the right thing prickles a little.*

It had been a fairly quiet Saturday of playing canasta and charades for Sophie, Patton, and Puff. That is, until Maximus showed up and started the great war by knocking the Fluffington family estate all wonky. Shortly thence came the meow heard round the world.

20

Something Important to Say

Miles didn't seem like he much wanted to talk about the fight on the way home, which left Circa struggling to fill in the blanks for herself. True, practically everyone in Wingate wanted to pound Stanley, and true, Stanley deserved a good pounding. But even if Stanley had flicked something at him, was that enough reason for Miles to flatten him? To get so bloodied over some Stanley junk?

"Mom!" Circa called out when they approached the house. Mom appeared almost instantly at the studio door.

"You need to help Miles," said Circa. "He's hurt."

She wondered how Mom was going to try to back out of the tough task of patching Miles up. To Circa's surprise, she didn't.

"Oh me, come on in here," Mom said, looking at his torn clothes. "What in the world happened?" Mom dabbed at him the way Dad did for her when she'd cut her arm on her lighting equipment.

"Stanley Betts," said Circa, and that was explanation enough for Mom.

"Hey, Circ, I've got to go home," said Nattie after Mom

had escorted Miles inside. "I promised I'd help with Durret tonight."

Nattie seemed a bit shaken, probably from the blood and the spit and the five TV channels' worth of cussing, Circa thought, because she sure felt the same way. Only now that the crisis had calmed, Circa couldn't quite decide how she felt. Usually, she instantly hated to see anyone bleed, but in a weird way, she felt kind of relieved to have seen the red of Miles's blood. That if he was really Shopt, somehow he was still just as human as them.

"You know what that boy makes me think of?" said Nattie, pulling Circa from her tangle of thoughts.

"What?" said Circa.

"He reminds me of a mushroom," said Nattie. "You know, like when you flip it over and it's got those things that look like the pages of a book hidden underneath there?"

"Yeah?" said Circa.

"Well, it's like he's got some sort of hidden story himself," Nattie said.

Circa fought back the sudden urge to spill her own version of Miles's hidden story. She nodded her agreement and turned to go inside.

"We need to find out when the full moon's going to happen," Nattie called back over her shoulder.

"Yeah, whatever, Nat," said Circa.

That evening at the table, Mom, Circa, and Miles shared a meal of fried chicken and macaroni and cheese, seasoned with conversation that was mostly a tap dance around the uglier details of the afternoon's ruckus. Miles ate while balancing a baggie of ice on his sore knuckles. Circa was itching to hear the whole story of what had happened, but she couldn't risk Miles spilling it and souring Mom completely on Maple Grove. If that happened, she might not let them even go back.

All through dinner, though, Circa's mind kept wandering back to that electrical outlet and to Stanley's cruel words. By dessert time, she'd decided she absolutely must plead her case for the Memory Wall. It had, after all, been days since they'd discussed it, and Mom did seem to be handling things a little better.

"Mom, you really need to go up there to Maple Grove sometime," Circa said boldly. "I think you would like the people. And you could see where their wall was . . . *is* going to be."

Without a peep, Mom stood to clear the dishes from the table. Circa felt her cheeks go hot and pressed on. Miles scraped up one last bite from his plate and shoveled it in.

"And plus you would love Nurse Lily," Circa said. "She's really sweet and great at taking care of everybody. Even at handling Stanley."

Mom began filling the sink with soap and water. "Circa," she said.

"And she's *so* excited about the wall," Circa interrupted.

Mom stopped still without turning around. She turned off the water and sighed. "Circa," she said. "I thought we had an understanding on this."

Circa felt miffed and desperate. "And you could take a relaxing walk by the little fish pond and smell the flowers," she continued, as if Mom hadn't spoken. "Without even really talking to anybody too much if you don't feel like it."

Circa poked Miles in the leg. "Say something," she mouthed.

"Um, yeah," said Miles, his mouth half full. "And you can tell Stanley not to flick cigarettes at us."

Circa poked him harder. "Not like that," she whispered.

Mom grabbed a sponge and began wiping a plate. She wasn't taking the bait. "I think we're all finished here," she said. "No need for you guys to help clean up."

"Great. Just whatever," said Circa, rolling her eyes at Miles, who shrugged and nodded her toward the studio.

"Me and Miles are going in there," she said, feeling her blood go hotter and hotter.

Mom packed up the remaining food as Circa and Miles headed to the studio.

"Nice," said Miles as the door closed behind them. "You poke a hole in my leg for talking about the fight, when you're the one who even brought the place up."

Circa took a deep breath. "I'm sorry," she said. "I just wanted to give her a reason to want to go up there, not something that would make her *hate* the place. After what *you* said, I'm lucky she didn't ban us from going there forever."

Circa picked up one of Great-Aunt Ruby's dried-up ink bottles from off the shelf. She felt just as angry red and crumbly inside.

"Man, you sure weren't kidding before," Miles said. "Your mom really doesn't want anything to do with that Memory Wall project."

"It's because she says it hurts her too bad," said Circa. "She blames all the restored pictures in this studio for killing my dad. You've seen how she hardly ever even comes over to this side of the room."

Miles looked across the dozens of images crammed onto the walls. "That's a tough battle, Circa," he said.

Circa shook the bottle to hear the flakes of color knock around inside. "You know that thing that happens when you've got something you want to say and then it just escapes your brain?" she said. "But you know that it was something important and it drives you crazy?"

"Look who you're talking to," said Miles.

"Well, I feel like that's what happened to my dad," Circa said. "That he had something important to say with that Memory Wall but didn't get to."

"Yeah. I know what you mean," said Miles, kicking the beanbag chair into shape. "But listen, for what it's worth, I really do bet Stanley was making all that junk up today. About the fountain and stuff."

"Thanks," said Circa. "I really, really hope you're right."

Miles arranged the beanbag around him. "So you didn't say. How was the visit today? Before the, um, incident."

"It was all right," said Circa. "Nattie liked it."

Then she thought for a minute. "Surely Lily would have told me if they had decided to put a fountain there instead."

"Did you get to see the captain?" said Miles.

"No," Circa said, not wanting to tell Miles about the unsuccessful poster bait. "Still not a pixel or a peep."

Circa fell back into Dad's chair and gave it a spin. "So why'd you do it?" she said. "Why'd you clobber Stanley today? Was it truly just because he flicked a cigarette at you?"

Miles dropped into the beanbag. "You really want to know?" he said.

"Really," said Circa.

Miles put his elbows to his knees just like the way he was sitting when Circa first met him. She thought about how that seemed like forever ago.

"He insulted your family," Miles said. "You, your mom, your dad. And, well, I just lost it."

"And you flattened him," said Circa. "Defending *us*?"

"I flattened him, but not near as flat as he deserved." Miles shrugged. "Who do I know any better than the Monroes?" he said.

Circa cooled down inside. Miles had not only calmed her worries, but had managed to make her feel safe too. No one but Dad had ever been able to do that. She decided that even if she couldn't yet tell Miles fully about her Shopt beliefs, then she could still secretly do a test with him. Something fun that might just serve up a thinnest-ever slice of justice as a bonus.

"Come on," she said, wheeling Dad's chair to the desk. "I have an idea. Go grab that yearbook off the shelf over there. The red one with the silver writing."

Miles got up and handed Circa the book. She flipped to a page in the middle, lifted the lid on the scanner, and carefully placed the book facedown. On the computer, she clicked to scan the page into Photoshop and waited for the hum of the machine to finish. As soon as it did, the resulting image popped up on the monitor. Among other people, there in the middle was Stanley Betts's big senior picture. Circa cropped the photo so it was just Stanley and not the rest of the junk on the page.

Then she turned to Miles. "So what do we do to him?" she asked.

Miles's face got full of mischief.

"Nothing too cruel," said Circa, thinking about nests and warts and purple glasses. "You know, in case it comes true or something."

Miles gave her a sidewise glance. "Comes true?" he said. "You accidentally inhale some of that paint in those jars?"

Circa paused, tempted to spill everything, wondering if it was the right thing to do, if maybe telling him was the one way to get Dad's message out. Only she couldn't see putting more hurt on Miles after the day he'd had.

"Ha," she said. "Had you going, right?"

"Yeah, sure," said Miles. "Now. Moving on. How about snakes coming out Stanley's ears?"

"Hmm. Still too cruel," said Circa.

"Circa, it's pretend here."

"I know," she lied.

"Swollen nose?" said Miles.

"He's probably got that already."

"An angry neck tattoo?"

"No. He'd like that."

"A jillion fire ants, then?" he said.

"Good idea, but too hard to Photoshop," Circa said.

"I think you're underestimating your skills," said Miles. "How about dental work?"

Stanley glared from the screen like he was mocking her. She felt her skin crawl, like he was right there in the studio smoking and spitting and cussing the Monroes.

"Dental work it is," said Circa, tempted to make teeth disappear, go crooked, or turn a putrid green. Instead, she settled on coloring the top two middle ones a very unattractive shade of creamed corn.

Miles watched every click of the mouse, every swish of the paintbrush tool, every zoomed-in, edited pixel, until Stanley's nasty smile had been made over.

"I meant what I told you before," he said. "Never mind what your mom says about it. You're getting really good at this," he said, making Circa proud.

"I'll save it as 'Jackola,'" she announced, and then printed out a copy for them to take turns laughing over. As Miles held on to the photo and admired its artistry, Circa was alarmed by the raw places on his knuckles. Inside, she hoped and prayed there wouldn't be any repercussions from the day's Miles versus Stanley bout.

21

Pink Lady

The next morning, something that sounded an awful lot like a repercussion knocked at the front door.

"Circa, go see who that is," called Mom from upstairs.

Over breakfast, Circa and Miles were discussing whether Great-Uncle Mileage would ever catch up with his long-lost nephew, and the adventure that might ensue when he did.

"Of course I have to answer it," said Circa. "She's probably still lying in bed."

"Come on. Give her a break," said Miles.

Circa stuffed in a last bite of granola bar and went to peek out the front room window.

"It's a woman in a suit," she reported up the steps. "She's holding a clipboard."

The woman knocked again.

"Go ahead and answer," called Mom. "I'll be right there."

Circa was surprised to hear the hair dryer come on. She opened the door.

"Hello, young lady," the woman said somewhat mechanically. She wore an official-looking ID badge that was obscured by a big jangly necklace. Circa noticed she had clumps of not-smoothed-in face powder poised to fall right off her nose.

"Is your mother or father home?" the woman said, nervously clearing her throat every other word.

"My mother is," said Circa. "She'll be right . . . Oh, here she is."

Mom came rushing down the steps, trying to gather her half-dry hair up into a clip.

"Mrs. Monroe?" The woman stuck her hand out stiffly. "I'm a representative of the Georgia Department of Child Services. We were contacted by the local police. It is my understanding that you have a lost child here?"

"Oh, um, yes, we do," said Mom. "A found one really."

Circa backed herself slowly into the kitchen. "Miles," she said. "It's some lady from the state of Georgia, something about child services. You don't think she's out here because of the fight, do you?"

"How am I supposed to know?" said Miles, looking worried.

"Miles? Circa?" called Mom. "Can you come in here, please?"

The two of them walked into the living room, Miles never taking his eyes off his own feet.

"Let's everybody sit down, I guess," said Mom, clearing stacks of mail off the furniture.

Miles and Circa sat together on the couch, while Mom and the woman in the suit took the chairs opposite them. Circa noticed right off that the woman's face was shockingly pink, even through all that powder, and that she seemed very uneasy. In fact, she looked like she wanted to bolt right out of the room, way more so than even Mom or Miles. The woman kept on clearing her throat like there was a popcorn kernel stuck on the back of her tongue. Circa would have felt sorry for her, had she not suddenly been struck by a sickening jolt of familiarity in the woman's face.

Circa waved to get Mom's attention as the woman bent to dig through her giant purse for something to write with.

"Look familiar?" she mouthed to Mom.

Mom nodded yes and shrugged, then Circa poked Miles to ask him the same thing. As soon as Miles looked up from his feet and concentrated on the woman's face, his eyes grew wide with recognition.

"Miles," said Mom, "this lady is here from the Department of Child Services. She's going to try to help figure your situation out. This is . . . pardon me, miss, but I didn't catch your name."

"Linholt," said the woman. "Barbara Linholt."

The room fell so quiet, you could have heard a shriveled flower petal drop. Circa, Mom, and Miles all gaped in disbelief. Mrs. Linholt cleared her throat and went right on talking.

"Miles, your case showed up on the bottom of my list for this week, and then my boss came in and said she'd seen a poster of you at the coffee shop and on our building this morning. So I decided to make you my top priority instead."

Everything was coming out like *blah-blah-blah* to a dumbstruck Mom, Circa, and Miles, though, which must have been obvious, because it wasn't long at all before Mrs. Linholt stopped herself midsentence.

"I know what you're thinking, Mrs. Monroe," she said.

"And yes, I am the same Mrs. Linholt who pitched a minor hissy fit about the photo you guys were restoring for me. As soon as I pulled up and saw that you were the Monroes of Studio Monroe, I knew this would be a tense visit."

She moved her badge from under the necklace. "I hid this before I came in," she said.

Mrs. Linholt looked all sorts of frazzled. "Forgive me for being flustered," she said, patting at her pink face. "I suffered some painful windburn from the tornado.

"Thankfully, most of my family were inside the park bathroom when it hit the reunion," Mrs. Linholt continued. "But the trauma, oh the trauma. This is my first day back at work since that day, and I'm a little scattered to say the least, so please bear with me."

Mom cocked her head in astonishment.

"Anyway," Mrs. Linholt said. "Mrs. Monroe, I feel so uncomfortable sitting here like this after I fussed with your husband so. Please pass along my apologies, and do tell him I'm willing to compromise and pay him half of his fee."

Mom shot a blank look of disgust at Circa, which Circa in turn shared with Miles. Fortunately, this woman in their living room mentioned nothing of the fight with Stanley. Unfortunately, she'd also been oblivious to other, much more crucial information.

She doesn't know about Dad, thought Circa. How in the world could she not know?

"Whew. Now that that's been said," continued Mrs. Linholt. "I've got quite a few questions I need to ask Miles before the state can determine where—"

"He died," interrupted Mom sharply. "He's dead, you know."

"Excuse me?" said Mrs. Linholt.

Circa and Miles both sunk low into the couch.

"My husband. He was killed delivering *your* reunion photos. That *you* demanded he bring. I just thought you might need to know that."

Mrs. Linholt covered her mouth to muffle a little squeak of alarm, but Mom wasn't near done with her yet.

"And let me ask you this, Mrs. Linholt," she said. "Do you even recognize this boy here? This boy who hitchhiked a hundred miles from the very site of your picnic? This boy who apparently wasn't invited to hide out in the bathroom with the rest of your family?"

Mrs. Linholt made a squeaky gasp. "Well. Mercy," she said. "He does look a tad familiar. But, well. Mercy. I don't know why. You see, I've been through a terrible—"

"Ordeal?" said Mom through her teeth.

Mrs. Linholt immediately began scritch-scratching her pencil across her clipboard, murmuring to herself and checking boxes superfast. She was speed-reading interview questions and coughing the answers to herself at full tilt. "Physical exam. Check." Cough. "Police notified. Check. Temporary accommodations." Cough. "Check. Psychiatric evaluation . . . Has he had one, Mrs. Monroe?"

Mom shook her head.

"Okay, no worries then," Mrs. Linholt said nervously. "As a courtesy, I'll just set that up myself."

"Is that absolutely necessary?" said Mom, her jaw so clenched it was hard to understand her. "The psychiatrist thing?"

Mom had suffered much trouble with those doctors over the years. Circa knew she wasn't going to take this one easily.

"Yes, it has to be done before placement is decided," said Mrs. Linholt. "And considering that all this should have been handled the day the boy showed up, I'll call right now and arrange it." She opened up the huge giraffe-pattern purse at her feet and frantically juggled out a cell phone covered in silver sparkles.

Placement? wondered Circa. She looked at Miles to see if he'd caught that word too, but instead he seemed instantly and completely mesmerized by the phone in Mrs. Linholt's hand. In fact, Circa noted that Miles never took his eyes off the phone the whole time Mrs. Linholt barked into the phone about paging an available psychiatrist. She was demanding in that way the Monroes had been quite familiar with to get what she wanted, glancing up occasionally at the three sets of eyes glaring at her, and practically threatening the person on the other end that he'd *better* send someone out today.

As soon as she pressed to hang up, Mrs. Linholt gathered her things and stood to leave.

"The state of Georgia is sorry for your loss, ma'am," she said as she scrambled toward the door, like she was scared Mom would pounce on her. "The psychiatrist on call will be here ASAP. After that, we will notify you of a decision concerning the young man." Mrs. Linholt left even pinker than she came.

No sooner had the door shut than Mom excused herself to the kitchen. Most likely for more than half of a bad-day pill, thought Circa, as she and Miles remained in a total slump on the couch.

"Man. That was awful," said Circa.

Miles didn't say a word, but instead appeared to be in some kind of daze. A stupor of sorts. The look, as it turned out, of a memory waking up.

"Circa." He turned to her and said slowly, "I talked to your dad."

22

The Gush of a Memory

Circa's jaw dropped open. "What do you mean you talked to my dad?"

"On the phone," Miles said. "The day of the storm."

Circa scooted as close to Miles as she could. He began to spill the story in pieces as it came to him.

"I had walked up to the clearing and asked that lady, Mrs. Linholt, if she would help me," he said. "She pointed me over to a cooler full of lemonades and told me to sit down, as she walked away and made a phone call. I thought that the call was to help me, even though it sounded like she was fussing at someone on the phone. After that, she just left me sitting there while she started putting food out on a picnic table. So while she was working, I snuck her phone—that glittery one—out of her purse and I called the last number on there. It was a man that answered, and the first thing he said was *Studio Monroe*."

Circa got chills upon chills. *Dad.* She remembered that last mysterious phone call Dad had gotten as he walked out the door that afternoon.

"I couldn't remember anything," said Miles.

"Even before the storm?" marveled Circa.

"Even before," said Miles. "I was scared to death. I told him I needed help. I begged him to please come get me. The man said he would come, so I found a spot where I could sit up against a brick barbecue and rest while I waited for him. Then I got weaker and weaker, and the wind starting to blow harder, and there were people across the way arguing about whether to pack up or not. But that woman, she was insisting that they wait it out in the bathroom. Next thing I knew, I was knocked to the ground when the big wind came. I woke up in the shelter of a big tree propped on top of the brick pile. The reunion photo was on the ground beside me, so I picked it up and got as far from there as I could."

Miles went radiant as the gush of a memory filled him up.

"So to *finally* answer your question, Circa," he said. "No, I don't think I ever saw your dad. But, yes. I did meet him."

The thought of Miles and her dad talking to each other, even if briefly, did Circa's heart some good. If a nasty like Barbara Linholt had been the reason Dad had to be out in the storm, Circa could at least be proud that he'd also gone to try to help someone worth helping. Especially someone with no memory.

"Are you sure that's all?" she said.

"What do you mean?"

"I don't know," she said. "I just keep thinking you might have a message or something, like from my dad to me."

"How could I?" said Miles. "I told you I didn't even see him."

Circa struggled to think of a way to say what she was feeling inside. "It's just that I thought maybe there'd be a message from him built in or something," she said, immediately wishing she'd thought of a better way to say what she was thinking.

"What do you mean, built in?" said Miles.

"Nothing," she said. "Nothing. Forget it."

"So why did Mrs. Linholt pretend not to know you today?" she asked instead.

"I don't think she was pretending," said Miles. "She probably didn't recognize me because she never much paid attention to me in the first place."

"Huh. Maybe so," said Circa, suddenly distracted by a fresh question that needed asking. "Miles," she said. "Did that woman look really pink to you?"

Miles smiled. "Of course she looked pink to me," he said. "Super pink. I thought she had on too much makeup or something. Or else she was really embarrassed, which she should have been."

"Yeah, well, I have another theory about it," said Circa, bubbling up inside.

Mom came back in holding a fistful of tissues and gulping a glass of water.

"But I'll tell you later," Circa whispered.

"Mrs. Barbara Linholt," scoffed Mom. "Talk about someone being in the wrong job."

"Like Stanley Betts," said Circa.

"I just find it hard to believe someone like her is capable of having a child's best interest at heart," Mom said.

"Mom, listen to this," said Circa. "You won't believe it, but you know that second phone call Dad got that afternoon when he was leaving? The one he acted so weird about?"

"Yes?" said Mom.

"It was Miles," said Circa.

Mom had to sit herself down.

"That sparkly phone just made him remember," said Circa. "He said he walked up to the reunion place, where that mean Mrs. Linholt wouldn't even help him. She pretended she was helping, but she was really just calling to fuss at Dad. Then Miles snuck her phone and called Dad too."

"I told him I couldn't remember anything," Miles said. "Not even who I was. I thought he would just hang up, but he was nice to me. Like he understood."

"That's Todd Monroe, all right," said Mom, squeezing herself into the available space at the end of the couch. Circa could tell she was trying not to cry in front of them.

"Maybe that's why I felt like I should come to Studio Monroe when I saw the stamp on the back of that picture," he said. "Because Mr. Monroe had treated me nice."

"Miles, do you remember anything else about him?" said Mom. "Did you ever see him?"

"No, ma'am."

"How about before you got to the reunion? Are you remembering anything before that?"

"No," said Miles. "But maybe this means I will."

Or maybe not, thought Circa. Mom laid her head back into a squishy sofa pillow, like her pill had taken hold quick. Circa patted Mom on the knee and was overcome by a fit of restlessness. "Can Miles and me go to the studio for a while?" she said.

"I suppose so," said Mom. "But help me listen for the phone, okay? Mrs. Linholt's going to be calling about this psychiatric thing."

"Okay, Mom."

Circa couldn't get Miles into the studio and shut the door fast enough.

"So what's this theory you've got on the pinkness?" he said.

"Look at this," said Circa, finding the crumpled, smeary Linholt Reunion photo that Miles had brought with him where Mom had left it on the desk.

"They *all* look pink in this," he said.

"Right," said Circa. "But now look at this one." Circa dug up the original photo from the middle of a stack on Dad's desk.

"A lot less pink," he said.

"Exactly," said Circa. "You see what I'm saying?"

"Not really," said Miles.

"Well, that awful Linholt woman insisted that my dad pinken them up in their photo," Circa explained. "So he did, and you saw what happened to her face."

"Okay . . ." said Miles. "Still not real sure what you're getting at."

Circa felt like she was about to turn inside out. "Well, how about this," she blurted. "What would you say if I told you that those purple glasses didn't even exist before I Shopt them onto a picture of my dad? And that nest outside my bedroom window, the one with the mama bird that pooped on Nattie. What if I told you that it didn't exist either until I Shopt it into a photo?"

Miles got the crinkle. "I'd say you're the one who needs the psychiatrist," he said.

"No, really," she said. "And it might even work in reverse, too."

Circa lowered her voice. "Listen, don't tell Nat I told you this, but the other day she had me Photoshop a wart off her face, and after I did . . . poof. It was gone."

Miles looked skeptically at Circa. "How long have you been thinking about this?" he said.

"All week," said Circa. "That's why I didn't want us to do anything too cruel to Stanley, in case it came true."

Miles narrowed his eyes at Circa. "I don't buy it," he said. "What about all that other stuff you've done? The Sphinx and the skywriting and the pretzel? Not to mention that big stack of crazy stuff your dad did."

"I don't know about all that yet," she said. "With the Internet down, I haven't really been able to do any research. Plus, I don't know if it's like a Monroe family magic thing, or just that computer or something."

Circa's mind was racing. "Not to mention," she said, finally taking a breath. "Maybe not all of it comes true, but only *some* of it."

Miles went completely still.

"I even tried to test things out myself the other night by putting a—" Circa felt the weight of Miles's stare and chickened out on the details. "By doing something to Nattie's yard," she said.

"Did it work?"

"Not sure," said Circa. "But even if it didn't, maybe there's a good reason why. I just don't know about it yet. I mean, it's not like any of this makes much sense, right?"

"You got that right," said Miles. "Circa, those purple glasses were bent and scratched like they really were old. They didn't just appear."

"I know," she said. "But remember, the picture of Dad that I Shopt them into was from way back when he was skinny, when he could wear that T-shirt you've got on," she said. "That was like ten years ago. So maybe the glasses appeared as already ten years old."

"Okay, now you're just being silly," said Miles. "Come on, let's get on with it and just do a Shopt something. I want to hear what finally happens when Great-Uncle Mileage and his long-lost nephew meet up."

Circa slapped the desk in frustration. "But maybe I'm *not* just being silly." She nodded toward the Shopt folder. "And like you said, think about if it is a Monroe thing, and that my dad had the power too. Think about what that would mean."

Circa could hardly wait any longer to prove herself. She was about to suggest that they both put her own Shopt powers to the test immediately, when with a *whap!* the front door to Studio Monroe slammed open.

There stood Nattie huffing and puffing. "Two things," she said. "I just saw out my window . . . a man, a tall, serious-looking man . . . getting out of a car in front of your house."

Nattie caught her breath. "You guys don't think he's here about the fight, do you?"

Leonard suddenly wished he'd checked out "The Wind in the Willows" instead. Now Lenny desperately hoped the library had the sequel, "Un-vanish Your Head." Or at least his secret second-best choice, "Vanish the Rest of Me Too."

23

Three Snaps

Circa ran to look out the studio window, but the man must have already made it to the porch. Shortly after, Mom stepped into the studio. "Miles, the psychiatrist is already here," she said, slow and solemn, like she was announcing the executioner's arrival. "Come on into the kitchen. This Dr. Jones says he can do the evaluation here."

Miles gave Circa a defeated shrug.

"Sorry," Circa mouthed to him. She was sorry about him having to go through with whatever a "psych eval" entailed, but mostly sorry that their Shopt wonderings had been cut short.

"It's okay," he said. "Maybe he'll help me remember some more."

"I sure wish that Mrs. Linholt wouldn't do us any more of her favors," Mom said under her breath as she rubbed twenty minutes' sleep from her eyes. Then Miles and Mom disappeared into the kitchen and shut the door.

"Doctor?" said Nattie. "What's going on, Circa?"

"Oh, Nat, this woman from the state of Georgia came

today," said Circa. "She's the same terrible Linholt woman who made my dad take those pictures to that stupid reunion. And get this . . . she even met Miles there that day. He was lost and scared, but she wouldn't even stop to help him."

Nattie's face tightened up into a scowl.

"She didn't even know my dad died," said Circa. "She just came in and said Miles was on her list of lost kids to come check on, but she didn't recognize him at all. I thought my mom was going to strangle her."

"Oh no," said Nattie.

"For real," said Circa.

"So now she's in charge of helping Miles?"

"Yeah. Messed up, isn't it?" said Circa. "She said something about Miles having to get a psychiatric evaluation before his *placement*."

"Placement?"

"I know," said Circa. "I wondered too. But Miles didn't even hear that part. You know why?"

"Why?"

"Because he was too busy remembering something," said Circa. "Nat, are you ready for this?"

Nattie nodded.

"Miles talked to my dad on the phone."

"What?" gasped Nattie. "How?"

"That day," said Circa. "Before my dad left. Miles took that woman's phone and called here asking my dad for help."

Nattie's eyes grew huge. "No way," she said. "And your dad went there to help him?"

It was the first time Circa had ever seen Nattie get so teary.

"I guess he tried," she said, feeling her own throat get squeezy.

"Placement," Nattie pondered aloud. "I thought they were supposed to find his real family."

"They didn't," said Circa.

"So what happens in the evaluation?" Nattie said, moving closer to the kitchen door.

"I don't know," said Circa. "Miles seemed to think it might help him remember some more."

Nattie pressed the side of her face up to the door. "I can hear the man talking," she said. "He's asking a bunch of questions."

Circa played back Nattie's entrance in her head. "Wait, Nat," she said. "Didn't you say there were two things you were going to tell us?"

"Oh yeah," said Nattie. "It was that I'm sorry for the stink."

"Huh?"

"You mean you don't smell it?" said Nattie.

"Smell what?"

"This." Nattie held up her foot. "A big pile of it in the middle of our yard. I had to run in here so quick I forgot to wipe it off."

"Dog poo?" said Circa, stirring inside. "Wait a minute, Nat. Do you know what this could mean?"

"Yeah, I know what it means," said Nattie. "It means I'm some kind of major poop magnet."

"Maybe that," laughed Circa. "But you know what else?"

Circa sat in Dad's chair feeling full up with a strange mix of snug secrecy and nagging desire to share something big with her best friend. After all this, surely it would be okay if Circa shared just a taste of this thing that was eating her up inside.

"Nat, you know all that stuff I said the other night about things appearing kind of mysteriously?"

"Sure," said Nattie. "The miracle thing."

"And about a person, or two people, maybe having a hand in that?" said Circa.

Nattie nodded.

"You want to know what I was talking about?" said Circa.

"Duh. Yeah," said Nattie, crossing her arms and turning to lean her back against the door.

"Remember when I said the word *Shopt* in the car last week when I was showing Mom that nest picture and you were wondering what that meant?" Circa glanced over the back of the chair at the Shopt folder safe in its spot. "Well, *Shopt* means Photoshopped," she said. "Like the things we do to edit photos."

"You mean like wart removing?" said Nattie.

"Exactly," said Circa. "Only for me and my dad, well, it's kind of always been more than that. The thing is, Nat—I'm not positive about this—but I think that some of the Shopt things are coming true."

"What do you mean?" said Nattie. "What things?"

"Like that nest in my tree," said Circa. "That was the first thing I noticed."

"Oooh, how is the nest?" said Nattie. "Any hatchlings yet?"

"No, Nat. Listen," said Circa.

"Okay. Sorry."

"What I'm trying to say is, when I took the picture of that tree, I'm pretty sure there wasn't a nest there at all. That's why I Shopt one in, just to test out my skills. But then, that night, there it was . . . the real deal sitting right there on the very branch I drew it on."

Circa had Nattie's full attention. "Why didn't you tell me?" she said.

"Because a long time ago I promised my dad that I'd keep the Shopt a secret. Only now, it seems like that's impossible. It seems like they're making themselves known.

"So listen. There's more," said Circa. "Then after all that, there were these purple star glasses that appeared out of nowhere in a box upstairs after I Shopt them onto an old picture of my dad. And remember your wart disappearing the other day? I think that it happened then too."

"But I thought my wart fell off," said Nattie.

"I did too," said Circa. "But now, I don't know. And then, today, there's the pink woman."

"The who?"

"Mrs. Linholt," said Circa. "She made my dad pinken her whole family in the reunion picture. And even after a whole month, that woman couldn't be any pinker than she was today."

Circa paused. She had to know what Nattie was feeling about all this. Nattie slid down the door into a sitting position and stared at Circa with a raised brow.

"And you called *me* a nuthatch?" she said.

"I know, I know," said Circa. "I keep telling myself it's crazy too, but I just can't stop wondering about it all."

Circa bowed her head. "That's why I asked you to look out your window the other night," she said. "That picture of Ernie Brown the dog was a test. I put a dog in there to see if it would really happen."

"Oh," said Nattie sadly.

"But I really did think you would enjoy having the picture as a present," said Circa. "And if the dog had appeared, I was going to give him to you."

"But there wasn't a dog," said Nattie. "Did *you* see a dog?"

"No," said Circa, "But it could have pooped and run off, right?"

"Yeah, but wouldn't I have seen it run off? Or heard it?" Nattie gave her a flat look. "I'm sorry, Circa," she said. "I mean, this is a neat story and all, but do you really think that stuff could happen? I mean, like, scientifically?" Nattie set the picture down. "Besides," she said, "nuthatches can build nests really fast, you know."

"I know it doesn't make sense, Nat," said Circa. "But like you said, anything can happen. And a lot of things don't make sense, right? Like the platypus?"

Nattie pressed her ear to the door again. "So then try something right now," she said. "Do something to that poster picture of Miles, and then when he's done with his appointment, he'll walk in here and we'll see if it worked."

"Oh, Nat, I don't know," said Circa. "I'd feel funny doing something to Miles."

"Circa, you edited *my* face."

"Yeah, but you asked me to. That's different."

"Come on, Circ. Just do something tiny."

"Okay, let me look," said Circa reluctantly, twirling the chair around and waking up the computer.

"The doctor is talking about hypnotizing him," Nattie said.

Circa opened the picture of Miles.

"Something about counting backward from a hundred," Nattie continued.

Circa searched Miles's face for something to edit subtly, yet still have it be noticeable.

"The doc is going to wake him up with a special sound when he's done," said Nattie.

Circa decided to erase a small scar from his chin.

"The special sound will be . . . *tree sap*?"

Circa zoomed in so much that the scar looked more like a pixelated gash.

"No, no," Nattie corrected herself. "The special sound will be *three snaps*."

"Of course you thought it was tree sap," said Circa, sampling Miles's skin tone with an eyedropper tool and then setting to work painting out the scar, one pixel at a time to get it perfectly precise. She couldn't help feeling guilty about it though, messing with Miles like they had done Stanley. Even if it was an improvement, it still felt like a major shmoo of a thing to do. All the while, Nattie listened at the door. After a few more minutes, she left the door and stood next to Circa's chair to watch her finish up.

"I don't think it's going well in there," Nattie said.

"How do you know?" said Circa, erasing the last speck of the scar.

"Just by the sound of Miles's voice. It sounds like he's super upset," said Nattie, bending close to inspect Circa's work. "So you really meant all that Shopt stuff you were saying, huh, Circ?"

"Yes," she said. "I *do*."

Circa hovered her finger over the mouse button in hesitation, then clicked to save her changes. "We'll be able to tell right away when he comes in whether the scar is there or not," she said. "Now you just go back and listen for the three snaps."

Once a week, the famous Lookmobile would come around tooting its horn. For a mere ten cents, one could take a five-minute look into the future, at the wars, the heroes, and the discoveries, playing out live and in full color before one's eyes. Today's special . . . 1963.

24

On the Chin

Finally, there came three distinct snapping sounds from behind the door.

"That was it," said Nattie. "He's awake."

"Good," said Circa. "I bet they're almost done. Now get away from there so Miles doesn't clobber you when he comes in."

Nattie got up and stood next to Dad's chair, which Circa had already swiveled toward the kitchen in anticipation of Miles's return . . . specifically, the return of Miles's chin. Despite the fact that the talk on the other side of the door had long since dwindled to just a quiet discussion between Mom and the doctor, it seemed like forever that they waited. Circa grew impatient to know what was going on. Had Miles accidentally stayed hypnotized? Did he pass out? Had the man in some sort of head-doctor way discovered that Miles had no story to find?

While Nattie resumed her eavesdropping, Circa watched out the front studio window for the doctor to leave the house. When she finally saw the man step off the front porch and head toward his car, Circa gave a wave for Nattie to clear away from the door again. At least five minutes passed, but no Miles.

"Come on," said Circa. "Let's just go in there."

The girls opened the door and stepped into the kitchen. There they found Mom, and only Mom, sitting at the table. She was staring at the empty chair across from her.

"Hey, girls," Mom said, tap-tap-tapping a business card on its edge nervously. "The doctor's gone, but Miles went upstairs with a bad headache."

"Oh," said Circa, disappointed. "So how did it go?"

Mom didn't answer. She just stared ahead with the same hazy-eyed look she'd had in the hospital. Circa hoped Mom hadn't said anything senseless in front of the psychiatrist. Or maybe he was used to that, she thought.

"I better go," said Nattie. "Let me know what you find out, Circ." Nattie slyly pointed to her own chin. "Okay?"

"Find out about what?" said Mom.

"How it went with Miles," Circa answered swiftly, telling herself that technically it wasn't a lie. "Just come to the studio after supper, Nat," she said.

Once Nattie was gone, Circa took a seat at the table. "What happened, Mom?" she asked. "Is Miles okay?"

"He's all right," she said. "But the evaluation didn't go so well."

Mom leaned in close to speak more quietly. "The doctor really put Miles through it," she said. "He even hypnotized him to try and help him remember, but Miles just got upset when he was under. When he woke up, he couldn't even tell us why."

Circa could tell by Mom's purposeful deep breathing that there was something even bigger bothering her.

"What else happened?" she said.

Mom picked at the corner of the business card. "The doctor seems to think that before Miles is assigned his placement, that we need to take him to the scene of his first memory," she said. "In order to help him remember farther back."

"To the reunion place?" said Circa. She couldn't imagine Mom agreeing to put herself through that. "So are we going?" Circa wondered if the trip might make Miles remember the message from Dad.

Mom got up to magnet the card to the fridge. "I can't even begin to think about that right now, Circa. I'm having a real hard time being Sunny Backdrop today, if you know what I mean."

Mom sat back down.

"What?" said Circa. "You know about that name?"

Mom nodded. "Your crazy mom notices more than you think," she said.

"Mom," said Circa, trying to make out the words scribbled on the doctor's business card. "What did that woman mean when she talked about Miles's *placement*?"

"I guess she was talking about where he'll stay until his condition changes," Mom said. "According to the rules, it sounds like the state was supposed to be taking care of him from the start." Mom cleared her throat dramatically "Let's just pray Mrs. Linholt isn't making that decision herself," she said.

Circa made out that the card on the fridge had an appointment date scribbled on it. *June 16th, Dr. Jones, Psychiatry.* She felt glad that Miles had a follow-up appointment scheduled. Maybe that meant *placement* would have to wait a couple weeks. The word itself was such a black cloud.

"Circa, why don't you go on upstairs and check on Miles. Make sure he's all right," Mom said. "I've got a call I need to make.

"Oh, and here you go," she added, handing Circa a couple of Tylenols and a water. "Give this to him for his head."

On the way up the stairs, Circa so trembled in anticipation of seeing Miles that she almost spilled the water. Would the scar be there, or would it be gone? And how would she look at his chin without giving away what she had done? When she approached the guest room, Miles rolled over onto his side and faced the opposite wall.

"Hey, Miles. It's me," she said.

"Hey," he answered without looking.

"I brought you something for your headache," she said.

"Thanks."

"But you have to sit up to take it," said Circa.

Miles rolled onto his back and scooted up against the bed pillows. Circa handed him the medicine and the water. As he tilted his head back to swallow it all down, despite how puffy his eyes were from being upset downstairs, Circa was far more concerned with another detail. That scar, red and diagonal and shiny as ever. Still right there on his chin. Defeated, Circa slumped on the cedar chest at the end of the bed.

"Blew it," said Miles.

"What?" said Circa.

"Blew it," said Miles. "I blew another help-the-lost-kid session."

"Man. Sorry," said Circa, distracted by wondering if there was maybe a simple explanation why this Shopt change hadn't worked.

"A million more questions I couldn't answer, and then the guy does this hocus-pocus hypnojunk that must have made me blubber like a doofus from the way they were looking at me," said Miles. "And on top of that, I snap out of it with nothing but a brain ache."

Was there a difference between it and the other picture changes that had seemed to come true? Circa considered.

"And to make things more embarrassing, the guy printed me like I was some kind of criminal," said Miles.

"Printed you?" Circa said.

"He had to get my fingerprints, because Mrs. Linholt was so frazzled out she forgot," he said. "He didn't even have a kit, so he took out a little half dried up ink pad and made me put my fingerprints across his business cards."

Miles held up one hand's worth of smudgy black fingertips to prove it to Circa. Then it suddenly hit her. That's it, she thought. *Printed*. The other pictures had been printed. The Miles one had not. Even the dog one hadn't been printed until days after Circa had Nattie look out her window. Maybe that's why Nattie didn't see anything that night. Maybe it appeared only yesterday.

Phew, thought Circa. There was still hope for the Shopt powers.

"Are you even listening to me?" said Miles. "You're acting like you're on another planet or something."

"I'm here," said Circa. "Just thinking is all. . . . Shouldn't they have done all that at the police station?"

"I guess the sergeant was too worried about his Code Thirty-two to remember," said Miles. "Let's just hope I wasn't some sort of major creep in my past life."

"I doubt it," said Circa. "Even if you are a casserole thief and a jerk flattener."

Miles ignored the joke altogether.

"So what does all that junk from today mean?" asked Circa. "What happens now?"

"I don't know," he said. "But it can't be good. They'll probably lock me up like that kook at the jail."

"No. Don't say that," said Circa.

Miles folded a pillow and propped it under his neck. "The doctor told your mom she should take me back to the scene of the reunion," he said. "And she didn't seem too thrilled by the idea."

"I heard," said Circa, rubbing the head on one of Great-Aunt Ruby's cherub figurines. "Sounds like it was a Sergeant Simms Code Thirty-two kind of moment down there too."

"Yeah," said Miles. "What was it? *Can I just get me an oatmeal cream pie and start this fail of a day over?*"

"I think it was a honeybun," Circa said, but Miles didn't even smile. Circa thought maybe he could use a little touch of magic to lift his spirits.

"I told Nat about the Shopt stuff," she said.

Miles peeked out from behind a pillow. "You showed her the folder?"

"No. But I did tell her about the mysterious stuff. I just had to."

Miles sunk back behind the pillow.

"You want to meet in the studio tonight and test it out?" said Circa. "I mean, after your head gets better?"

"Why not?" he said all muffled.

"Good," said Circa. "Just come down whenever."

Circa went to her room, aiming to call Nattie and report her findings on the chin scar. But when she picked up the phone, Mom was still on the line. Circa held her breath and listened.

"That's great," said Mom to whoever. "If you would, just send the info to the house and we'll give it a try."

Circa realized that holding her breath had been a bad plan, when it meant she had to exhale twice as big.

"Circ, is that you on here?" Mom said. Circa panicked and hung up, as soft as she could. She tiptoed downstairs to continue listening in the foyer just outside the kitchen, but soon as she'd made it, Mom was saying her thank-you and hanging up.

"Who was that?" Circa asked as she pushed through the double doors.

"Oh, just some info gathering," said Mom. "Nothing for you to worry about." Mom looked all sorts of weary. "I'm going to—"

"I know, I know," said Circa. "You're going to take a nap."

Mom shuffled from the kitchen without argument. Circa looked at the phone sitting on the table and thought about Miles and that sparkly phone of Mrs. Linholt's. Instantly, the redial button began calling to her. As soon as she could hear Mom padding around her bedroom directly above, Circa grabbed up the phone and pressed redial. She'd planned on just hanging up as soon as she found out who Mom had called . . . until an all-too-familiar, skin-prickling voice answered.

"Thanks for calling the MG," he said. "S'up?"

Stanley.

At first, Circa was disgusted that Stanley had answered the phone, but the ick turned less icky when she realized what that actually meant. That Mom had called Maple Grove. On purpose. Was she planning a visit? Had she called to discuss the Memory Wall? Circa remembered what she'd overheard on Mom's call. About sending a packet to the house. Getting the ball rolling. Could she be talking about the pictures?

"Helloooo. Not getting any younger here," said Stanley.

"Stanley, put Lily on the phone."

"Who is this?"

"Get Lily."

"Shrinkie Pinkie?"

"Get Lily *now.*"

"Say please."

Circa wanted to vomit at the thought of saying please to Stanley, but she had business to take care of.

"Please."

"Hang on," he said. "And oh, be sure and tell that empty-headed stray of yours that I'll look forward to helping him move in."

Circa felt her heart sink like a stone. What did he mean, move in? She could hear the scratches and bumps of someone wrestling the phone away from Stanley on the other end.

Another call beeped in on the Monroe line. Circa clicked over. "Hello?" she said impatiently. "No, Nat, nothing changed. Hey, Nattie, I gotta go. Bye."

Circa clicked back over to a voice saying frantically, "Hello? Circa?"

"I'm here," said Circa.

"Baby, don't pay him no mind," Lily said in a fluster.

"Lily, what was he talking about?" said Circa.

"Your momma didn't tell you?"

"No."

"Well, I guess there's no harm in me telling," said Lily. "She and I just spoke about your friend Miles."

Oh no, thought Circa. She imagined Miles behind a colored door for the next eighty years.

"I told her that—" began Lily, but Circa interrupted.

"You mean that call wasn't about the Memory Wall?" she said.

"No, baby."

The lump of dread in the pit of Circa's stomach doubled in size.

"Lily?"

"Yes, ma'am?"

"Are you guys putting up a wall fountain?"

There was a terrible silence on the line.

"And that's why you haven't been giving me any pictures?"

Circa could hear Lily draw in a breath.

"Yes, baby," said Lily. "Please don't be mad with me, Circa. I didn't know how to tell you without giving you more pain. It's just that the Memory Wall idea was your daddy's thing, and he was doing all that fine work for us for free, and I didn't think much of anybody could live up to that kind of talent or kindness."

"But I was going to try," said Circa, her eyes filling with tears. "Lily, I was going to try."

"I know that, precious girl. We just felt with him gone on to heaven that our Memory Wall might well need to be—"

"To be dead," said Circa.

"Oh no, baby," said Lily. "Please don't—"

"Okay then, bye," interrupted Circa. She was shamelessly aware that she'd just hung up on Lily. She was also certain that she'd heard enough.

25

Kinfolk

Circa sat motionless in the dim, quiet kitchen that still smelled faintly of the doctor's cologne, overcome with a sensation of loss far heavier than anything she'd felt all week. Why couldn't she just press redial and have it be Dad that answered, like Miles got to do on Mrs. Linholt's phone that day? She wondered what she'd say to him if she could. "Dad, there's no more Memory Wall. I'm so sorry I let you down." Circa found herself whispering these things aloud, until the added weight of her words was too much to bear. Then she fled to the comfort that waited on the other side of the wooden door.

Circa slumped herself low into Dad's chair and considered never ever leaving it again. She did one slow swivel around and surveyed the room, considering the unfairness of it all. All that amazing work of Dad's covering the space, and yet the one big thing he really wanted to do was about to be rinsed away by a wall fountain. All those people's memories down the drain.

Circa stopped her spin at the big monitor, her knee bumping the keyboard and awakening the Shopt picture of Miles across the screen. She thought about how hard she'd worked to erase some of the hurt from Miles's face, only to find out that more had just been put on him. If she printed the picture and the test was a success, how was she going to explain to Miles that she had taken it upon herself to change his face? After all, if Dad had taught her anything, it was that photo work was about helping people on the *inside*. As her guilt mounted up, Circa swiftly closed out the picture and dragged it to the trash. Instead, she would do a Shopt test that would help Miles on the inside, not a dumb thing that would hardly make a difference anyway, like removing one of a hundred scars.

Circa wondered what in the world she could do as both a test and a help to Miles. The potential Shopt magic suddenly seemed to be all she had left to distract her from her own unrestorable life. There had to be something simple that she could do well, something that would do some good if it were to come true. Maybe something that would even help him remember. She considered what Nattie had said about the power of a full moon, how the notion of it helping Miles get his memory back seemed ridiculous when Nat first mentioned it, but now suddenly it felt like pure inspiration. Without hesitation, Circa unzipped Mom's big camera from its bag, carried it out to the driveway, and waited for the thick clouds to part. The moon wasn't even nearly full, only halfway there. But Circa planned to fix that.

Once she had a good shot of the half moon, Circa rushed back in and popped the memory card into Dad's computer. She turned on the iPod to play Dad's song as a familiar Shopt accompaniment. Then she opened the pic and immediately went to work as the music began.

Oh Lord, keep your eye on me.
You know how foolish and reckless I can be.
Light up my way, so I can see.

For over an hour, Circa carefully completed the work. She meticulously pasted, painted, erased, shaded, and smoothed the half moon into a full one. As she worked, she could hear the home phone ring time and time again. The machine kept answering, but the person hung up each time without leaving a message. Finally, the fourth time, Mom must have picked up.

Circa put the finishing touch on her full moon, a special lighting effect that made it glow brighter than she'd ever seen before. Once it was saved, she printed out a copy. The picture proved even lovelier in her hands than it was on the screen, and Circa felt a mesmerizing mix of pride and hope as she gazed at it. So mesmerizing, in fact, she didn't notice that both Nattie and Miles had entered the studio from different directions behind her. The two of them silently converged around Circa and nearly startled her from the chair when they stooped to join in the moon gazing.

"Man, you guys," said Circa, spinning around. "You totally scared the wits out of me."

"Didn't mean to," said Nattie. "You were just so into the picture, I didn't want to interrupt."

Miles nodded in agreement.

"Circ, you sounded upset on the phone, so I came over soon as I could. You okay?"

"Not really," said Circa. "But I'm working on it. How's your head, Miles?"

"Better," he said. "No thanks to that ringing phone."

"I know," said Circa. "What in the world?"

Nattie wasn't speaking. Instead she was staring not-so-subtly at Miles's chin.

"What?" he said, wiping at his mouth. "I got something on my face?"

"Oh, no, you're fine," said Nattie, turning ten shades of embarrassed. She followed up with an *aw man* look at Circa.

"Anyway." Circa rushed to change the subject. "You guys like my moon?"

"Your moon?" said Miles.

"Well, *half* mine," said Circa. "I changed the half moon into a full one."

"A test?" said Miles.

"Yep," she said. "I realized that the Shopt thing doesn't seem to happen unless the picture is actually *printed*."

Circa winked at Nattie in explanation of the abandoned chin test.

"And that picture was taken tonight, so all that's left is to see if anything has happened out there."

Miles and Nattie exchanged a skeptical look.

"Okay, fine, I'll play along," said Miles.

"Me too," said Nattie, following his lead. But Circa knew good and well that Nattie was halfway to becoming a believer in this platypus of theirs.

"Well, then, what are you waiting for?" Miles said to Circa. "Aren't you going to go check out the window?"

Circa suddenly got fluttery inside.

"In a minute," she said.

Nattie picked up the picture and admired Circa's work.

"I know why you made the moon full," she said in kind of a singsongy way.

"How come?" said Miles, making his way toward the window.

"Because I thought a full moon might make your memory come back," said Nattie.

"And because Great-Uncle Mileage *loves* a full moon," said Circa, scrambling out of the chair to try to beat Miles across the room. But Miles was already at the studio window looking out.

"I'm not feeling any memory magic yet," he said with a smirk. "But it's way too cloudy now to even see if the moon's different."

"So we just wait for the clouds to move, to see if Circa's brand-new version is up there," said Nattie, searching nosily around Dad's desk.

Circa and Miles stood side-by-side at the small window waiting for the thick clouds to crawl their way across the sky as Nattie picked up the Shopt folder and begun thumbing through its contents.

"Hey, Circ," said Nattie. "If this Shopt power of yours turns out to be true, will you make me a new hat?"

"Sure, Nat," laughed Circa. "I'll make you a fancy one."

"Since hers got pooped on," said Miles.

Nattie shot over a look Circa could feel through the back of her head. "I *knew* he saw it!" she said.

Miles and Circa stood at the window and smiled at the low, thick sky.

"Hey, Circa," said Nattie. "How come you never showed me all these before?"

Circa turned to discover Nattie sitting on a spot she'd cleared off of Dad's desk. She was making her way through the stack of Shopt pictures one by one, stopping to read each and every story.

"What are these?" said Nattie.

Circa got squirmy at the sight of her friend holding a folder full of secrets that the Monroe family had kept close for years, but not so much that she made Nattie stop. Sorry again, Dad, Circa thought, as her discomfort was suddenly eclipsed by the need to revisit the images herself. Circa walked over and joined Nattie, clearing off a spot right next to her friend and hoisting herself up. Nattie was in the midst of the group of photos Circa had done with Miles, the adventures of Great-Uncle Mileage, baby soldier.

"It's a collection of Shopt," explained Circa. "I did these and wrote stories to go with them."

"Good, isn't she?" said Miles, without taking his eyes off the sky.

Circa watched for Nattie to react to being the last in the room to know the secret. To her surprise, Nattie's face lit up. "Good's not the word," she said. "These are amazing."

Instantly, Circa felt like fifty pounds of secrecy had been lifted from her shoulders. As she and Nattie went through the photos together, she took great pride in having to point out to her friend the things she'd added.

"We're not done with the adventures of Great-Uncle Mileage, though," she told Nattie. "He still needs to find his long-lost great-nephew."

Circa looked over at Miles.

"Okay, so the moon thing's gotta wait," he said, leaving his post at the window. "What's the next test?"

Circa was weary of waiting for results. "Let's just do something easy and fast and obvious," she said. "Like change my hair color or something."

"Oooh!" said Nattie. "Let it be me, Circa. Put a streak in mine."

"But if it works, your mom will kill me," said Circa.

"Please," said Nattie. "I won't even tell her it was you."

"All right," said Circa. "If you promise. I'll take a picture of you with Mom's camera, then we'll edit it and see what happens."

Circa hopped off the desk to unpack the camera again. Miles took over her spot on the desk next to Nattie. Together, they enjoyed the Shopt while Circa got the equipment ready.

"Hey, Circ," said Nat. "What about these other pictures? The ones with the stuff scribbled on them."

Circa stopped her digging. "Be real careful with those," she said. "My dad made them for me."

"You mean you didn't do these too?" said Nattie, and Circa was thrilled to no end that someone would assume that.

"No," said Circa. "Dad was the very best at the Shopt."

Circa inserted the memory card into the camera and cleared the sky picture off of it just before the battery died. Then she made her way to Mom's side of the studio and found a marbled blue backdrop suitable for a portrait, while Nattie and Miles shared one Shopt wonder after another.

"So I don't get it," said Nattie. "The nest, the glasses, the people-pinkening stuff you mentioned. You called all that Shopt too, right?"

"Right," said Circa. "Really kind of like little-bitty Shopt, I guess."

"So then what's the difference between all that little stuff and this big stuff?" she said. "I mean, if you and your dad had this special power, wouldn't some of these things come true too?"

"Yeah," Circa said sheepishly, joining them again at the desk. "I've been wondering about all that too."

Circa felt funny about being the only one in the room who knew how very important this Shopt test was going to be. For her, and especially for Miles.

"Like what about this guy in the parade here?" said Nattie. "What if sparks really did shoot out of his trumpet?"

"Come on, Nat," said Circa, but her mind tingled at the prospect.

"Yeah, Circa," said Miles. "Remember you told me that day how they found the piece of plaid at the water's edge? The bagpipe waterfall thing?"

"Or this fisherman," said Nattie, flipping to the next photo. "Maybe he really did catch a disco ball."

"Yeah, wouldn't it be so cool if it really did all happen?" said Miles. "Then Great-Uncle Mileage could really come find me. Boy, would he have some stories to—whoa. Wait a minute," said Miles, pausing Nattie at a particular photo. "I haven't seen that one."

Circa froze. It seemed like Miles moved in slow motion as he picked up the Shopt version of the Linholt Reunion photo. Circa couldn't believe it. She'd totally forgotten she'd put it back in the folder. She'd been so careful to hide it before, and now here it was in all its storyless glory for everyone to see.

"How come you never showed me this one?" Miles said to Circa. "I didn't know your dad Shopt the reunion picture."

Circa swiftly took the photo from his hands. "Because I thought it might upset you to have to look at that place again," she said. "That and, well, I can't stand it that my dad never got to tell the story of this one."

Miles looked over Circa's shoulder. "Wow," he said. "That one's packed full of stuff."

He wrenched the picture back again from Circa's tight grip and studied it. "Oh," he said slowly. "Now it makes sense."

Circa's heart jumped into her throat. "What does?" she said, watching Miles's every move.

"Why you asked me if I'd seen a beaver and a giant potato," he said.

Circa deflated.

"But, you know, that baby's pretty cool too," said Miles with a chuckle. "That one of Great-Uncle Mileage's kinfolk?"

"You spotted the baby?" said Circa in disbelief. "How in the world?"

"Give me it," demanded Nattie, stretching and straining to see the details. "Let me look."

"You forget how much time I had to study the original version of that reunion photo," said Miles. "I practically had every Linholt memorized."

Circa stared longingly at the colorful scene. "My dad said the story of this baby was a real good one," she said, her voice trembling. "He was going to tell it to me when he got home."

Miles handed the photo over to Nattie and closed the Shopt folder.

"Oh, man," said Nattie. "I'm sorry, Circa."

Circa went back over to look for Mom's spare camera battery. She suddenly felt blanketed by the need to find out about the Shopt power, and right away. To get closer to what it was Dad wanted to tell her. To know that baby's story.

"So this is where the reunion was?" Nattie said. "Where the tornado happened?"

"Yeah," said Circa, digging through the camera bag.

"And where you were?" Nattie said to Miles.

Miles nodded.

"That's so weird," said Nattie.

Circa looked up from her search. Miles reopened the Shopt folder and began to flip back through it. All the while, Nattie dwelled on the reunion photo.

"So how old would that baby be if he was real?" asked Nattie.

"Come on, Nat," said Circa, fumbling clumsily to change out the camera battery. "Forget all that."

"No, really," said Nattie.

"The one I had said 1998 on it," said Miles. "So I guess it would be a teenager, right?"

Nattie glared at Miles. Circa felt her hands go sweaty.

"Think about that," Nattie said.

"About what?" said Miles.

"About if this Shopt power is real and works the way Circa says it does," said Nattie. "Then that would mean this baby would be about thirteen, right?"

"Sure, Nat," said Circa nervously. "Now come on, put it down and let's take your picture."

Nattie's voice grew more serious. "And just like the nest and the glasses, this person would have appeared out of nowhere, right? Right when the Shopt version was printed, you say, Circa?"

Circa bugged her eyes out at Nattie, trying desperately to send her a mental *shut up* across the room. But Nattie was unstoppable.

"And he would have shown up where?" she asked.

"The reunion," said Miles, dropping the folder once more to his lap. His voice had become icy cold.

The studio stood still in time as Nattie's unspoken suggestion came crashing down. Visibly spooked by her own observations, she looked to Miles for his reaction.

"Circa, please tell your friend she's way off base," said Miles.

Circa just stood there in silence, a tiny flame igniting inside her.

"Tell her," said Miles.

But try as she might, Circa couldn't speak a word. She could only stand in quiet support of Nattie's observations.

"No way," Miles said. "You've lost your minds." He squirmed in the spotlight of the two girls' stares. "You think that baby is *me*?"

26

The Message

Miles went white and looked like he was going to throw up.

"Seriously," he said. "Are you guys kidding me?"

"I'm just saying," said Nattie.

Miles crossed his arms and scowled. Circa's insides churned. If scientific Nat had come up with this theory totally on her own, then it must be true.

But when Nattie saw their reactions, she completely changed her tune. "Come on, I was just kidding around," she defended.

"How about you, Circa?" said Miles. "You don't believe that I'm Shopt, do you?"

But Circa wouldn't deny it. She *couldn't* deny it.

"Great," said Miles, hopping off the desk. "Not only do I have no memory, but now the reason I don't is because I'm not even real to begin with, right?"

"But it's not like that," said Circa. "Nobody said you weren't real."

"So tell me what's real about it, Circa?" said Miles, his face turning red. "About being some sort of nonhuman pixel freak?"

"But you *bled*," said Circa.

"So that's supposed to make me feel better?" said Miles. "What? Have you thought about this before tonight?"

Circa shrugged timidly.

"Miles," said Nattie. "I really didn't mean—"

"Forget it, Nat," said Miles. "Just do like me and forget it."

Miles made a beeline for the kitchen. "Fail of a day," he said as he turned to look at Circa once more before slamming the door behind him.

Circa's first instinct was to run after Miles, to make things right. But that instinct was mashed flat by the rolling ball of wonder inside her.

"Let's not mess with this stuff anymore," said Nattie, spilling over with regret. "I just got carried away is all, and now this whole thing's really creeping me out."

Circa fixed her eyes on Nattie. "But what if it's true?" she said.

"I really was mostly kidding with him," said Nattie.

"But *what if it's true?*" Circa repeated.

"Snap out of it, Circa," said Nattie. "We just hurt our friend."

Circa was beyond snapping out of it. "What if the Shopt thing *is* real, and what if that baby *is* Miles?" she said. "Nat, I've been wondering about this for days. I've been *dying* to tell somebody. And then you go and figure it out on your own. Don't you see what a big deal that is?"

Circa found Dad's photo magnifier and set it on top of the reunion picture, looking closely at the details of the Shopt baby.

"It all makes sense," she said. "How familiar he was from the beginning. The crinkle, the snoring, the smile. He was totally built out of Monroe features."

"Circa, quit it," said Nattie. "You're making him sound like Frankenstein or something."

"And his scars," continued Circa. "They could just be mistakes Dad made on the picture. All the little rough spots."

"You're really creeping me out, Circa," said Nattie. "You need to get Miles back in here and tell him we didn't mean it."

"But don't you realize what this means, Nat?" said Circa, rising up from the viewer. "If the Shopt power can make a whole fresh person appear, then imagine what's possible."

"You don't even know what you're saying," said Nattie.

"I do too know," said Circa. "I'm saying that if this thing is true, then there might be a way to change other big things too."

"Like what?" said Nattie.

Circa felt like she'd crashed into a wall of truth. That was it. The message. The one Miles had brought from Dad. It wasn't something Dad had said. It was truly something he'd built inside Miles. It was so clear now. Dad wanted to come home, and Circa had the power to make it happen.

"Like changing a dad getting killed by a tornado," she said, about to burst with possibility. "I mean, if a person can be totally Shopt into existence, then why can't a Shopt thing also *save* someone's life?"

"Oh, Circa," said Nattie, chewing hard on a braid.

"I'm serious, Nattie," said Circa.

"Don't you think this thing has gotten way out of hand?" said Nattie. "Let's just quit it, okay, and go have some peanut butter pie or something. I can eat the crust and you can eat the filling, and we'll give Miles his very own piece."

"How in the world can you think about pie right now?" Circa said even louder. "Don't you see what all this could mean, Nattie? Don't you see?"

She walked over to the monitor, picked up the wooden box that held her father's ashes, and set it down hard on the desk.

"This," she said. "*This*, Nat." Circa's voice began to quake. "This is what's left of him."

"Circa—"

"Don't you get it?" said Circa. "I don't need ashes, Nattie. I need my dad. My mom needs my dad. And those people at Maple Grove need more than a stupid fountain wall to give them their memories back."

Nattie fumbled for the Shopt folder and held it up.

"At least you've got these," she said desperately. "You said yourself that your dad made all this special stuff just for you."

"And now I've got the message too, Nat. The Shopt message. Miles is here for one reason . . . to show me that I can bring Dad back. That's it, Nat. That *has* to be it."

Circa picked up the reunion photo. "There must be something here I could do," she said. "Something I could change in this picture to make him come back."

Nattie grabbed Circa's wrist.

"Circ, don't," she said. "You're putting your head into a hive."

"Quit it," said Circa, jerking her arm away. "What does that have to do with anything?"

"It means you're going after something that's really sweet, but I'm worried that you're only gonna get stung bad. And I don't want you to—"

"Oh, Nattie, you and your dumb nature stuff," snapped Circa. "Why don't you save it for the Science Academy?"

Nattie went silent.

"Don't be such a shmoo," said Circa.

Nattie climbed off the desk. "Bye," she said sadly, but Circa didn't even look up from the photo until she heard the front studio door squeak open.

"Wait! Nat! What about the streak in your hair?" Circa called out, but Nattie was already gone.

"Fine. Whatever," muttered Circa. "I've got all the proof I need anyway."

She launched Dad's Photoshop and opened the original Linholt Reunion photo. Her head wild with longing, she wondered if she could edit just one small detail that would change what happened to Dad somehow. To restore not just his legacy, but to actually restore *him*. She remembered what the preacher had said at Dad's memorial service, that "the comings and goings of souls are best left up to God." But wasn't God the one who had approved this miracle in the first place?

What can I change? Circa wondered as she frantically darted her eyes from one side of the Linholt photo to the other. Then suddenly, she had an idea. *The tree,* she thought. The tree that Dad crashed into. Maybe it's in this picture. Circa considered the possibilities. If she were to remove all the trees from the photo, would that mean Dad's Jeep would have had nothing to hit? Would that bring him back?

Without hesitation, Circa began carefully removing tree after tree from the grove. It was detailed, painstaking work, but she was fueled by adrenaline and by Dad's song, which she turned up as loud as she could stand it on Dad's headphones. "One of these days, I'll come back," the man sang, boosting Circa's determination. Every few minutes, a shred of doubt formed inside, but Circa would simply shake it off and concentrate on erasing another tree.

It was only when her eyes got bleary from removing leaves and bark, one zoomed-in pixel at a time, that she had to stop and rest for a moment. As she did, Circa took a fresh look at the photo of Dad and Mom and baby her that was stuck to the monitor. For the first time ever, she focused in on her tiny hands in the picture, how her missing pinkie was totally hidden behind Mom's arm. She remembered Miles asking her who that lumpy baby was and thought again about how Mom and Dad had kept her a secret until the day she was born. Then, for a moment, it began to soak in . . . what it must feel like for someone to tell you that you're less than real.

Difficult as it was, Circa knew she had to ward off the cold shiver of possibilities she'd never considered before and stay focused on more pressing life-and-death matters. She powered on Dad's printer and clicked FILE: PRINT on the treeless reunion picture, trembling with anticipation as she wondered how exactly it would happen. Would Dad sneak up on her just like she used to do to him? Could she spin around in the chair and exclaim, "Well, lookee who's here?" Would that moment become their new favorite time of day?

When the printer responded with a paper jam error, Circa opened the cover to tug a crumpled piece of photo paper free and, in doing so, sent another paper flying off the desk onto the floor. She bent down to pick up the paper and recognized it immediately as the folded-up Shopt photo of the soldiers and their surprise baby friend. The first shot ever captured of Great-Uncle Mileage the baby spy. Opening up the picture filled Circa with even more guilt about the way she'd treated Miles. But then all at once, she was struck by a far more troubling realization. She yanked her earbuds out and stared at the picture in horror.

The baby. That poor baby that Circa herself had so poorly Shopt into this picture.

If Miles was indeed the Linholt Reunion baby, then this soldier pic could very well mean there was *another* real Shopt person. That this baby could very well be an old man wandering lost out there somewhere. And not just old and lost, but missing a right arm that she never even bothered to give him. Circa couldn't believe she hadn't thought it all through better than this. She shuddered to think about what terrible things might have happened to Miles if he had never found Studio Monroe. And what a twice-as-terrible ordeal a scared, old, one-armed man with no history would have to endure.

Circa felt herself go weak all over. What have I done? she whispered to the little soldier.

Lois had always looked to her books for enlightenment before, but that day found herself suddenly tempted by the wisdom of the giant, floating, pig-faced sunflower.

27

All Those Pages Underneath

Circa quickly refolded the picture and stuffed it into the Shopt folder, but the thought of the abandoned soldier baby haunted her every move, making her tremble as she attempted once more to print the treeless reunion picture. Just when she was about to click PRINT, Mom walked into the studio.

"I saw the glow of the computer from under the door," Mom said.

Circa could tell by the tone of Mom's voice that her pill was wearing off. Mom pulled up a stool and sat beside Circa at the desk, the first time she'd been this close to Dad's computer in weeks. Still, Circa looked straight ahead, fearing she'd come unglued if she looked her mother in the face.

"Miles still sleeping?" Mom asked.

"Um. I guess," said Circa. Her heart was a spinning compass. Hope. Misery. Wonder. Regret.

"What you working on there?" said Mom. "Is that the reunion picture?"

Circa tried hard to compose herself. "Just some Shopt stuff," she said, rehovering the pointer over the PRINT button.

"Hey." Mom gently brushed Circa's ragged ponytail away from her face. "Are you shaking?"

Circa let go of the mouse and sat on her hands, just like she'd seen Miles do that day on the porch. "Sort of," she said, staring at the treeless photo on the screen.

"Circ, what's going on?"

"Nothing," she said. "I've just been sitting in here thinking, and I got kind of sad is all."

"About Dad, or Miles?" asked Mom.

"Both," said Circa. "Plus somebody else maybe."

Mom scooted closer. "Tell me," she said.

Circa felt like a dam about to burst. "Mom," she said. "You won't believe me if I told you."

"Try it anyway," said Mom.

"Well . . ." said Circa. "You know the Shopt, right?"

"Of course," Mom said.

Circa rubbed her feet together nervously. "Well, I believe it could be real," she said. "I believe that some of the Shopt things that Dad and me did might have come true. Like the purple star glasses. And the nest with the bird that pooped on Nattie. And pink Mrs. Linholt. And well, um . . . Miles."

"Miles?"

"Yes, Miles," said Circa. "Think about it, Mom. He came from that reunion. He's a teenager. He doesn't remember anything before the time Dad printed that Shopt picture for me. He has those marks all over him. And Mom, he's got that crinkle."

Mom just shook her head.

"Mom, don't do that. I *know* you've seen that crinkle."

"Yes, but—"

"What I'm trying to say is, and this is the part you're really not going to believe," said Circa, "I think the baby that Dad Shopt into the Linholt Reunion picture is Miles."

Mom crossed her arms over her middle and sat fixed in silence.

"I'm not saying I understand it," said Circa. "Or that it makes any sense. But I've been thinking about this for days, and I just didn't want to tell anybody before I knew it was true. But the facts are almost too weird for it *not* to be true, you know? And then Nattie went and said it tonight too. And then, well, I got to thinking about all that and how if a Shopt thing was powerful enough to make a whole person show up, then why couldn't a Shopt thing bring another person back?"

Circa felt herself welling up.

"So I tried it, Mom. I tried the best thing I could think of. I took all the trees right out of the reunion picture, so it would be like there never was anything there for Dad's Jeep to hit. I thought it could maybe bring Dad back. That he might just show up like Miles did."

Mom closed her eyes. In thought maybe, or in a prayer for strength. "Oh, my baby . . ." she said.

"But wait, that's not it," interrupted Circa, her voice growing more frenzied. "Because then I was trying to print the no-tree picture, and I found that first photo I tried to edit with the poor soldier baby in it and now I'm afraid there's a whole 'nother Shopt person who's lost because of me, and can we please try to find and help him somehow?"

"Sweet girl, you're not making sense," Mom said tenderly.

"Here he is," said Circa, indignant, holding the soldier

234

picture too close to her mom's face. "We need to find him, Mom. We need to rescue him. Dad would want us to."

Mom took the photo, folded it back up, and set it on the desk. Then she closed her eyes like she was summoning a response. "Circa, baby, listen to me," she said. "You have been under more stress in the last few weeks than most people have their whole lives. You've lost your father, put up with a half-functioning mother, and had to rescue a stranger. And that kind of stress on a body can make things seem like something they're not."

But Circa was unmoved by Mom's doubts. She looked again at the gathering of Linholts on the screen. From the oldest to the youngest, they all seemed to be mocking her.

"Mom, let me just print out this picture," she said. "And we'll see what happens."

"Circa, do you really believe what you are saying?"

"Maybe Dad'll come right back," Circa said as she reached for the mouse. "Maybe he'll walk right in here and he'll be singing."

"Circa—"

"And maybe he'll help us go find Great-Uncle Mileage."

"Circa!" Mom raised her voice. Then she leaned across the desk and held down the power button on Dad's computer until there was no more. No more photo, no more computer noise, no more power. She swiveled Circa's chair around and looked her daughter square in the eye. "Answer me, baby. Do you really believe these things you are saying?"

Dizzied by a swirl of grief and anger and hopelessness, Circa broke down into a fierce flood of tears. "Yes," she sobbed. "I really do. I really do believe that Miles is Shopt and maybe even so am I and that Great-Uncle Mileage is alive and that you just killed the one thing that would bring Dad back home."

Circa strained to reach the computer button. "Turn it back on, Mom," she cried. "Turn it back on. I have to do it again."

Mom leaned in fast and gathered Circa into a big, tight hug. Circa could feel her begin to cry as well.

"Why did he have to die?" Circa cried into Mom's shoulder. "He wasn't done yet."

"I know, baby, I know." Mom straightened up and wiped her face on her sleeve. Then she took hold of Circa's hand.

"There's something important I need to tell you," she said.

Circa looked intently at her mom's face. She held on to one last hope that this was going to be the big reveal of the Monroe Shopt magic secret.

"Before you came along," Mom began, glancing over at the family photo, "your dad and I wanted a child so very badly, but we'd faced years of trouble and heartache with trying to have one. We kept the news about you quiet until you made your appearance, because we wanted to make absolutely sure of things before we allowed any fanfare." Mom took both of Circa's hands in hers. "You were the answer to our prayers, Circa.

"But even then," Mom said. "We always wanted to have another child."

"You did?" said Circa.

"We did," Mom said. "But we had the same troubles as before."

"Oh. I'm sorry," Circa said, feeling Mom's hands squeeze tighter.

"Me too," Mom said. "I feel like that's maybe why I've struggled with my depression over the years." Mom dabbed at Circa's cheeks with her cuff. "But then you know what?" she said. "One day, at a moment when you and I were both sinking fast, a strange boy showed up on our porch. And that boy, in his short time here, did something beautiful for us. He gave us something to focus on other than our grief. And no matter where he goes home to, I'll always be grateful to that boy for being another answer to a prayer."

Mom grabbed both of Circa's hands into hers. "And I do believe with all my heart that your dad had a hand in that," she said.

Circa felt her tears retreating for the moment. Could this mean Mom had become a believer in the Shopt powers?

"But not in the way you think." Mom continued. "Let me tell you more about Miles." She drew in a deep breath. "Circa, I'm just going to shoot straight," she said. "Miles is not Shopt. Miles is a ward of the state of Tennessee. His real name is Corey James."

Circa felt like she'd been punched in the gut, and hard.

"What do you mean?" she said. "How do you know that?"

"Those calls that kept ringing and ringing earlier," said Mom. "They were all from that Mrs. Linholt. When I finally answered, she told me they'd heard from the authorities in Tennessee. Miles's fingerprints had matched some on record.

"He has no living family," Mom said. "He's been living in a boys' home that's under investigation for numerous counts of abuse. The state matched up his fingerprint records, and Mrs. Linholt got the call at the close of day."

"But I don't get it," said Circa. "He was where Dad died."

"That's because he had run away from the boys' home into north Georgia," said Mom. "He wandered up to the reunion, probably for some food or something."

Circa combed over everything Miles in her head. The "post-traumatic stress disorder." The running in his sleep. The terrible hypnotism.

"Oh no," said Circa. "All those scars . . ."

Mom nodded slowly. Circa felt an empty space inside where her hope of big magic had once lived. She felt the tears come again, only they were extra bitter ones this time. Tears that you get when you've lost a dad not once, but now twice. And maybe even lost a brother at the same time.

"What's going to happen to Miles now?" she cried. "Will he have to go back there?"

"I don't know," said Mom. "Mrs. Linholt said that she plans to come take him into custody of the state tomorrow. I imagine they'll want to put him in some kind of psychiatric hospital in Tennessee. She said they can't put him in the foster care system while he's still got the memory problem. She said it's too much of a risk."

Circa got the all-too-familiar feeling of important things crumbling around her.

"You mean they'll just make him live with some strangers?"

"*We* were strangers to him once," said Mom.

"Yeah, but not really," said Circa.

Mom nodded in agreement.

"Mom," Circa sputtered. "I really can't explain it, but for some reason I really don't want Miles to leave us. Like he belongs here or something."

Mom smiled sadly. "I feel the same way, Circ," she said. "I've felt that way ever since his first night here."

Circa had to replay what Mom had just said. "Then why were you going to send him to Maple Grove?" she puzzled.

"Maple Grove?"

"You called up there and talked to Lily about Miles."

"Only to see how we could help him," Mom said. "Since the hypnosis didn't work. I wanted to see what Lily recommended, since you said how well she cares for those people up there."

"Oh," said Circa, stunned and relieved at how wrong she had been about her own mom. "Does Miles know any of this yet?" she said. "About who he really is?"

"No, I wanted you to know first," said Mom. "You've been around him more, and I thought you could help me figure out the softest way to deliver the news."

"Can I be the one to tell him?" said Circa.

Mom hesitated. "Are you sure you want to do that, Circa? That's a heavy thing to have to tell someone."

Circa nodded. It had to be her. "I'll do it now," she said.

"Okay then," said Mom. "But before you go, let's talk about this Shopt business for a minute."

"I know, it's not real," Circa said, her mouth fighting hard against the words, her brain clinging to one tattered scrap of belief. "Mom," she said, "are we going to the scene of the—" Circa stopped herself. Of course they weren't. Now Mom had an excuse not to go.

"Of the ordeal?" said Mom.

"Can we?" said Circa, with little hope of a yes, of the remote chance of finding any of the other beautiful things Dad had Shopt into that reunion picture. "In case it really will help

Miles remember . . . I mean you know, the good stuff he might have in there."

Mom hesitated. "Mrs. Linholt is coming in the morning," she said. "There's just no time to do that, Circ."

"But what if no one *ever* takes him there, and what if that was the one thing that would give him his memory back?" said Circa.

Mom didn't answer. Instead, she just put her hand on Circa's shoulder. "Come on," she said. "Why don't you go have a talk with Miles. I'll wait down here if you need me."

"Okay," said Circa, wishing hard that you could yank a person across a fear that the person couldn't push herself through.

Circa passed through the kitchen and made her way upstairs to say so many things that needed to be said to Miles. First and foremost, of course, being an apology from the bottom of her aching heart. With every step closer to his room, she felt worse about the way she'd treated him, after all he'd been through already.

"Miles." She began speaking before she even crossed the threshold of the guest room. "I'm so—"

Circa stopped dead in her tracks and dashed back to the top of the stairs. "Mom!" she called out frantically.

"He's gone!"

28

Missing Found Person

Mom ran to the bottom of the steps.

"His window's open," said Circa. "And his backpack's not there. I even looked out across the backyard in case he was hiding, but none of the grass is smushed."

"He had to have climbed down the trellis," Mom said. "Why in the world would he do that?"

"Come on," said Circa. "We've got to go find him."

Mom grabbed tight to the banister. "Circa," she said. "It's late. For all we know, he's been gone for a while now. I don't think we should go driving around hollering for somebody at this hour."

"Of course you don't," snapped Circa. "You'd say that no matter what time it was."

"Circa, that's not fair. You know I've gone above and beyond my own comfort time and again to make sure Miles is okay."

"So then why would you stop now?" Circa said. "When it's prickly?"

"That's not fair, Circa," said Mom. "Think about it. Miles has run away from places before. He'll be okay. And he knows the way back here."

"But you said yourself how much he means to us."

"And I meant it," said Mom.

"But how can you be so sure? Can't we just—"

"No, Circa," said Mom, her voice shaking. "What you've got to understand is that Miles handles his fears by leaving. And I handle mine by staying. And neither of us is right."

"But I *don't* understand," said Circa.

"If he's not back by the morning, we'll call and report it to the police," Mom said as she watched anxiously out the front room window. "I just can't figure why he'd run again," she said. "It had to be for a reason. Maybe he was listening in on my phone call or something?"

Circa sat on the top step and put her head on her knees. "I know the reason," she said.

"What is it?" said Mom. "Do you think he's remembered something?"

"No," said Circa. "He's gone because of how I treated him."

"How could you say that?" said Mom. "You've been nothing but kind to Miles since he got here."

"Until tonight," said Circa. She could still see the dirt on the steps from Miles's first day there. Aching inside, Circa stood back up and went to her room.

"Hey, Circ," called Mom from below. "Don't blame yourself for this. Miles is a troubled boy, but he's also a survivor. I'm sure he'll be all right."

"I hope so," mumbled Circa, closing her bedroom door behind her. Tempted to climb down her pine tree and go search for Miles herself, Circa headed straight for the window and opened it wide, only to discover that her escape would be impossible. For there on the best climbing branch sat that big, clumsy nest, and there in that nest now wriggled three newly hatched baby birds. Taking a bit of comfort in their company, Circa pulled up a chair and joined the tiny family at the window, quietly waiting and hoping for her friend to return.

She stayed there and watched for hours, even after the hard windowsill made her elbows ache. *Because sometimes doing the right thing prickles a little*, she heard her dad say. She longed for him to tell her that it was way past her bedtime. All the while, the constant peeping of the nuthatches made her feel terrible about being ugly to Nattie, and she wondered if Nat would ever share a honeysuckle with her again. But mostly, she wondered if she would ever get to see Miles again.

To drown out her own thinking, Circa tried again and again to sing softly the song Dad loved, but each time, the opening words of it proved almost too much to bear.

It's way past midnight. Everyone's asleep.

Outside the window it's quiet on the street.

By the third attempt, Circa was nearly at her wit's end with sadness and guilt. In desperation, she looked to the sky and began to mutter a prayer like any other.

"Oh, Lord," she said tearfully, "Keep your eye on my friends."

Then, suddenly, a shadowy figure approached on the street below.

Mary Jo would hereafter be famous for dredging up the long-lost key to love and happiness. Someday she would even polish up the key and pass it along to her grandchildren. But for today, for this one shining moment, she was just plain giddy to be wearing that glorious jellyfish hat.

29

Parting Clouds

It was four twenty-one in the morning when Miles wandered onto the driveway, his backpack slung over one shoulder. Circa had become near delirious with exhaustion and regret, but she still scrambled down the stairs, out the door, and into the yard to greet him.

"Where have you been?" she said breathlessly. "I've been watching for you all night."

"Yeah, I saw," said Miles. "Your light's the only one on the whole street."

He sat down on the front porch, in the exact spot he'd been when Circa first saw him. She planted herself on the other side of the porch steps.

"Miles," she said. "Wait. Before you answer me, please just listen for a minute. I'm so sorry for what happened in the studio tonight. I just got kind of crazy with the Shopt idea, and I guess it sort of made me not think about who I was hurting."

Circa looked at Miles's hunched profile.

"I put my head in the hive," she said.

Miles leaned back wearily on the porch column.

"That's why you ran, isn't it?" said Circa.

He nodded.

"You're *not* Shopt," Circa said.

"Good to know," said Miles.

Circa gathered up the strength to spit out a bitter truth. "You want to know who you really are?"

Miles looked at her, his tired eyes showing a flicker of anticipation.

"My mom got the call," said Circa. "Your real name is Corey. Corey James. And you came to Georgia from Tennessee."

Circa watched Miles's face carefully, to see if her revelation rang any bells for him. He looked just as staggered as she had been by the news.

"You ran away from a boys' home . . . where kids were being hurt," Circa said, her voice trailing off. She longed to be able to tell him a wild Great-Uncle Mileage tale instead of this sorry one. "Sorry to dump all that on you," she said.

The two of them stared out into the weeds.

"Wow," he said. "Imagine a life so awful your brain completely blocks it out."

Circa squeezed her knees up tight and laid her forehead on them.

"You know, I've kind of had a feeling all along that there wasn't much good to be found in that load of forgotten stuff," said Miles to the air.

Circa couldn't bear to imagine Miles's past suffering. "So where did you go tonight?" she said.

"I didn't really know where I was going," said Miles. "But I felt like I had to get out. And I just ran toward town."

Circa's guilt pressed down hard on her shoulders.

"But then I got a little ways away and something weird happened," said Miles. "There was this old man and his dog sitting on a park bench on Third Street. He was the only one around, and he kind of spooked me when I first noticed him there, so I crossed to the other side of the road to avoid him. But then he called out after me as I walked by."

"He was just sitting out there in the middle of the night?"

"I know. It's weird," said Miles. "I figured he was a homeless guy. Anyway, he called me over and asked me to sit for a minute, so what did I have to lose, right? And besides, from what I could see of him, he looked pretty harmless."

"From what you could see?"

"Yeah, he was wrapped all up in a plaid blanket, with his face mostly hidden, like it was the dead of winter or something," said Miles. "He never really even looked at me. He just asked me all about who I was and where I was going. His voice was kind of weak and scraggly, like it was an effort to talk. And the dog was bundled up, too, but panting like anyone would under a blanket in the summer. The man said the mutt had wandered up just like me.

"I kind of unloaded on the two of them," he said, "since they weren't doing much of anything but listening. I told the man what little I knew and what lots I didn't, and about you guys, and about why I left."

"You told him about the Shopt stuff?" said Circa.

"Yeah, sort of," said Miles.

"Who was he?" Circa asked.

"He never told me," said Miles. "The crazy thing is, his voice sounded kind of familiar."

"Huh," said Circa. "What do you think he was even doing out there?"

"I don't know," said Miles. "All he said was that he liked to come outside to enjoy the moonlight."

Circa paused to look at the sky.

"What light?" she said, but soon as the words had come out, her heart quickened as she saw that the thick clouds were on the move. She held her breath in anticipation for what seemed like minutes as the clouds parted to reveal nothing less than a big, bright, glorious . . . *half* moon.

"What's going to happen to me?" said Miles, crashing Circa's attention back down to earth.

She hesitated big. "Mom says Mrs. Linholt is coming to get you in the morning," she finally said.

"Man," said Miles. "I sure didn't think I was coming back here tonight just to get taken away."

"I know," said Circa. "Do you wish you hadn't come back?"

Miles shook his head slowly. "You know how you hate it when kids say your parents bought you from the circus?" he said.

Circa nodded.

"Well, I wish your parents had bought *me* from the circus. I'd rather live here as a freak any day than go back to being Corey James . . . whoever he was."

Circa's gut twisted up tight. She searched her own pain for some way to commiserate with Miles. "After you left the studio tonight," she said. "I got all crazy about the Shopt stuff. Like real bad. Like I actually thought I could use the power to make my dad not dead."

Miles eyes widened. "You did?"

"I know," she said. "It's nuts. And get this . . . I even wondered if I might be Shopt too."

"Whoa," said Miles.

"Yeah," said Circa. "I guess what I'm trying to say is, if it had all been real, then we at least could have been freaks *together*, right?"

Miles didn't answer.

"But don't worry. Now I know. It's not real," she said.

"Yeah?" said Miles, tilting his head back on the porch column and looking up at the sky. "Or remember? Maybe it's only *half* real."

He looked at Circa and grinned. She realized it was the first time she'd seen the crinkle all day.

Circa smiled. "Well," she said. "Did the moon at least make you half remember?"

"No," he smiled. "But it did help me see your street sign."

Miles looked at Circa. "Even if *none* of the Shopt stuff is real, it doesn't make it any less special, you know," he said. "I mean, the way that all those pictures in that folder made things better."

Miles shrugged. "For me at least," he said.

"Yeah. For me too," said Circa, watching the curtains of clouds close up again.

"You know, it was Mom that made us wait here instead of going out after you," she said. "I was mad, but now I'm glad we waited."

"Your mom is stronger than you think," said Miles.

"Easy for you to say," said Circa. "She doesn't seem to have any trouble taking care of you. It's me that's the problem."

"There might be good reason for that," said Miles. "Maybe it's because I see what she can do, and you see what she can't."

Circa felt a sting inside. "So what made you come right back?" she said.

"Because the old man said I needed to stick around," said Miles. "He told me I had a job to do."

"Really?" said Circa. "That's what changed your mind?"

"I felt like I'd run into him for a reason," said Miles. "So I guess that was enough for me."

"*A job to do?*" said Circa. "What do you think he meant?"

"No clue," said Miles, shaking his head.

"Hey, Miles," Circa said tentatively.

"Yeah?"

"What color was the dog?"

"Hard to tell," he said. "He was mostly under the blanket too. Maybe brown? Why?"

"Nothing," said Circa. "Habit, I guess. All I know is you better go on in and tell Mom you're back . . . before she wakes and calls the police about you."

"All right," Miles said, standing and dusting the dirt off his legs. "You coming?"

"In a few," said Circa. "There's something I've got to take care of first."

As soon as Miles was inside, Circa searched the yard for the plumpest pinecone she could find. Then she walked over to Nattie's front yard and lobbed it at her bedroom window, hitting it on the first try. Nattie came to the window, rubbing her eyes.

"Circa?" she called down. "Is that you?"

"Nat, I need to say something," Circa began. "And try not to fall asleep."

Nattie stretched big and leaned out the window to listen.

"I was wrong, Nat," she said. "I was wrong about the Shopt, I was wrong about Miles, and I was wrong about saying your nature stuff was dumb. You've been trying to be sweet to me, and I've been way too spaced-out to care. The thing is, you are really great at something, Nattie. And I'm not even talking about nature-ish stuff. I'm talking about friend-ish stuff."

Nattie put her elbows on the windowsill. "So you're not trying to forget me?"

"What do you mean, Nattie?"

"I mean, you're not going to forget me when I'm over there at the other school?"

"No way, Nat." Circa hadn't known anyone to try to forget something good on purpose.

"Even when people start calling me names for being the new, bug-loving kid with the hat and the big hair and the white shiny sandals?" Nattie said.

It had never occurred to Circa that Nattie was just as scared about the whole change as she was. "Oh, Nattie, come on. That's silly. Nobody calls *you* names."

Circa felt a pang of guilt. "Oh," she said sheepishly. "Except me."

"Yeah," said Nattie. "So what about that shmoo thing?"

"I was wrong about that too," said Circa. "Will you please forgive me?"

"Or course," said Nattie, smiling sleepily.

"Thanks," said Circa. "Now you can go back to bed."

Circa turned to leave, but stepped right back as Nattie was closing her window. "Oh, and the baby nuthatches have come out," she said. "Better be thinking of some names."

"Sure will," said Nattie.

Circa noticed that the air had taken on a dewy just-before-daylight feel, which urged her to speed up her step as she approached her own front door. Even if they were both half asleep, she wanted to spend as much time with Miles as she possibly could, for in just a few short hours, Mrs. Linholt would be coming to take him away.

Every birthday cake, a different word showed up in the smoke of the blown-out candles. So far this year, Josephine had collected Nicka, Nacka, Dicka, Dacka, and Choo Choo. She recorded each one on a crumpled piece of paper hidden under her bed, hoping that one day the words would all make sense.

30

Mrs. Linholt Can Wait

It was Saturday, nine thirty a.m., and Mrs. Linholt would be at the Monroe house in half an hour. Unable to sleep, Circa and Miles had spent the rest of the night seated at the kitchen table spinning pie-fueled, near-nonsense tales of the day Great-Uncle Mileage and his nephew finally got to meet. But now that Mrs. Linholt's arrival grew close, Miles was glumly gathering up his backpack from the floor, Circa was pacing the kitchen solemnly, and Mom was in the front room putting the finishing touches on what looked to be a note.

"Come on, guys," Mom said. "Or we're going to be late."

Circa wondered how Mom could be so casual about rushing Miles to his departure. She and Miles went into the front room to find Mom curling a piece of tape to stick to the back of the note.

"Circa, please stick this to the front door for me," Mom said. "I'm going to grab me some just-in-case stuff from the kitchen."

As soon as Mom was out of sight and rattling a medicine bottle, Circa and Miles huddled to read the note. It said:

Mrs. Linholt,

Sorry for your trouble, but we've decided to take a little last-minute therapy trip with Miles, per the doctor's orders. I'll be in touch when we return.

Laurel Monroe

Mom reappeared in the kitchen doorway. Circa and Miles looked at her in astonishment.

"Like I said, doctor's orders, right?" Mom said with a shrug. "Mrs. Linholt will just have to come another time."

Mom stuffed a bottle of water into her purse. "Now let's get on out of here, in case the woman's extra eager to do her job this morning," she said. "Not to mention before I lose my nerve."

As Mom and Miles made their way to the driveway, Circa lagged behind to press the note to the door. Then she ran to join Miles in the backseat as Mom started the car.

Mom took a deep breath and threw the car into reverse. "To the ordeal," she said, followed by zero false starts, zero running back inside.

"But Mom," said Circa. "I thought we weren't . . . I mean, I thought you couldn't . . ."

"Yeah, me too," said Mom. "But sometimes doing the right thing stings a *lot*, right?"

Mom started down Delp Street. "It's kind of like when I carried your eleven-year-old self up the stairs to your bed the other night," she said. "I had to shut my eyes and ask your dad for some strength."

"You mean, 'A little help here, sweetie?'" said Circa.

"You got it," Mom said. "I've said that to him a million times this week. So I thought maybe one million and one might help today."

Circa nodded and smiled. She'd never known her mother to initiate a road trip. She wasn't sure what had changed, but somehow, for some reason, all lights were green. Mom was pushing through, and Circa felt proud. Even so, she couldn't help dwelling on the reality of what lay ahead. The trip was a victory for Mom, sure enough. And it had bought them one more day with Miles. But what then for him? she wondered. And what kind of sadness would be waiting for all three of them at the reunion scene?

"Mom . . . what if Miles doesn't even *want* to remember?" said Circa, watching his reflection as he gazed out the side window.

"Then he can tell me to turn this car around," said Mom.

"It's okay, Mrs. Monroe. Thank you," said Miles, as if he knew the trip wasn't really about remembering at all.

As they made their way through the streets of Wingate and onto the main highway, it troubled Circa to be so anxious about going somewhere, and it made her wonder if this was what Mom felt like all the time. As they passed one highway sign after another in growing anticipation, Circa felt even sadder, knowing this was the last drive Dad ever made. Every blurred mile of grassy roadside brought her closer to tears, until Mom spoke up and broke the silence in the best possible way.

"Miles," Mom said, "I've been thinking about this an awful lot over the last few hours, and I want you to know something."

Mom looked at Miles in the rearview mirror.

"I want you to know that, if I have anything to say about it, you won't be going anywhere with Barbara Linholt. And for the record, I plan on having a *lot* to say about it."

Miles suddenly looked a thousand pounds lighter, like Great-Uncle Mileage himself had swooped down in his plane and lifted a weight right off of him.

"Not going with her *ever*?" he said.

"Ever."

"Not back to Tennessee?" said Circa.

"Not to anywhere," said Mom. "In fact," she said, "I plan to do my best to make you a permanent part of the Monroe family."

Circa could see Mom smiling in the mirror and Miles crinkling right back at her. She began to feel pretty crinkly herself.

"Hey, bro," she said with a punch to his arm.

"Forgive me," said Mom. "I keep calling you Miles, when I guess I should be saying *Corey*."

"It's okay," he said. "I actually prefer Miles."

"Miles it is, then," said Mom.

"And Circa," she continued, "I've got something to say to you as well."

Circa prayed she hadn't saved the bad news for last.

"You know," said Mom, "I've been hearing about all the photo work you've been doing lately."

Circa looked inquisitively at Miles, and he gave her a guilty shrug.

"After you left the studio last night, I stayed behind and took a look through the Shopt folder," said Mom. "I saw some old favorites in there, of course, but then I noticed some new ones."

"Mom, we were just goofing—"

"No, now let me finish," said Mom. "I was going to say that I noticed some new ones that were every bit as good as the ones your dad had made."

"Oh," said Circa with a curl in her voice.

"I've been so distracted I hadn't taken notice of your work," Mom said. "But now, I have to admit that I've been wrong. Circa, it is undeniable. You truly do have your father's gift."

Circa puffed with pride.

"So much so, in fact, that I think you should definitely have a go at the Maple Grove photos."

Circa bolted upright in her seat. "But what about the fountain?" she said. "Lily said they were putting a wall fountain up."

"I imagine that fountain can go anywhere," said Mom.

"Maybe they can knock it over and reflatten Stanley with it," said Miles.

But Circa paid no attention to Miles's comment. She was busy enjoying the flicker of a dream coming back to life.

"Wow. Thanks, Mom," she said. She mouthed a thank-you to Miles, and he replied with a nod of congratulations. Circa felt so warm, it was almost like Dad had just climbed right into the car with them. The feeling carried on for nearly the rest of their ride, until they crossed over into Denfork County, where the worst of the tornado devastation had happened. In stunned silence, Circa, Miles, and Mom marveled at how quickly the scenery around them had changed from businesses and homes to unrecognizable heaps of things.

"Guess there are lots of folks' lives in need of restoring, huh?" said Mom.

Circa and Miles both nodded in agreement, struck by the sporadic scenes of destruction along the roadside. Just past a tractor turned upside down, Mom slowed the car and veered off the highway at the next exit.

"This is the place," she said.

Moments later, Mom pulled into a little paved parking lot next to a wooded picnic area. Once they were stopped, Miles wasted no time getting out of the car to go explore.

"Be careful," said Mom. "It might be kind of dangerous with all that damage over there."

Miles gave her an affirmative wave and disappeared among the bushes.

"What if he doesn't remember anything by June sixteenth?" said Circa. "Will they try to send him away?"

"June sixteenth?" said Mom.

"The date on that appointment card on the fridge," said Circa.

"Oh, that wasn't for Miles," said Mom. "That reminder was for *my* appointment."

Circa couldn't believe what she'd just heard, after all those years Dad had tried to arrange that very thing, but it sure made her glad to hear it.

"Dr. Jones feels certain he can help me with my own struggles . . . in a much less drowsy, nightmare-free way," said Mom.

"Good," said Circa. "But Mom, what made you be able to come do this *today*?"

Mom looked to the little rectangle of gray sky in the sunroof. "You're asking the wrong person," she said.

The two of them climbed out of the car.

"Mom," Circa said as she shut her door. "What really made you change your mind about the Memory Wall?"

"I told you already," Mom said. "It was that talent of yours."

"Was that it?" said Circa.

"That and maybe just a couple extra nudges," Mom said.

"From who?"

"Well, when Miles came inside early this morning, he found me in the studio and told me in no uncertain terms he thought you were ready to continue your dad's work. That I had been paying attention to what you couldn't do instead of what you could. That you and your dad were ready to *say something important*, I believe is how he put it. Powerfully sweet, considering he thought it would be one of our last conversations," she said.

Circa felt her heart swell with gratitude. "What was the other nudge?" she said.

"Hmm, well, the other one is a bit of a mystery," said Mom. "While you were upstairs waiting for Miles last night, someone from Maple Grove called the house. He whispered to me that he had some friends that were very much in need of that wall."

Circa searched her brain for who the caller might be. She knew it wouldn't have been Stanley.

"Was it Hank-not-the-Mayor?" she said. "Did he mention his intestines?"

"No," Mom chuckled. "No mention of those."

"Did he say who the friends were? That might narrow it down."

"He only said *friends*," said Mom. "Then he told me that we had a job to do, and after that he just hung up."

"Huh," said Circa, as they neared the clearing. "Maybe it was Joe the food— Wait, did you just say *a job to do*?"

But Mom didn't say a word. Instead, she just stopped still as a statue at the outskirts of the picnic area. Circa noticed immediately what had caused her mother's reaction. There, at the entrance to the clearing, were the obvious marks of an accident. The Jeep had long since been towed away, but the tire ruts in the grass and the fallen tree remained. It was a gut-wrenching discovery, and within moments of seeing it, Mom went totally white and had to sit down in the grass. Circa joined her at once, feeling woozy with grief herself.

Totally oblivious to Mom and Circa's discovery, however, Miles wandered the area in the distance and searched, like he was playing a game of hide-and-seek with his own memories. There were so many smaller trees crisscrossed on the ground, he had to jerk his leg free with every step. Speechless and sickened, Circa and Mom sat leaning against each other on the grass while Miles lifted twisted metal chairs and splintered picnic tables off a big pile of damage at the other side of the clearing. Circa wondered how much more of this she could stand, when Miles suddenly shouted, "Hey! I found it!"

Circa and Mom got up and held hands as they carefully wove their way to where Miles was in the distance. They found him standing next to a half-crumbled brick barbecue grill. Propped diagonally across the top of the grill was the leafy end of a big, fallen tree.

"This is where I was," he said. "Right before I heard everything start crashing. Only this tree wasn't here when I first crouched next to the bricks."

There was such rubble piled over the fallen tree, Mom and

Circa had to stoop to see the small, person-size hiding space under the trunk.

"Look at that," marveled Miles. "The tree landed across the grill and kept all these tables and stuff from crashing down on me."

Circa glanced around and shuddered at the heap of destruction that surrounded them. Then she looked back at the tree. Her eyes followed the length of it all the way back to the entrance of the clearing.

"Mom," she said slowly. "Look at this tree."

"Amazing," said Mom. "It saved his life."

"No, Mom, I mean look at the *whole* tree."

Mom and Miles both took in the entire length of the tree, from where they stood all the way to its splintered trunk at the entrance of the clearing. There were tire ruts deep in the ground at the base of the stump.

"It's the one Dad hit," Circa said, an oil-and-water mix of anguish and amazement coursing right through her. "That's the one that saved Miles."

"You mean your dad—" Miles stopped midsentence and just stood gaping at the small triangle of shelter. "He *did* come help me."

Mom wrapped her arm around Miles and started to cry, but Circa suddenly found herself more full of inspiration than tears. She studied the tree, all the way from its jagged break to its soft green canopy of shelter. As she did, for the first time ever, she considered how a person's purpose here on earth might not be made up of a thousand past or future *thens*. How it might be all about just one *now*, when he was there at that very moment someone really needed him. Even for Dad, who was right here to rescue a desperately lost, hurting boy . . . a boy who would in turn rescue Circa and her mom when it was time for Dad's own soul to go.

She thought about the song Dad loved and could almost hear him poorly belting out the lyrics. "Oh Lord, keep your eye on this place." Circa touched her hand to the coarse bark of the fallen tree. As she did, she wondered if Miles was the answer to Dad's prayer. And if Dad was just maybe the answer to Corey James's prayer.

"Wow" was all that Miles could utter.

"Come on," said Mom, smiling tearfully as she patted Miles on the shoulder. "I think we've seen enough."

"Wait. Not yet," said Circa.

While Mom and Miles searched for a safe pathway out through the mess of debris, Circa stepped high up onto a righted picnic table and turned in a slow circle, searching all around the clearing, longing to find any of the wonderful things Dad had added to this picture. She stopped when she heard the sound of something being flapped by the wind in a tree limb above. It looked to be a piece of paper caught on a branch barely within reach, and she stretched to grab it free.

Circa smoothed out the paper and took one look that made her heart spill over with sadness. It was another one of the Linholt Reunion photos, all pinkened, but otherwise plain as ever. Nothing tangled in the trees, no sly potato, and worst of all . . . no baby. Looking at the place in the photo where that Shopt baby should have been made Circa try to imagine life without Miles, and she couldn't stand the thought. Circa pressed the print to her belly and shuddered at how she'd tried to Shopt out all the trees, including one very important one, from the clearing.

"You know," said Miles from behind her. "The beaver would have been long gone by now anyway, right? Mrs. Linholt probably turned the potato into salad. And the watch, well, the wind might have blown it to who knows where."

"Botswana," said Circa.

Miles hoisted himself up onto the table. "But the missing baby, well, I can't really say."

"I can," said Circa, dropping the picture and letting it float to the ground.

Circa looked Miles in the eye. "The baby grew up to be a real hero," she said.

"Heroic as Great-Uncle Mileage?" said Miles.

"Even more so," said Circa.

Mom came stumbling through the picnic fragments to the table.

"Mom," said Circa, holding out a hand to help her up. "I was just thinking, this place could really use some candy vines."

Mom took in a deep breath.

"I don't know," she said, so doubtfully that Circa was afraid her comment had just made things worse.

Then Mom wiped her eyes and said, "I was thinking more along the lines of a *Kapow!* bush."

"Or a koala bear," said Miles, with a crinkle.

As the three of them steadied themselves side-by-side on that wobbly picnic table, Circa marveled at how a dad could magically make things okay, despite being missing from the picture.

She grabbed on to Miles's and Mom's shoulders and looked to the sky.

Thank you for the thens, she thought. And thank you for the now.

31

A Job to Do

Circa could feel her heart beating in her earlobes. The festivities at the Maple Grove Residence were just getting started, but August sixth had already far exceeded her once-faded, wildest dreams. From Circa's perch on the bricked edge of the walking path, at the center of the atrium, it appeared as though a hundred people had shown up for the unveiling of the Studio Monroe Memory Wall. She stood as still as her nerves would allow as Nurse Lily tried again and again to pin a corsage to Circa's new dress without sticking her in the shoulder. As Lily fiddled with the big pearly straight pin, Circa surveyed the entire scene from just above the crowd's heads.

All around her, a delightful mix of residents, family, and friends milled about. There was Ms. Rempy and her slurring parrot, Hank-not-the-Mayor and his digestion, Maki Lee carrying the branch she'd decorated for Circa, and even the Nelsons, wide awake and holding hands in their side-by-side wheelchairs. There were church friends, neighbors, and schoolteachers. Even Sergeant Simms from the police station was there. She was sorry to note that there was also Stanley Betts, standing right next to the stage with a broom in his hand. Lily had instructed him not to leave her sight, so all he did was stand there looking surly and sweeping the same crumpled napkin back and forth. Circa had secretly hoped to see him smile at least once, so she could check if just maybe his teeth were a little Shopt yellow.

"Oooh," said Lily. "Somebody already needs a nap."

Through the glass wall between the atrium and the lobby, Circa was tickled to both see and hear the Boones' arrival, as little Durret was indeed in the midst of a small tantrum. She watched Nattie and family walk straight over to Mom, who was greeting one person after another in the lobby and sharing with each of them the stories on the Memory Wall behind her. Even Circa had to admit the wall was a grand thing to behold, and as it should be, for she had worked tirelessly for weeks restoring to perfection the images of her Maple Grove friends and the town they called home. Mom had even done her own special part, paying a visit to the center in July to make a new portrait of each resident—all but one, that is—to include with the older pictures on the wall.

After Mom introduced the Boones to the display, she directed them over to a food area, which was really Lily's desk draped in a purple velvety cloth covered with all manner of cheeses and fruits. To Circa's delight, Mom had picked up everything herself at the store and as a surprise, she'd even tried to slice the apples into thinnest-evers. Naturally, Circa kept it to herself what a poor job Mom had done. After all, it was worth eating thickest-evers for the rest of forever to see her mom smiling regularly.

"Lily," said Circa, her eyes fixed long-distance on the swath of purple fabric. "I sure do wish Captain Mann would have come out today."

"Don't I know it," said Lily, finally getting the corsage situated. "But you and me just might need to set that wish aside for a while, baby."

It had gotten so crowded in the atrium that Circa hadn't even noticed Nattie weaving her way through, until she'd bounded onto the bricks and done a huge fake sneeze onto Circa's carnation.

"Nattie!"

"Sorry, Circ, I just had to do it," she said. "Did you know that the Europeans used to use the carnation to treat fevers?"

Nattie patted the big flower.

Circa rolled her eyes. "Poop magnet," she muttered.

"No, seriously, it's true," Nattie said, "But mainly I wanted to tell you what an amazing job you did on that wall."

Circa felt herself blush. "Thanks, Nat. That's real sweet."

"Amazing job, that is . . . for a total *shmoo*," said Nattie, taking a leap off the bricks before Circa could swat her. Nattie nearly collided with Miles, who was making his own careful way toward the stage carrying three glass-bottle Cokes.

"Here comes our boy," said Lily. "Your mom tells me he's doing better and better."

"Yes, ma'am," said Circa. "Him and my mom both are. They go to see Dr. Jones every Monday."

Circa smoothed her dress. "His memory has been coming back to him real slowly, but the doctor says that's a good thing," she said. "Miles and I call it one pixel at a time."

Circa watched Miles carry the bottles high over people's heads.

"He's even going to start school with me in a couple weeks."

"Glad to hear it," said Lily. "Be nice to have a big brother around, huh?"

Just as Miles approached, Circa eyed Stanley pushing his broom right into the path of Miles's feet. There was no time to warn him though, so all Circa could do was squench her eyes and brace for the trip. When she didn't hear a crash, she opened her eyes to see Miles stopped in his tracks, glaring hard at his nemesis. He said only one thing.

"Beat it, jackola."

Stanley drew back the broom and looked to Lily for support.

"Sounds like great advice to me," she said.

A scowl came over Stanley's face, and with a dramatic jerk of his arm, he flung his broom into the pond, sending fish darting off in every direction.

"I'm out!" Stanley hollered as he stomped and swore his way through the parting of the crowd, to the lobby, and right out the door. The guests closed right back into the gap after he was gone, and except for a few whispers and a "Hallelujah!" from Lily, it was like nothing had even happened.

"Yes," Circa said to Lily emphatically. "It sure is nice to have a big brother around."

Miles handed Circa and Lily each a Coke as Ben-the-Councilman, the next best thing to Hank-the-actual-Mayor of Wingate, stepped onto the bricks alongside Circa and commanded everyone's attention. Miles and Lily hopped down, leaving Circa and the councilman alone up there in the atrium's natural spotlight. Circa gulped her drink so fast it fizz-burned her.

"Ladies and gentlemen," the man boomed way louder than

the small crowd demanded. "I'm certainly not the star of this event, so I'll be brief as an elected official can be. We have come here today to celebrate the unveiling of a wonderful tribute to the men and women of the Maple Grove Residence. An ever-present reminder not only of these residents' storied pasts, but of Wingate's rich history as well. And it is my understanding that this tribute makes its debut today because of the efforts of a persistent, talented, and hardworking young lady, Circa Monroe."

The crowd erupted into applause that made Circa go warm all over.

"I'd also like to say," said the man, "it has been brought to my attention that this young lady, together with her partner in training, Miles, plans to restore storm-damaged photos for local tornado victims as Studio Monroe's next project." The crowd applauded again. "Would you like to say a few words?" he whispered out of the corner of his mouth.

Circa felt her knees go wobbly, but she nodded anyway, and the man stepped off the bricks. Circa cleared her throat and swallowed big as the claps died down. Then she locked eyes with her mom, who stood on tiptoe at the back of the gathering.

"Um. Thank you. But it wasn't just me," she said, as Lily motioned for her to speak louder. Beneath her, Circa felt her dressy shoes teetering on the bricks. "I just finished what my dad started is all.

"He used to . . . my dad, I mean . . ." she said, "he used to tell me that a good photograph could make one *now* speak for a million *thens*."

Circa looked to her feet, her throat feeling too tight for more words. Just then, someone began pushing and excusing his way to the front of the crowd. It was Miles, and he planted himself firmly in a spot where Circa could see him nod her on.

"At his funeral," she said, "the preacher told us that the comings and goings of a person's soul are best left up to God."

Circa focused on Miles until the others blurred around him.

"And now I know that even if God lets somebody's life be short, there could still be one *now* that makes the coming and going of his soul totally worth it."

Circa bowed her head and buckled her knees. She noticed that the crowd had fallen silent except for some sniffling. So very silent, she thought she could hear the small tinkle of a bell from over on her right. Circa turned her head to look toward the sound as her audience dabbed their eyes, and she nearly gasped in surprise at what she saw at the edge of the atrium. It was a purple door swung wide open, revealing the backlit silhouette of a stooped old man.

Circa suddenly felt speechless. "Thank you," she clumsily blurted out, as Lily rushed to relieve her with some additional words of gratitude. Since all eyes had been on her, Circa seemed to be the only one who noticed the new guest. She stepped off the brick wall swiftly into the waiting hugs of a dozen people, her own mom included.

"I've never been more proud," Mom said. "And I know your dad is loving every moment of this."

"Thanks, Mom," said Circa, stopping to give her a proper hug, all the while keeping her eyes on the man waiting in the doorway.

With Lily still speaking to the crowd about Maple Grove, Circa slowly approached the man who stood leaning at the threshold of his room.

"Captain Mann," she said.

The man in the doorway reached up and tipped his hat. It was an army captain's hat, just like Lily had described, and it was covered with medals of all colors. The man's shoulders were wrapped in a red plaid blanket that was so big it hid most of the rest of him.

"Hello," said Circa. "I'm Circa Monroe."

"So I've heard," the man said. "You've made quite an impression today, Circa Monroe."

The man's voice was weak and scraggly, but somehow soothing. Circa studied the lines on his weathered face, drawn to one deep forehead crinkle in particular. It made Captain Mann seem every bit as strangely familiar to her as Miles had that May afternoon on their front porch.

"Can I get you something to eat or drink?" she said. "Some crackers or cheese or something?"

"No, thank you," he said, shifting his weight with a grimace. "But could you maybe find me something to lean on?"

"Sure," said Circa, promptly looking around for something to fit the bill. "Hang on."

Circa saw the back of Miles's head in the crowd. He was holding Stanley's broom upright next to him. She squeezed through and tugged at the back of his shirt.

"Come on," she said. "And bring the broom."

"What's up?" said Miles.

"You won't believe it," she said. "It's Captain Mann. He's come out!"

Circa and Miles wove their way back over to the man, as Lily wrapped things up and directed the visitors to take a tour of the garden. Circa handed over the broom, and the old man gripped it like a hiking stick.

"Much appreciated," he said.

"Captain Mann," said Circa. "This is Miles. You remember, the boy on the poster I wanted you to meet?"

The man tipped his hat at Miles the same as he'd done before, but Miles just stood there gaping. He seemed twice as surprised as Circa was to see their long-invisible friend make an appearance.

"Captain Mann," said Circa stiffly, filling in the silence. "We're so happy that you've decided to come out and meet us for the first time at our celebration."

Miles cleared his throat to interrupt.

"Um . . . Not for the *first* time, Circa," he said, with a widening grin. "Or even the *second* time, really."

Circa noticed that Miles had a look of recognition on his face, but not a sickly one like he'd given Mrs. Linholt months before. And certainly not like the look he'd had so many times over the summer when a bad memory would come back to him. Instead, it was more like the satisfied expression of a mystery being solved. She glanced over at Captain Mann to see his response, but all he did was get a twinkle of mischief in his eye.

"Maybe Captain Mann has come out to look for the moon," said Miles. "Or just maybe he's going to take the van for a joyride and pick up a lost hitchhiker."

Circa went as white as her carnation.

"No way," she said to the man. "You mean you're the one—"

The old man shifted his weight again and made some grumbly growly noises. Then he swiftly handed the broom right back to Miles.

"Young man," he said gruffly. "Don't I recall saying you had a job to do?"

"Yes, sir, you did," said Miles, and off he went just like that, sweeping crumpled napkins across the room with him.

"You know," Captain Mann said, breaking the silence of Circa's wondering, "I'm familiar with this Studio Monroe of yours."

He turned and nodded toward the dresser on the other side of his dimly lit room, where there sat two photos propped against the mirror. One of them Circa instantly recognized as Miles's poster. The other one had been put there in place of her old chicken-on-a-bicycle drawing. She could see just well enough to identify the photo. Just well enough to make her knees go weak.

"It can't be," she muttered. "The soldier picture."

The Studio Monroe stamp that was reflected in the dresser mirror confirmed her suspicion. It was the original restoration of the old soldier photo she'd put that baby into on the day of the storm, on the very same day Captain Mann had shown up. How could it be? thought Circa, the once-doused thoughts of magic welling up all over again inside. She thought about that poor, incomplete baby she'd once fretted so about. About how old he might be if alive today, and how skilled he might be at escape. Circa grew so entangled in a fresh, sticky web of wonder, she hardly noticed that Captain Mann had begun to get wobbly in the knees himself. As he reached out to steady himself against the door frame, the blanket fell from around his shoulders and crumpled at their feet, startling Circa from her trance.

"Oh!" she said. "Hang on, Captain. I'll get it."

Circa stooped to gather the blanket off the floor. When she did, she was struck by yet another captivating detail about

Captain Mann. What he'd been hiding under the blanket, or better yet, what he *hadn't* been hiding was now plain as day. Captain Mann, she discovered, was in possession of not just one, but *two* good arms. As Circa struggled to stand up under the unwieldy heap of wool and relief and curiosity, the old man reached out to help her, wrapping his knobbled hand gently around hers. The second their hands touched, Circa took a small step back, somewhat staggered by the sensation that came.

"Oh my," said Captain Mann. "Are you all right?"

"Yes, sir. I sure am," said Circa, her face lighting up with a tender smile as she realized that this bizarre feeling, after all, was nothing new to her. This strange, unshakeable sense of connection that raced from the crinkle of her brow all the way to her missing pinkie finger.

Circa heard a distinct whimper from the other side of Captain Mann's room. "So . . ." she said curiously as she peeked in. "I don't suppose his name is Ernie Brown?"

"Whose name?" Captain Mann whispered.

"Oh, sorry," Circa said slyly. "I just thought that might be a good name. For the dog, that is."

"What's the big idea?" said Captain Mann. "You trying to get me booted out of this place?"

He pulled his door shut behind him.

Circa laughed. "Come with me," she said. "I want you to see something."

Taking Captain Mann by the arm, Circa led him through the crowd into the lobby, trying to match her own shuffle speed to his. Then together, they stood front and center opposite the immense collage-style display of photographs that came to life in the glow of a dozen spotlights.

"This is the thing I told you about before, the Memory Wall," she said. "These are all the other Maple Grove people. And their stories."

Circa realized only when she felt the warmth that a small crowd of residents had gathered behind the two of them. She and Captain Mann looked back over their shoulders and saw Maki do a little bow, Miss Rempy blow a kiss, and Hank-not-the-mayor flash a purple smile.

Circa and the captain turned their attention back to the wall. "That photo right up there in the corner is me and my dad and my great-aunt Ruby," she said. "We had all rolled our hair up real crazy. Even my dad. Look, we're all squished into that bed in your room. Nurse Lily snapped the picture without us even knowing it."

"Marvelous, just marvelous," said Captain Mann. Circa saw his eyes go shiny as he took in the wall from corner to corner. "Only it makes me wish I had something to add to all this."

"But I think you do," said Circa. She glanced around the lobby, now brimming with smiles and loud, tangled stories of then and now.

"And maybe I can—" she said. "I mean, maybe *we* can help you reach it."

At first, nobody really knew where the boy had come from. Both Miles and Corey, both lost and found. A pixelated baby. A 13-year-old wanderer. Not a Linholt. Not yet a Monroe. Just looking for answers . . . and himself becoming an answer to a prayer like any other.

Thank you, Dad.
Love, Circa

Acknowledgments

Thank you to everyone at Disney-Hyperion for giving me the privilege of telling this story, and to Lisa Yoskowitz for using your talents to help me tell it without all the junk getting in the way. Thank you, Joanna Volpe, for your inspiration, hard work, and belief in my writing. Thank you to readers, teachers, librarians, and friends, for being ever excited about new tales.

To all of the "Linholts". . . Bryan, Lainey, Pat, Mike, Cindy, Susan, Greg, Sheri, Jack, Glenda, Jason, Valerie, Wyatt, Cody, Abigail, Marshall, Terrie, Andrea, Clint, Max, Sullivan, West, Jan, Perry, Spencer, Graham, Tripp, Tamara, Jacob, Mary Katherine, Adam, Ellie, Katelynn, Emerson, and, last but not least, Baby Foofy. I love you all like family.

Thank you to Kevin Welch, for your awe-inspiring gift of songwriting. Your "A Prayer Like Any Other" moves me as much as it does Circa.

To all of the people (and animals) depicted in these photos, thank you for letting me subject you to my Shopt whims.

And above all, thanks to God for the gift of then, now, and forever.